Loving Mister

Stratford

Loving Mister Stratford

Stratford

The Stratford Family

KELSEY SWANSON

This is a work of fiction. Names, characters, places, and incidents are products of the author's imagination or are used fictitiously and are not to be construed as real. Any resemblance to actual events, locales, organizations, or persons, living or dead, is entirely coincidental.

No parts of this book may be used or reproduced in any manner whatsoever without written permission, except in the case of brief quotations embodied in critical articles and reviews.

Cover Design by Erin Dameron-Hill, EDH Professionals

For every Neurodivergent who has felt misunderstood.
You are just as deserving of your Happily Ever After.

Chapter One

London, August of 1823

Simon Stratford didn't ask for much.

He was, by all accounts, considered extremely low-maintenance, especially as far as second sons of earls went.

He never spent more than he was allotted; he didn't run up exorbitant tabs on drink or women.

He never worried his family ill by disappearing on binges for days at a time.

He stayed out of trouble and kept mostly to himself.

He'd always earned the highest marks in school, graduating at the top of his class at University.

All he asked for in return was a little bit of peace—a concept those few friends who'd stuck with him throughout the years seemed to have difficulty grasping.

Whereas his family had long ago resigned themselves to acceptance of his unrelenting drive to focus on his projects, his friends, however, were still boisterous, randy young men chomping at the bit for excitement, coin burning through their pockets, and wholly unable to comprehend how Simon did not share in their desires.

After graduating from University, Simon had taken rooms not far from St. Jame's Square—a bachelor's flat simple enough for his tastes and needs, but with an address his mother felt was befitting enough of his station. Simon didn't care what it looked like, he just wanted somewhere quiet to perform his work. Peace and orderliness reigned supreme in his little alcove of London.

That peace was currently being interrupted by the persistent pleading of his friend, Rafael Hart—Rafe to his friends and the young Viscount Blackwood to everyone else. Apparently, Rafe's most recent paramour had convinced him to escort her to the premier of a new play headlining some famous French actress. Simon hadn't bothered to pay attention to any of it: the title of the play, the Frenchwoman's name, or even that of Rafe's temporary toy.

Rafe had managed to obtain four tickets at the last minute—he no longer had a box of his own at the theater—but, as it would happen, every last one of his other hell-raising friends was busy that evening and couldn't accompany them on such short notice.

"Don't make me go alone," Rafe practically whined; in fact, Simon would wager that it would have been considered a whine had any man other than Rafe elicited such a groan. One tended to be given an extreme amount of leniency when he was as aesthetically pleasing as the broadsheets continually proclaimed Rafe to be. "You know how I loathe the theater."

"You're not alone, you'll have Lady Fancy with you."

"Felicity," Rafe corrected. "And her cousin is in Town from Cornwall, so she'll be attending as well. We need another man to help even our number and attempt to expose the chit to a bit of culture."

"And I'm clearly your last resort," Simon observed drolly, to which his friend rolled his hazel eyes.

"I know you're not truly insulted, Sim. I'd been doing you a favor by trying to *avoid* extending you the invitation. It just so happens that your luck has run out, my friend."

Simon finally looked up from the orderly stacks of papers and notes, books and quills, pots of ink and blotting paper laid out atop his oversized desk. Rafe looked so hopeful...not unlike an annoyingly, deceptively innocent-appearing puppy. He would mess on the rug as soon as you turned your back, then be just endearing enough that you didn't strangle him.

Not for the first time, Simon wondered at the sensibility of his decision when all those years ago at Eton he'd allowed Rafe to save him from verbal, mental, and physical torture, thereby entering into some sort of unspoken social contract accepting him as a friend. What had kept the two of them together over the years was a mystery to all, even the parties involved. Simon supposed there was something about Rafe that kept him more in touch with the outside world than he would have were he allowed to remain solitary; as for Rafe, Simon liked to think he was drawn to the steady, constant presence Simon presented. Simon was never hard to find and it had been remarked that he was very good to talk to...well, more people tended to talk *at* him than *to* him.

Rafe, had been one of the consistent few to willingly seek out Simon's companionship, and Simon did suppose he owed his friend a bit of reciprocity...especially when he looked at Simon as if any hope of bedsport with that theater-minded beauty lay squarely in his hands.

All Simon had to do was sigh and Rafe knew he'd won. His obscenely handsome face split into an excited grin.

*****

The audience at the playhouse that evening stood on its feet in an ovation for the principal actors. The waves of applause were nearly deafening, accompanied by the occasional collective cheer as a favorite took a bow. The French actress had proven to be quite entertaining. It wasn't difficult to tell that, even beneath the layers of stage makeup, she was more than passably pretty and there was no denying her powerful presence on the stage. Simon, himself, didn't often attend social events—let alone plays—unless there was some form of bribery or coercion involved, but even he in his relative ignorance could admit that he'd enjoyed the performance. He added his polite applause to the din echoing off the dark wood walls and swaths of burgundy fabric cascading from the ceiling to create the stage's curtains.

This West End venue, The Mask and Lyre, was not quite as large or as grand as Covent Garden or Drury Lane, but it was still a respectable locale and the principal working actors were considered some of the best in London. Judging from the glittering gems and luxurious fabrics rustling in the golden candlelight, Rafe and his latest paramour hadn't been the only ones drawn there by the performance. The audience was as much a display and performance as those actors taking their bows upon the stage. Simon shifted uncomfortably in his formal evening kit and wondered, not for the first time, why, exactly, Rafe had insisted upon his attendance. He'd claimed it was to serve as an escort to his paramour's cousin, but the girl had begged off with a headache at the last minute. Though Rafe had shot him a deeply apologetic glance, he hadn't offered to release Simon from his obligation. This reasoning was beyond all of Simon's comprehension.

It wasn't as if they'd paid Simon much mind during the performance…and certainly not with the woman's tongue in his friend's ear. Simon barely suppressed a shudder and shifted away in his seat, turning his attention back to the crowd of other ladies and their escorts chattering gaily in their bunting-swathed boxes. Inane. All of it. Simon sighed heavily and barely resisted the urge to check his pocket watch. The play was over. He'd be home soon enough. His fingers fairly itched for his quill.

Unfortunately for Simon, Rafe (ever the charmer) managed to convince a stagehand that they belonged backstage with the rest of the close friends of the performers and theater benefactors.

"Must we?" Simon muttered under his breath. The stairway leading to the lobby and freedom had been tantalizingly close. One step backward and he could have been happily swept away by the tide of bodies heading in that direction.

Rafe glanced at his mistress—quite easy to spot in her unnaturally pink gown—as she chatted with another woman at the entrance to their rented box. "Yes, we must, Sim. Lady Felicity was overjoyed when I told her we'd be going backstage." No doubt she'd been titillated by the thought of stealing into an area normally deemed unfit for women of breeding—dipping her toe in the forbidden waters, so to speak.

"You're certainly going out of your way to win her favors."

"Yes well," Rafe lowered his voice conspiratorially; "if you ever find a woman who can do the things she can with her tongue, then, by all means, I will bend over backward for you to ensure you get your dessert." He clapped Simon on the shoulder in a brotherly fashion. "Now…shall we?"

Once backstage, Rafe and…Fanny?…mingled with the crowd as if they truly did deserve to be there, whereas Simon was certain he stuck out like a burlap sack amongst the silk and satin. He'd never managed these situations well, and in the close quarters of the maze of back hallways and narrow rooms, the bustling crowd of actors still on a high from their performance, he felt supremely uncomfortable. He didn't have the same social anxieties as his sister, Lily, who tended to experience a crippling panic whenever she found herself in a crowded room; his anxiety stemmed from something else entirely. Simon felt as if he were a blatant interloper, that (as they usually did) someone would spot him for the imposter that he was, recognizing that he didn't fit in with their society's norms and mores.

To make himself less conspicuous, Simon took a few steps backward into a darker area of the room in which they'd congregated. It appeared to be some sort of storage area with props and tall pieces of mismatched scenery organized in some inscrutable fashion known only to the madman who had coordinated it. It reeked of sweat, paint, wood polish, with the mellow undertone of beeswax and stench of tallow, but there was plenty to watch, a myriad of people to observe. His eyes scanned the fascinating collection of guests, actors, and other theater employees.

Men in pristine black coats flirted shamelessly with half-dressed actresses wearing little more than petticoats and loosely lashed robes. Underlings scurried to and fro with notes and paper-wrapped bundles of roses, lilies, carnations, and other fragrant blooms to be delivered to various performers; others went about their duties, seeming rather unfazed by the crowd as they tied ropes, hauled props, and dashed about carrying piles of costumes.

Simon stepped back to avoid a collision with one such runner when the din was interrupted by a small yelp of pain. He immediately froze, confused, and searched for the sound's origin. Finally looking down, he found a woman clad in a garish orange-and-blue gown, kneeling on the floor, shaking out her fingers he'd just crushed beneath the heel of his polished boot.

"Are you alright?" he asked, still trying to puzzle out what she was doing on the floor. Should he apologize for stepping on her? Would that be too rude to blatantly point out her behavior, which happened to be odd enough for even Simon to notice? Should he ask what in the world she was doing down there?

But when she turned her head to look up at him, however, Simon's mind did something it never did: It stopped.

Odette momentarily forgot her smarting fingers as she looked up, and up, and up into the handsome face of the stranger who had quite possibly just broken her hand. He was clad in formal black and white—obviously one of the benefactors of the troupe or the play, perhaps even just a wealthy member of the audience with prominent friends—with polished black boots and dark blonde hair cropped close at his temples and slightly longer on top. His incredible blue-green eyes were set slightly wide on his elegant face, but they were complimented by his slashes of straight, sandy brows and cheekbones that looked as if they could cut glass. His nose was straight and well-formed. Her eyes drifted to his mouth—the lower lip fuller than the cupid's bow arch of his upper lip—and it took her a moment to recognize that those lips had formed words intended for her to hear and respond.

And she'd missed them.

"I—I beg your pardon, what did you say?" She hoped the cacophony of the room would make up for her atrocious lack of listening skills.

"I asked you if I might help you to your feet," he repeated, not demonstrating so much as a hint that he noticed her slip.

"Oh! No, thank you."

She smiled.

He simply blinked down at her.

"No?"

She replied with a shake of her head. "You see, I seem to have dropped one of my earrings and I've borrowed the pair from someone. If I cannot find it, then I may as well make my grave right here and now."

"I see." His piercing eyes seemed to take her in, assess her one inch at a time. He was so serious, so analytical. The fact that he didn't laugh at her was impressive enough; when he crouched down beside her, she nearly expired. He was mere inches away, smelling of parchment and, faintly, a clean-scented pomade. "What does this earring look like?"

Odette turned her head to show him the one that remained in her left ear. "They're sapphires. I didn't want to wear them, but she insisted."

"Who is 'she'?" he asked somewhat absently as the tip of his gloved forefinger brushed the lobe of her ear to view it better in the dim lighting.

"My—my relative," she replied, trying not to shiver at the strange sensation of having a man touch her ear. "I am a relation of one of the actresses. She insists that I dress up for these performances and parade around backstage, though I find it extremely uncomfortable."

"That would make two of us," the man muttered, now concentrating on scouring the floor.

Odette could hardly believe that he was helping her, let alone that he was now down on all fours with her in the corner of an after-show event on opening night. Good God, what would people say if they saw the two of them?

What would her mother say?

She barely stifled a bubble of hysterical laughter.

Odette had lived her entire life in the formidable shadow cast by Stella Auclair, the French actress known for her exquisite, fragile beauty; Odette had never felt quite up to snuff when compared to her. They were only sixteen years apart in age—her mother having been impregnated and abandoned shortly after entering the theater. Thanks to the generosity of her fellow thespians, she'd managed the impossible and maintained her career despite being a mother; she'd even become one of the most sought-after female leads in London with her flair for the dramatic, her ethereal looks, and enviable ability to memorize lines and directions more quickly than anyone. This, coupled with her mother's crippling fear of aging out of the major roles, meant Odette had always been forbidden from calling her "mother," or even the French, "*maman.*" When in the company of others, Odette had always been urged to address her as "Stella"—the Anglicized version of her name, Estelle. As such, their relationship had been more of close female relatives or companions rather than that of mother and offspring. It had suited Odette in some respects but left her hollow in others.

She'd never been privy to her father's identity; the story seemed to change each time Odette had asked. Once, he was a deposed Italian prince, then he was a wealthy American tycoon. As Odette grew up, however, she realized (more likely than not) he had simply been a handsome, silver-tongued actor who'd seduced the young, lovely French girl so desperately longing to make her debut on the stage. All of this meant that Odette had grown up with a very confused idea of what it meant to have a family.

When she'd come of age, she'd spent most of her time away at school. And when she returned to her mother, she had spent her time accompanying her to events and watching the performances like the dutiful daughter of a woman who refused to acknowledge her maternal status.

Though she'd been sent away for her education and finishing, Odette's earliest memories were of watching her mother apply her makeup before going on stage; the intricate costumes and paste jewelry; and the deafening roar of applause when her mother finished. Odette used to clap her hands over her ears.

Her childhood playmates had been some of the children hired as set hands or runners, a few of whom had grown up and made names of their own working in the business; one of them had even starred alongside her mother in this particular performance. Garret Frost had risen to near stratospheric success these past few years; it had been quite a pleasant shock for Odette to see him so successful when she'd returned for a visit, and, knowing of his humble beginnings and difficult past, she couldn't have been more pleased for her friend.

As soon as she'd been of age, her mother had shipped her off to the most exclusive, expensive boarding school she could find; all under the guise of wanting to give her daughter the opportunities she'd never had. Odette still had no idea how her mother might have afforded such an education, but she certainly must have skimped and scrounged every last penny, perhaps even sold some of the gifts provided by one of her faceless admirers or protectors over the years to do so. While Odette's childhood had been largely following her mother's career, moving around a great deal and often having to go without; her early teenage years had been during her mother's ascension into notoriety. She'd quickly procured them stable living conditions and arranged for Odette to have an education worthy of a proper lady.

Unfortunately, all Odette's manners and schooling seemed to fly away as this odd man's brilliant eyes met hers. When he'd been standing above her, she'd have sworn his eyes were more green than blue;

up close, however, they seemed to be an impossible mixture of the two—a mesmerizing, swirling vortex of complex nuances of color.

Odette swallowed hard.

"You don't care for the theater?" she finally croaked. His long fingers plucked up a scrap from the floor before flicking it away, reminding her that she was supposed to be searching for her lost earring.

"Normally? No. I'll grant that tonight's performance was rather more entertaining than I expected. Viscount Blackwood convinced me to accompany him tonight."

A viscount? This man was well-connected, though she'd suspected as much from the fine quality and cut of his clothing. Though he dressed simply, there was no disguising the fact that what he wore was expensive and was impeccably tailored.

"Is it the people? The production?" she couldn't help but ask. She may not have enjoyed being the daughter of a performer, but that didn't mean she couldn't appreciate the hard work of the actors, the beauty of a particular production, how moving a brilliant story could be. "Why don't you care for the theater?" She watched as he lifted the corner of a bit of tarp covering a piece of scenery, searching for the glint of a gemstone in the dim lighting and finding only disappointment.

"A bit of everything, I suppose. Then there are the inanities—the social customs one is expected to adhere to, which I believe to be terribly exhausting and contrived." His speech was so formal, so proper. His inflection was aloof; his diction was elegant, but there was an impatience about his tone. She didn't feel as if this was necessarily directed at her but at the topic. He was obviously a man who knew what he liked, and it was just so. His eyes met hers once again. "I find the spectators are as much in a play of their own as those onstage. They've their roles and their costumes; I don't doubt that some have even rehearsed their lines. It's all so premeditated. Were the theater solely a form of entertainment without the social aspect, perhaps I might enjoy it more."

She opened her mouth to reply but gave a little yelp of surprise instead when he lunged toward her, reaching beneath the lace-trimmed hem of her skirt.

Seemingly entirely oblivious to what he'd just done, he held out to her the glittering sapphire earring in the center of his large palm. "*Voila*," he said, a small tilt to his lush lips.

"*Merci*," she breathed, accepting the bauble from his warm palm and safely affixing it once more to her earlobe.

The man stood and reached down to help her to her feet.

As she straightened herself out, flicking wrinkles from her orange skirts with their blue floral print, she realized just how tall and lean this man was. Her head reached his chest in such a way that his chin would barely graze the top of her head were they standing that closely to one another. He was slim, but broad of shoulder, with long limbs and a strong stance. She, by comparison, felt rather mousy with her dishwater blond hair and roundish features. He was elegant in all the ways she lacked. And, from the way he was assessing her so pointedly, she had a feeling he was keenly aware of this fact.

Simon couldn't stop staring at the woman before him. Now that she was standing, he got his first truly uninhibited look at her, and he was taken aback by some foreign sensations.

He liked what he saw.

A great deal.

She had sweet, generous curves which conveyed both a femininity and a hardiness he found most appealing. Not only this, but her bright blue eyes glittered like paler, more brilliant versions of the earring he'd just helped her locate. Her lips were voluptuously full and made her easy smile even more charming. She was captivating in a way that was unfamiliar to Simon.

Just how long had it been since he'd had a woman?

Far too long, judging by the urgent stirring in his loins that usually served as his indication to handle his baser needs.

"I don't believe I caught your name," she finally said, a coy smile on those delectable lips of hers.

Right. Social basics.

"Mr. Simon Stratford," he offered, bowing over her hand almost mechanically. Several moments passed. He did not release her hand, nor did he bother to inquire after her name. She seemed unperturbed, offering it up instead.

"And I'm Miss Odette Leroy." Her presentation of the name was in the flawless French pronunciation, "lur-wah", and the movement of her lips was utterly captivating.

The way she looked at him was very strange to Simon. She didn't frown at his social slips. She didn't mock him. She didn't sneer. She was kind and warm. He almost didn't know how to react to this.

"Would you care to sit with me, Mr. Stratford, since it seems that we two are wallflowers at this event? Perhaps we can keep one another company and everyone else will leave us alone."

Simon could only nod as he accompanied her to some nearby crates and they settled in.

It didn't take Odette long to realize that Mr. Stratford wasn't one to talk. He seemed to hesitate before almost every one of his replies, as if the answer was infinitely important and he had to weigh it over in his mind before presenting it for her inspection. He took such care with every response that it made her feel special—like she was someone worth talking to, that her responses and opinions mattered. There were a few occasions where he made odd comments and observations about things and she soon realized that his mind appeared to be working several steps ahead; especially when he fell into a few minutes of silence. He was immensely thoughtful and, she believed, truly fascinating.

Many women of her status and situation would flatter and humor the second son of a prominent earl, hoping to flirt their way to a coveted invitation or something else of even greater value. Odette, however, found genuine enjoyment in their conversation. Once she overcame the unbelievable reality that such a handsome, well-born man was paying attention to *her*, they fell into a companionable rhythm. Even their silences as they observed the others milling around backstage had been pleasant. She enjoyed the richness of his chuckle. She was enchanted by the quirk of his alluring mouth. And when he smiled at her…her heart stopped.

Whatever this was—whatever she was experiencing—Odette knew she would do best to avoid placing too much stock into it. She'd likely never meet Mr. Simon Stratford again.

This knowledge was likely what bolstered her nerves, allowing her to relax and simply enjoy the time they did have together in a way she'd never before experienced.

He didn't know if minutes or hours passed, but Simon, oddly enough, found that he didn't mind. However long it was, he and Miss Leroy sat in companionable conversation. She seemed particularly adept at filling any awkward silences he may have generated. Rather than take a lack of response from him as disinterest, she seemed pleased enough to forge ahead. Even so, there was nothing self-centered or egotistical about this behavior; instead, she seemed to be doing him a favor rather than enjoying hearing the sound of her own melodic voice. Once or twice, much to Simon's surprise, she was even able to encourage him to converse quite fluently. Normally, people didn't hold his attention for this long, let alone relative strangers.

It had to be something about her eyes or her smile, maybe the way she made him feel as if his opinion mattered. She inclined her body toward him whenever he spoke and tilted her head in his direction when she awaited a reply. It took him some time to figure out what it was about her: She made him feel comfortable. She settled his mind.

*****

Rafe ducked back into the carriage after seeing his paramour to the door of her home. Simon was a bit surprised that the carriage hadn't been sent off to carry him home alone; that Rafe hadn't spent the night (rather that he hadn't been rewarded with a night in her bed after going through the effort of this night at the theater), but Simon didn't question it. His friend dropped into the seat across from him with a sigh.

"Drinks at the club, then?" he asked with a cocked brow. Rafe could see it was on the tip of Simon's tongue to decline, but he forged ahead. "Come on, now. Just one or two. You don't even need to drink, you can just hold it and look handsome." Tight-lipped, Simon turned to look out the window. Rafe took this for assent and knocked on the roof to send them into motion.

This night was proving to be endless…

Once they were settled into the fine leather chairs at Rafe's exclusive gentlemen's club, a warmed brandy set beside each of them upon the inlaid table between their chairs, Rafe asked a question that had been niggling at him for the latter part of the evening.

"So, who was that girl backstage after the play?" He eyed Simon over the finely cut edge of his crystal glass as he took a sip. "I hardly ever see you in the company of women, let alone a single one who's managed to keep your attention for so long before; she must be very intriguing, indeed."

Simon, used to his friend's nosy interrogations and penchant for making everything about carnality after so many years, gave a little shake of his head.

"It wasn't like that. Her name is Miss Odette Leroy; I met her rather by chance," Simon replied, fondly recalling the unique circumstances of their introduction.

"Odette? That's a rather unique name—very French," Rafe commented and took another nip of his warmed brandy. "You do realize who she must be, don't you?" Simon didn't offer a response, so Rafe continued, "With that hair and name, I'd wager money on her being related to Stella Auclair, the female lead in tonight's performance. Someone backstage mentioned Miss Leroy's name in passing. I guess Mademoiselle Auclair doesn't like for it to be known that she has a daughter who is one-and-twenty, though the ruse seems to be more of a farce than anything at this point...a stroke of vanity on her part. Everyone in the theater knows Miss Leroy is more than a companion to Mademoiselle Auclair."

Simon's sandy brows rose in interest. The relative whose earrings she'd borrowed must have been her mother, the French star of The Mask and Lyre. If her mother was attempting to hide a scandal over having a child out of wedlock, or if she truly was disguising the fact that she had a grown daughter, then it made sense. Though Simon couldn't fathom why a mother wouldn't want to tout having such a pretty, kind young woman for a daughter.

"I wonder," mused Rafe as he stared into his glass; "It's common knowledge that her mother is an infamous courtesan—she takes the truth that actresses are freer with their wares and creative in bed to another level. What are the odds that the apple didn't fall far from the tree? Could Miss Leroy have set her sights on you as a protector?"

Simon frowned at his friend. It was hardly very fair to make the broad assumption that a woman's involvement in the theater made for looser morals—it was a slippery slope if ever he'd encountered one—but still... It made Simon wonder about Odette's unconscious sultriness, her confidence, and the ease with which she'd gotten him to converse. The last was no easy task, and all of these would be characteristics one would expect of an experienced courtesan—a woman used to enticing and entertaining men. And there was no denying that Simon had been both entertained and enticed, on top of intrigued and made to feel vastly interesting.

And yet, there had been a hint of innocence about Odette. He caught it in some of her body language, the way she'd been embarrassed at the circumstances of their first encounter. Simon didn't entirely trust his judgment on this, however, because he was the first to admit he wasn't always the best at reading social cues.

In all, he supposed this pondering was rather pointless because he doubted he'd meet her again.

"Is this truly what you wish to discuss?" Simon began, cocking a brow. "I hardly believe you'd prefer discussing a woman with whom I had a passing conversation, rather than the fact that you aren't in Freya's bed."

"First of all, it's Felicity—and I know you're being purposely obtuse at this point—'*Freya*'? You can't be serious?" Rafe snorted before his lips thinned to a line of discontent. "And second...it would seem she decided to terminate our arrangement. I should have seen it coming when I caught her looking quite cozy with the Earl of Wells."

"Ah," Simon nodded as if he understood being thrown over by a woman with whom he'd formed a physical attachment. He didn't need further explanation of the situation, however; he was perhaps one of the only individuals who had some understanding of just how dire the straits were in which the Blackwood Viscontsy resided. It was no surprise that a woman such as the widowed Lady Felicity Moore would jump at the chance to have a protector who could shower her with an obnoxious abundance of goods and baubles. For all his appealing looks, charm, prowess, social graces, and status as an ideal of the *ton*, Rafe was still a man with feelings. Before Simon could open his mouth to offer condolences, Rafe slapped his knees and signaled for another drink.

"Let's not dwell on this, shall we? I've already decided to call upon Lady Towbridge tomorrow afternoon—she's been dogging me for months. I may as well give the woman something to swoon over in earnest."

Simon shook his head, a small smile tugging at the corner of his lips. Thank God Rafe wasn't fragile.

Chapter Two

Simon was once again attempting to work on his research, comfortably ensconced in his warm, quiet rooms, when his elder brother, George, Viscount Sommerfeld, came to call.

George's personality couldn't have been more different from Simon's had they not shared a lick of blood. Early on, Simon had realized what a disappointment he'd been as a younger brother. Though he'd tried ad nauseam in his early years, he hadn't liked the same games or enjoyed the same pastimes as his more athletic, outgoing, golden lion of a brother. Thankfully, George had sought an even tighter bond with Jeremy Balfour, Baron Shefford, rather than torture or attempt to force Simon into changing his ways. This, of course, didn't mean that Simon was oblivious to the chasm that grew and yawned between him and his male sibling.

Despite their myriad of differences, however, these past few years had gone a long way toward making Simon feel more as if he were a part of the Stratford family rather than an interloper sent to observe and not quite comprehend their habits. George, it seemed, was finally beginning to see Simon as a valuable relation; unfortunately for Simon's work, this meant George dropped in a great deal more than he used to.

Currently, George and his wife, Meredith, were in Town for the Season. They'd been married three years already and it was easy for Simon to admit that he quite liked his sister-in-law. She'd managed to breathe humanity back into his brother. Before her, no one else had been able to pull George from the dark place into which he'd fallen following his terrible leg injury. Also to her credit, she'd always managed to listen to Simon with genuine interest. Meredith unfailingly made a point to ask Simon what he was working on whenever they saw one another. While George's eyes usually glazed over—as most peoples' tended to do when Simon began discussing his projects—she always managed to make him feel heard and appreciated. Simon also experienced real enjoyment watching the way Meredith was the only one capable of putting George in his place. His brother's moods were sometimes mercurial, though less so than in the past. Meredith seemed to know exactly what to say to manage her husband.

This time, however, George came alone.

"This is deplorable," his elder brother grumbled, poking around his woefully understocked sideboard. He leaned on his cane as he righted himself, balancing to take some of the weight off of his injured right leg. "I always had a healthy supply on hand when I used to keep my bachelor rooms in Town."

"You know I don't drink," Simon replied lightly without bothering to look up from the parchment spread out before him.

"It's not for you, more so for your guests." George trudged over to the only other chair in the room, an oversized leather-upholstered wing-backed chair set before the small hearth in the enclosed room.

Though George's limp was less pronounced thanks to the rehabilita-
tion he'd been enduring over the years, some days were still better
than others. It would seem that today was not a particularly good day.

"Have you considered the possibility that I don't stock my sideboard as a deterrent?"

George chuckled. Simon knew his complaints about the lack of
spirits was more for show than in truth; George had cut down on his
drinking drastically these past few years. Marriage to Meredith had
certainly changed him in many ways.

Simon sighed heavily and finally set down his quill, more than a
little frustrated that everyone seemed intent upon keeping him from
his research. Something he'd discovered only recently was that the
sooner he humored the intruder, the sooner they let him be. At the
pace he was currently moving, Simon was never going to meet the
deadline for the journal.

"To what do I owe this visit, brother?"

"Do try not to seem so put out," George replied, his lips tilting in
his characteristic half-smile as he fingered the silver lion's head cap-
ping his cane.

The ensuing silence, however, was uncharacteristic. Simon eyed
his brother, declining to speak first. Finally, George continued.

"I just wanted to get out of the house. The thought of my club was
unappealing—almost as much as interacting with Mother and Father."
George made a small, self-deprecating sound. "When I would have
normally gone to Jem; he, Lily, and the children are still in Kent. You
know how none of them care much for the Season."

And, with that, Simon was once again the last resort.

He heaved a sigh.

"Meredith is upset," George admitted; "and I, brother, am
helpless." The words were leaden in the air around them. This was a

problem with which Simon suddenly felt overwhelmingly inadequate to handle. "I don't know how to fix it." George focused on the garnet eyes set into the lion's head in his hands.

Even Simon could guess where this conversation was headed and it was infinitely uncomfortable—close as their family might be, this was on a personal level not commonly breached. Society had no such compunctions, however, and Simon was still privy to the whispers and gossip: Three years into marriage and there were no children. The expectations of a first-born, titled, English son were very clear: Live long enough to inherit, marry well, and produce an heir.

Though it would seem from George's words that *Meredith* was the one who was disappointed in their lack of an heir. Interesting.

Simon very much supported this venture, as it put him one step further away from having to inherit the Aldborough Earldom. The two years of George's injury and subsequent suffering had been terrifying for Simon in an entirely different way: That time had put him perilously close to having to relinquish his scholarly ambitions and focus on learning how to manage an estate. A rather large one, at that. He wasn't entirely cold-hearted, of course, he wouldn't have wanted George to die either. His death, however, would have been the end of George's suffering and only the beginning of Simon's.

"Is Meredith displeased with you?" Simon asked innocuously enough, to which George shook his well-groomed, golden head.

"Heartbroken is a more apt description…and I don't know how to make it better. I want nothing more than to give her everything her heart desires, but there are things clearly outside of my control. Nature is a fickle wench." Simon examined his brother's normally bright, mirthful green eyes. George was undeniably weary. He was a man who loved his wife with every fiber of his being and longed to give her the world, and, yet, he couldn't do the one thing that any man

—no matter his rank or wealth—should be able to do. He read all of this in the lines bracketing George's mouth, the creases at the corners of his eyes. Simon didn't doubt that this was a particularly painful blow to a man who, even five years later, still struggled with a crippling injury and feelings of inadequacy when compared to his peers.

"I suppose all you can do is be there for her; show her that you won't abandon her even if she cannot meet your expectations," Simon told his brother something he thought he'd like to hear were the roles reversed.

George finally met his gaze. "I don't care if she cannot bear a child, I just want her to be happy."

"Have you said this?"

"Well, yes—"

"Those *exact* words?"

George briefly narrowed his eyes at Simon before his lips split into a small smile. "Yet again, your blunt insight is surprisingly helpful." Seeming placated enough to move onto a less raw topic, George asked what Simon had been up to. "You certainly must have more going on than your books and your papers."

"I attended the theater two nights ago with Blackwood."

A twitch of George's brows told Simon he'd piqued his brother's interest. "And how was that?"

"The production was interesting enough. Blackwood gained us access to the backstage area with his winning charm." His lips tilted in a slight smile as he recalled, not for the first time since then, his strange first meeting with Odette.

"Oh? And who, in particular, made this venture so interesting?" George asked coyly, his nuance lost entirely on his brother.

"Just a woman." Too late, Simon recognized the trap into which he'd stepped. While he wasn't good at reading social cues, he sometimes forgot that others could still read *him*. He clenched his jaw and refused to elaborate; the smug smirk on George's face irked him deep in the pit of his stomach.

"I'm pleased to see you getting out in the world. I may not have always cared for Blackwood, but perhaps he's turning into a better influence now that you have both matured some."

Simon served George a droll stare at his hypocrisy. His brother had certainly been no saint in his youth, though Simon chose not to mention George's former notoriety for taking a new lover every month or so and leaving a trail of broken hearts in his wake. Hardly what Simon would deem a good influence.

George glanced at the small ornamental clock set above the hearth.

"Is that the time?" George stood with a grunt and steadied himself. "Don't forget that you need to be at Aldborough House at eight so we can all go together to the Prince Regent's birthday ball. You know how Mother insists upon us all arriving as a unit." The ostentatious mid-August event always called upon the best and shiniest of England's elite to pay homage to Prinny's ego and flair for opulence and overindulgence. It was still a few months ahead of the official Season, but that didn't stop the Prince Regent from demanding an early trek to Carlton House. Several of the more far-flung families would no doubt take up their London residences ahead of normal schedule to avoid all the back and forth and the expenses that would incur. Unfortunately for Simon, his family spent a great deal of time in Town, and the weight of the Stratford name and the Aldborough Earldom meant their attendance was no less than mandatory.

Simon silently cursed the further interruption, but promised he would do his best not to become too entrenched in his research and lose track of time…as he tended to do. He turned back to his papers and picked up his quill once more.

He didn't hear his brother saying he'd show himself out and the door clicking shut behind him.

Odette was red-faced and exhausted by the time she was finally deemed ready for the ball. Her mother had forced her to change gowns several times and her hair had been redone twice, all making her feel perfectly inadequate. She'd always suspected that she wasn't quite good enough in her mother's eyes because this was, after all, a very familiar pattern for her.

She didn't have the same fragile, willowy figure that was so en vogue.

Her hair never seemed to look as her mother wanted it to and her grace left something to be desired.

She knew her mother cared for her…she just wasn't very adept at showing it. She'd always tended to give Odette gifts in lieu of hugs or saying "I love you," which had been all she'd wanted as a little girl.

Now that Odette was of an age to attract a marriage, her mother had switched from controlling her from a distance to a more hands-on approach, all while with the intention of helping her to make the best match possible. Despite Odette's dubious parentage, lack of breeding, and her mother's reputation (of which she had no disillusions), the actress had some high hopes for her, indeed. She fostered those hopes in Odette's education, her sponsorship generously provided by a prominent countess with ties to the throne, itself (the origins of said sponsorship were not something Odette had ever been brave enough to question), and the (adequately) pretty facade presented when she was swathed in gems and expensive fabrics.

That evening, her mother had truly gone over the top with her demands, seeming to take this ball for the Prince Regent's birthday particularly seriously, which only served to make Odette even more uncomfortable and nervous than usual. It was all rather absurd to be so shaky when it was her mother who was supposed to perform an aria in front of hundreds of guests to celebrate. A woman of many talents, her mother…

After literal hours, the two of them were finally deemed ready, her mother satisfied enough to qualify Odette as "presentable," they left for the party.

It turned out to be the most stunning, opulent event Odette ever could have imagined, and then some. She'd previously been either away at school or too young to attend in the past, so her first en-counter with the type of soiree put on by the Prince Regent was mem-orable, indeed.

The party was attended by the greatest peers of the realm, politi-cians, and even some visiting royalty. The flurry of embroidered, glit-tering, and be-plumed gowns was stunning; the men were all sharp in their immaculate evening kits. Even though Odette had silently thought herself gaudy and over-dressed back at home, she felt dowdy amongst the most beautiful people in London. Where exactly did she, the illegitimate daughter of a French actress, fit in? More importantly, why was she being forced to do so?

There was to be dancing and dinner, followed by a grand cake crafted by the royal baker. The confection was rumored to take up two entire tables with its towers, tiers, bridges, and delicate spun sugar creations. Erected on the far side of the ballroom was a raised dais swathed in royal purple velvet drapes and a gold emblem with the Prince's seal. He hadn't arrived yet and, no doubt, he wouldn't until the crush of guests ended and all eyes would be on him as a glorious spectacle.

Upon arrival, Odette's mother was quickly drawn into a large ador-ing crowd, as usual, leaving her unnoticed and off to the side. She was accustomed to being viewed as a hanger-on or a hired companion to the bewitching Stella Auclair. There was a certain freedom in this anonymity that would not have normally been afforded to her had she had her mother's full attention—or been viewed as a more respectable lady.

Odette snatched her opportunity and slipped away to retrieve a crystal cup of punch for herself. The heat of the room was already stifling and there was still at least another hour of guests filtering into the space.

Taking respite in her brief freedom, Odette sipped her punch and meandered slowly, performing a languid survey of the enormous glittering room with its high, painted ceilings and gilt trim as she stayed on its perimeter. She finally paused at the base of a soaring Corinthian column, tilting her head back to take in its impressive height and berth, the intricate carving soaring above her head.

As she lifted her cup to her lips again, however, a man bumped into her shoulder, hardly bothering to spare a glance in her direction as he murmured a hollow, automatic apology. The drink sloshed over the lip of the crystal cup all over the hem of her skirts…and down the leg of a nearby gentleman.

"Oh my goodness! I'm so, terribly, horribly sorry!" she stuttered frantically, frozen from mortification.

A large hand with elegant gloved fingers held out a crisp white handkerchief to her, but its owner said nothing. It was then that she finally looked up to see the handsome, angular face of the man to whom she'd spoken at the theater the other evening. Mr. Stratford. As handsome as she'd found him during their original meeting, he was stunning in the bright golden light of the ballroom, dressed in his immaculate formalwear. Hoping she didn't seem too much like a gaping trout, she accepted his proffered handkerchief to wipe the punch from her dove-gray glove.

"We do seem to meet under interesting circumstances, don't we, Miss Leroy?" There was an unexpected hint of lightness to his tone and he seemed rather unconcerned with the mess she'd made, the un-doubted stickiness he must have been experiencing as the punch soaked through and ruined the fine fabric of his breeches.

An eagle-eyed servant arrived to clean the spill and Mr. Stratford took her elbow to gently guide her a few feet away.

"Mr. Stratford," Odette began, hoping her heated cheeks weren't too glaringly obvious; "Please accept my sincerest apologies for spilling on you—and the evening has only just begun."

He waved away her words. "It is only clothing. And no one will be all that surprised to see me arrive in stained clothing. At least it's not ink."

She couldn't stop her smile. He was charming without trying, judging from the seriousness of his expression.

"Might I inquire as to what you were doing hiding in a corner?" he inquired with a touch of what seemed to be concern.

"I could ask you the same," she retorted.

"Much like the theater, I'm not entirely comfortable at these large social functions. I do it more for my family. I doubt that anyone would notice my absence, but my mother insists. In the name of keeping the peace, I dress as she tells me to and I arrive when and where she says I must. It was much easier to cry off when I was at University."

"I can sympathize with that," she admitted, though not quite ready to admit to the shocking degree that their lives seemed to run parallel. "And what is it that you would be doing if you hadn't been forced to attend this ball tonight?"

His eyes seemed fixed upon her futile attempts to scrub the punch from her gloves. "I'd likely be working all evening on my research. I'm co-authoring a paper with a colleague—the mathematician, Sir Nigel Wright. The deadline for our work is approaching and every one of these interruptions is putting me further and further back."

Odette nodded as if she could understand the pressing need to attend to an occupation outside of societal and familial obligations. Of course, she would have *liked* to have had something with which to occupy herself, but her mother was far more concerned with ensuring Odette's future than allowing her to discover a hobby or passion.

From their few interactions, she believed Mr. Stratford to be supremely intellectual, favoring knowledge over these preening peacocks of the *ton* with their rituals and their complex pecking order. Even better, he seemed unafraid of admitting it. She could appreciate that; even more, she could respect it.

Odette's hands stilled as the seconds ticked by and he still did not (politely) ask the same question of her. Rather than allow the silence to continue, she casually responded as if he had asked her anyway. "I am currently re-reading *Pride and Prejudice* by Miss Austen, but I've lately taken to poetry and the odd piece of political satire as a way to inject variety between popular novels. I'd likely be spending my evening reading if I were not here."

He tilted his head and she had the sense that he was examining her very, very carefully. Those unique eyes of his stared straight into her soul, sending a chill traipsing up and down her spine. It was unfamiliar, but not unpleasant.

Before they could speak further, there was a shout of music to announce the arrival of the Prince Regent. As one, the massive crowd turned toward the dais and began to ripple in a wave of bows and curtseys. Naturally, Odette and Simon followed suit. Just as they'd both been trained to do.

Odette had only seen the Prince Regent in person once before. Her mother had insisted upon presenting her at Court when she came of age. There, amongst the titled, lovely young ladies of the *ton* crammed together and waiting for their turn to be announced and unleashed upon Society, she'd felt like an ugly duckling, indeed. Her mother had called in a great favor to find her a sponsor to present her. It had all seemed so vitally important to her that Odette couldn't say no, no matter her anxieties.

Odette had stood in line along with the other swans in the sea of white—pearls, feathers, lace, and satin clouds, all of them. She'd felt like an impostor and swore every one of those girls knew her for what she was.

The Regent, with his fair, flushed features and tall, paunchy build had been undeniably bored and disinterested, slouching low in his throne and waving each girl by with hardly a glance spared. When he'd heard her name accompanied by that of her unlikely sponsor, the Countess of Aethelton, his pale eyes had flitted over to her, taken her in from head to toe, and—she couldn't help but feel—found her coming up short.

That night, even across the crowded room of the party, Odette found him imposing and intimidating.

"I seem to have missed the mark on tonight's dress code," Mr. Stratford whispered for only her hearing. "Mother will be so disappointed in me."

Odette struggled to stifle a giggle when she realized he was referencing the Regent's elaborately tied cravat, his coat bedecked in superfluous medals and garish, clashing colors of his coat and waistcoat. It was all cut in the highest of fashions, trimmed in glittering gems and gold thread, but meant to flatter a figure much trimmer than the one Prinny was currently sporting.

"Odette!" She sobered and straightened instantly at the sound of her mother's voice. Her blonde head appeared around the column and Odette didn't miss the keen glimmer in her eyes as she took in the sight of her daughter speaking to a well-dressed man. "My dear, who is your friend?" she asked, extending her gloved hand with its glittering ring. This one wasn't made of paste, but a large yellow sapphire gifted to her some three years prior by a man whose name Odette couldn't recall.

"Mr. Simon Stratford," Odette offered, experiencing an odd pang in her chest as he bent over her mother's hand. It had felt so freeing to have this one interaction, this one acquaintance, away from her mother's ministrations and prying eyes, and here it had come to a swift and decisive end. "Mr. Stratford, Mademoiselle Stella Auclair. My mother." Though the last earned her a glare, Odette didn't mind. She couldn't have explained why, but it was very important to her that there were no false pretenses where Mr. Stratford was involved. It simply felt wrong—especially when he seemed to be nothing but full of candor.

Her mother's assessing gaze swept over Mr. Stratford's lean, tall form; she'd always prided herself on knowing everyone worth knowing in Town (especially everyone with a title or fortune) and it was clear she'd also recognized him as the second son of the Earl of Aldborough. She'd stood over her shoulder while Odette had been forced to memorize the more important families listed in Debrette's.

Her mother easily fell into her role of a charming actress, the one that earned her entrée into some of the higher strata of society despite her Frenchness and lowly origins, the tone that helped gain significant donations from the patrons of The Mask and Lyre, the sultry voice that kept her in fine clothes and gems.

"How kind of you to locate my wayward daughter for me, Mr. Stratford. She looked at him from beneath her long, dark lashes, her eyes rimmed with a seductive sweep of kohl to accentuate their striking paleness.

"She seems to have discovered my hiding place rather than the other way around."

Her mother loosed a low laugh and continued to hold onto Mister Stratford's hand as if to impress upon him how charming she found his comment. To her amusement, Odette realized she already knew him well enough to recognize there was no intentional humor in his comment. She pulled her lower lip between her teeth, trying not to smile when he looked questioningly at her. He seemed to struggle for something else to say.

"I…saw your performance the other night. I found it quite well done." He looked more than slightly taken aback when her mother caressed his arm as she thanked him for his compliment.

"You're too kind, sir! I'm honored to have such an admirer."

Again, he cast a searching glance at Odette, a blatantly baffled expression painted upon his attractive face. She offered him a sympathetic smile. She, of all people, recognized how her mother could be overly enthusiastic and Odette knew first-hand that it could be overwhelming to some personalities. Apparently, poor Mr. Stratford fell into that category.

"I'm terribly sorry, but you will have to excuse us." Only Odette could hear that there wasn't the barest hint of honest contrition in her mother's voice. "I've some acquaintances to greet and Odette should attend; wouldn't want anyone to claim I was remiss in my duties as a chaperone," she added flippantly and slipped her arm through

Odette's, barely giving her time to tuck Mr. Stratford's handkerchief back into his hand and cast him a little wave of gratitude.

Once they were a safe distance away and somewhat concealed by another clutch of partygoers, her mother patted her hand.

"You did well catching the eye of an earl's second son, but I believe we can do better, Odette—perhaps a first-born son with a much lesser title." To Odette's mortification, she could hear the gears and wheels of her mother's mind running furiously. "Then again…" she trailed off as she scanned the room; "Viscount Sommerfeld and his wife still haven't produced an heir after a few years of marriage…nor did the viscountess produce issue in her first marriage, and that one had lasted quite some time until the old baron's passing. Perhaps there remains a chance that Mr. Stratford or his offspring could inherit the Aldborough Earldom in the future…if the viscount doesn't tire of his barren wife and have the marriage dissolved upon the basis of impotency before then. Despite the unfortunate limp, he still appears remarkably robust; still young and virile." Her mother gestured with a tilt of one well-shaped brow to a tall, dashing blond man leaning lightly on a cane; he stood beside a smiling, beautiful, fire-haired woman—clearly the subjects of her mother's salacious one-sided conversation. "Or," her mother lowered her voice conspiratorially, "maybe the fault lies with him and no amount of wives will cure what ails him—perhaps his injury involves more than just his leg. All the better for the younger son, no?" She snapped open the hand-painted fan hanging from her wrist and fluttered the implement before her face in the fashion of a hummingbird's wing, giving Odette only glimpses of the cruel tilt of her painted lips.

Odette nearly swallowed her tongue, shocked into silence by her mother's curt discussion of such vile gossip. She was, as yet, unused to this cutthroat world of the *ton*, but even this felt as if it bordered on cruelty. Lately, her mother had been a great deal freer in divulging such knowledge as a means of better preparing Odette for the Marriage Mart now that she viewed her daughter as a woman. After all, how could she ever hope to snag the right husband if she didn't know the ins and outs of every one of her options…and opponents?

Odette chanced a glance over her shoulder back at Mr. Stratford and she was surprised (and more than a little thrilled) to find him watching her with his mesmerizing, intelligent eyes. Of course, her mother hadn't missed the tiny gesture.

"Perhaps," she mused; "you should encourage the attentions of Mr. Stratford. I've heard he's slightly odd, but he seemed stable enough to me. Even if it never comes of anything, there is always the chance that he could introduce you into the right circles. The entrée he and his family can provide could prove invaluable."

Odette's eyes turned down to her punch-stained gloves and she stopped listening to her mother's plotting. It turned her stomach to think of turning whatever warm feelings she experienced with Mr. Stratford into something grasping and sordid. They'd only had two interactions, but she'd left each one feeling…something. Something warm and comforting. Something she knew would make her smile long after the candle was doused and she was alone in the dark replaying the day's events.

She pasted on a pleasant expression, hoping it didn't seem too contrived and that all those years of watching her mother rehearse would pay off.

Later in the evening, George and Meredith located Simon in a corner of the ballroom. He'd been occupied counting the hours until he would be able to leave, but their interruption was not unwelcome. The dancing had begun and he was dodging his mother's eyes so she wouldn't try to force him into asking some poor chit to dance. With any luck, this conversation would help him kill some time and avoid the dance floor.

Simon smiled in greeting to his sister-in-law and pleasantries were exchanged.

"George told me you'd been to the theater recently. I've been trying to coerce him into taking me to the new production at The Mask and Lyre. How did you find it?" Meredith asked. Given his conversation with George, Simon might have expected a less polished version of her, though he'd always known her to present a stiff upper lip no matter the circumstances. As collected as she appeared, Simon noted the steady arm his brother kept at Meredith's back, providing her unwavering support both literal and unspoken. For all his disinterest in the affairs of others, Simon was capable of caring deeply for certain individuals; and he certainly hoped George was able to be whatever Meredith needed. She'd been that for George ten times over by now.

That evening, Meredith wore a high-waisted gown in hunter green, the pleated skirts revealing alternating darts of a paler shade of green to match the gossamer cap sleeves on her pale shoulders. Pearls and emeralds snaked around her neck and were woven throughout her flame-colored curls. His brother had chosen a singular beauty for a bride, but Simon found her intelligence to be far more fascinating and endearing than something so fleeting as appearances. Uncommonly perceptive, she'd always been deferential to and respectful of Simon's mannerisms…but this also gifted her with a tenacity to uncover anything to which she put her mind. It was safer for all parties involved if she wasn't privy to all but the barest of facts. Woe to all of them if she and their sister, Lily, were ever working in tandem; a right pair of Bow Street Runners, they were.

"Well enough," Simon replied brusquely, deliberately choosing not to elaborate.

"I think he was more intrigued by the crowd backstage than the actual performance," intoned George, to which Simon rolled his eyes—his brother's ribbing hadn't been lost on anyone in their little corner. Unfortunately.

Glancing between the brothers, Meredith perked up. "A woman caught your attention?" Meredith's indigo eyes twinkled in interest. "Who is she?"

Simon swore silently. This line of questioning made him instantly uncomfortable. He didn't like brushing Meredith off because she never did that to him; but if anyone could pry information out of him, then it was his sister-in-law…and George likely knew that.

Were Simon a man prone to irrational violence, then he would have liked to have throttled his brother right then and there. This had been precisely what he'd been trying to avoid. An interrogation had not been on his list of tasks to survive that week.

Instead, Simon opted for an easier explanation and scanned the room, spotting Odette. Quite remarkably, she seemed to be the center of quite a bit of attention at the moment. She was lively and graceful in her dewdrop-blue gown, its gossamer overskirts embroidered in silver thread and dotted with brilliants. The low neckline accentuated her generous curves, the soft pale slope of her throat and shoulders beneath more layers of filmy, fluttering fabric flowing like waves lapping at the pristine shore of her arms as she moved. She wore a delicate silver chain and a large, bright blue gem at her throat that danced as she breathed and glittered when she laughed. Her hair was piled atop her head in an artful sculpture of curls and silver ribbon. In a word, she looked breathtaking.

Simon tilted his chin in her direction as she was spun in the arms of the Prince Regent, himself.

"There," he said.

Meredith stood on her toes to peer over the crowd. "Where? What is she wearing?"

"Do try not to be so obvious, dear; we wouldn't want to mortify poor Simon in front of his first real paramour." George chuckled and placed a hand on his wife's shoulder.

"She's not a paramour," Simon commented drolly; "and she's wearing blue and silver."

"Blue and silver?" Meredith mumbled to herself over and over as her eyes scanned the crowd in the direction to which Simon had gestured.

"That's not her with Prinny, is it?" George asked suddenly, his green eyes widening as they fell upon Odette.

"Indeed," Simon said, a tone in his voice rather close to smugness. They'd probably believed he'd been lying or she had a hunchback or a fifth limb—to be fair, he didn't know with complete certainty that the last wasn't true, but he could make a reasonable guess that it wasn't.

There were several moments where all three watched as Odette moved in the center of the dance floor.

"Good on you," George finally said with a note of disbelief he wasn't quite able to disguise. Meredith placed a chiding hand on George's arm, likely hoping to stave off any further brotherly taunting.

"She looks like a very lovely young woman," she added to soften her husband's comment.

Simon smiled in return but said nothing, settling instead for watching Odette from afar.

Sensing his unwillingness to elaborate, Meredith skillfully steered George to another topic. "Are you up for taking another turn around the room yet, George? The evening is still young and there are yet many more hours of standing and milling and mingling ahead."

"Oh lovely," George replied dramatically but willingly held out his arm to his wife. His leg prevented him from partaking in the dancing, but he and Meredith had worked out a sort of routine over the past few years. She would dance when invited, but he would stand as a statuesque presence on the periphery of the dance floor, ready to scoop her back up as soon as the set was finished. Simon knew it was far from what George would have preferred, but it worked for them.

Both their bodies and their voices were swallowed up in the swelling crowd as Simon continued to watch Odette spin in the arms of the Prince Regent.

There was a becoming color high in her cheeks and her pale blue eyes were glittering. He felt inexplicably drawn to her, like a magnet with an opposing charge. He'd never experienced such a sensation—he'd only ever viewed women as a natural urge which he'd routinely resolved with the occasional visit to a high-end bordello catering to London's elite. Never before had he enjoyed speaking so casually with a woman, and he excluded Meredith from that number only because it didn't seem fair to include one's sister-in-law. Odette was amusing, slightly clumsy and charming. She seemed not to find him the least bit boring and had yet to make him feel like he was unpleasant to be around. It was…nice.

He was sincerely doubting it at that point, but, even if Blackwood was right and she might take after her mother's carnal appetites and looser morals, who was he to push her away? She fascinated him. She drew him in. She possessed some indefinable quality Simon simply couldn't ignore. Ever since their meeting at the theater, a tiny seed

had been planted and taken careful root in the caverns of his mind…
and ignoring it was not an option for him.

Odette was nearly breathless when the dance was finished and she
dipped into a low, carefully rehearsed curtsy to her partner. She had
hardly believed it when the Prince Regent interrupted her conversation with another guest and asked her to dance (the word "ask" was
used loosely…a prince did not ask for a dance, one simply accepted
without question or hesitation when he held out his hand). While
they'd spun with all the eyes of the *ton* upon them, he'd actually pep-
pered her with little inquiries—about her life, her education, whether
she was enjoying herself at his party. She'd never expected him to see
her or notice her, let alone ask her to dance or make polite conversation with her. It had been a heady interaction, indeed.

He was tall—taller than he'd looked from afar or when he'd been
reclining negligently in his chair at her debut—and the iciness of his
eyes set deep in his paunchy cheeks was unexpectedly keen. The
whole of England knew of this man's excesses and his mercurial tem-
peraments, his trend toward overindulgence, and the harsh treatment
of his wife, Princess Caroline, but he moved with surprising ease and
carried himself with the mien of a man who'd been born to staggering
privilege. There was no hint of cruelty or lasciviousness or volatility
in his interaction with Odette, only polite (if shallow) conversation
and the twists and turns of the dance as everyone else looked on. He
didn't smile at her and she would have feared he found her halting
answers unbearably dull, but his countenance was not unkind. It was
intimidating to be sought out and then become the unwitting center of
attention; to be yanked from the natural state of existence as an unre-
markable wallflower and deposited into the arms of the most powerful

man in the country. But Odette had done it. And she was rather proud of herself.

With the dance completed, he deposited her once more at her mother's side. The Prince Regent very shortly thereafter took his leave to replenish his energy for more dancing with food and drink, and Odette didn't see him up close for the rest of the evening. He danced several more times, though those were less graceful as his drinking increased.

Her mother, on the other hand, had acted quite unexpectedly. Odette hadn't expected her to be so reserved, especially after her daughter had been so very much on prominent display while in the arms of the guest of honor. She was oddly quiet, in fact.

That was, until Mr. Stratford emerged from the crowd, head and shoulders above the other men.

He bowed over Odette's hand and asked if he might pencil in his name for a dance—if she had any available, that was. To say Odette was stunned was an understatement. Other than the Prince Regent, her dance card was, as yet, entirely empty. Too taken aback to reply, she could only dumbly hold out her arm with the card and string wrapped around her wrist. As he used the dangling pencil to write his name in his chosen line, her mother caught her eye. Seemingly much recovered from whatever had struck her, there was a definite look of triumph on her face—markedly different from the mask she'd donned after the Prince Regent had taken his leave.

Unaware of the silent conversation between mother and daughter, Simon held out his arm to Odette and led her to the dance floor, moving with an uncommon grace and an elegance she hadn't expected.

"You dance beautifully," Odette couldn't help but extend the compliment as he expertly guided her around a turn.

He inclined his head in thanks. "I usually detest the spectacle."

"You're remarkably talented for disliking it."

"My fencing practice must be put to good use," he replied noncha-
lantly. "Similar muscles."

Odette silently agreed, feeling the smooth, powerful movements of
his lean body beneath her fingers; his impeccable posture as he guided
her across the floor. She was still lost in her silent admiration when
next he spoke.

"I should like to call on you if you'll allow me to." The words were
said so suddenly and with so little emotion that Odette wasn't sure she
heard the words correctly. She met his blue-green eyes and the sincerity she witnessed caused her to momentarily lose her footing. Thankfully, he easily recovered from her slip-up and disguised it as the skill-
ful partner he was.

Though her mouth opened and closed a few times, she couldn't
speak; no man had ever asked her such a thing before in the several
years since her debut; no man had been interested—either finding her
face or her personality lacking or believing her to be wholly unsuitable because of the accident of her birth. She couldn't blame them entirely. Despite her mother's best efforts, Odette could be polished and
dressed to perfection, but she would always be the illegitimate daughter of an actress.

A niggling part of her wondered if this could possibly be some cruel joke, but meeting Mr. Stratford's eyes put all of that to rest.

His remarkable eyes were truth personified.

This was a man to whom artifice held no attraction.

She hardly knew him—had only met him on two occasions—but
she trusted him. She could only describe it as a warm, comfortable
feeling filling her gut each time their eyes met.

Though his beautiful face remained impassive, something was
lurking behind his eyes, some vulnerability that she saw there and it

made her quickly nod her head in mute agreement, a heated blush covering her face like a veil. His gloved fingers tightened very slightly on hers and they continued into the next turn of the steps.

Before she knew it, the dance was completed and Mr. Stratford deposited her back with her mother. Even though he retreated for the remainder of the evening and her dance card was soon filled with names of other men curious to discover why she (of all the other young women in attendance) had gotten the attention of the Prince Regent, and they were seated far apart at dinner due to the order of precedence, Odette swore she could feel Mr. Stratford's eyes upon her through it all.

In the wee hours of the following morning when she lay awake in bed after they finally returned home, she recalled the highlight of her evening not as her dance with the Prince Regent, but hiding behind a column and a potted plant with a slightly odd, but still impossibly charming, Mr. Stratford.

Chapter Three

The next few weeks felt to Odette to be either a dream or some vicious prank.

In between his work, Mr. Stratford frequently came to call upon her at the West End flat she shared with her mother, though she couldn't have begun to guess how he'd learned of the address. Surely incomprehensible resources were available to those with the money to access them.

Although he maintained his reserved nature throughout, Odette managed to coax a smile or two from his handsome lips, confirming her suspicions that the gesture would brighten up his entire face. His eyes would crinkle charmingly and his normally staid expression became almost boyish in comparison to his usual air of almost aloofness.

As she came to know him better, however, she learned he was not aloof; rather, he was infinitely thoughtful and perceptive. He examined everything, weighed each of his words, and seemed to watch her with a keenness that made her skin tingle. He made her feel interesting; he made her feel heard.

Of course, she also came to learn that his manners were imperfect, though Odette knew it was not from lack of breeding or education. He seemed to miss some cues and she quickly recognized this was not done out of mal-intent or disrespect.

Once, when he accompanied her and her mother out to shop one afternoon, he failed to offer her his arm. The gesture wasn't unnoticed by her mother, who raised a brow. Not wanting her mother to think ill of him, Odette gently asked Mr. Stratford if he might kindly assist her. He all but jumped at her soft nudge back to social propriety and they resumed their excursion without further incident. He was obviously willing to adjust his manners and, indeed, seemed to *want* to dote, but simply wasn't all that certain *how*.

She made occasional inquiries into his work, but, rather than open up to her about it, he seemed to withdraw into himself—almost as if he was afraid to speak too much about his interests. He glossed over it, simply stating it involved mathematics one time, and answering that it built upon some of the work developing in France another. Were she less perceptive, then Odette might have feared he believed her too dim to understand; instead, she recognized his hesitancy was born from a life of being told he was boring or uninteresting.

How amusing she found it that Mr. Stratford believed *he* was the uninteresting one!

His visits gradually increased in length and frequency as he seemed to take pleasure in her company. To her delight, his touch would sometimes linger upon her arm and his eyes would follow her intently. No other man had ever looked at Odette in such a way and it thrilled her, but it also made her feel uneasy—as if this was not reality.

Had he been a more socially cunning or contrived man, she might have been inclined to believe that it was all a joke ("let's seduce the awkward daughter of the scandalous actress"), but she didn't sense a conniving, cruel bone in his entire body. She quite sensed that this was the last sort of prank he would play upon her or anyone else.

After four weeks of his visits and obligatory tokens of flowers and even a couple of books of poetry by some of her favorite authors (she had noticed early on that he was a careful listener and she had only to mention something once for him to pick up on it), her mother began to comment on Mr. Stratford's earnest interest.

"You know, my dear," her mother said one evening as she reclined post-performance in embroidered silken robes, sipping from a glass of claret; "this Mr. Stratford is quite taken with you. Perhaps more than you're even aware."

Odette flushed and looked down to her fingers where she picked at a loose thread on her skirt.

"And I can tell you're a bit smitten as well," her mother continued smugly.

"I thought you said I could do better than a second son of an earl," Odette said more icily than she'd intended. Somehow, along the way, she'd grown protective of Mr. Stratford. There was an innocence about him she wanted to shelter and nurture, like a dog who had been weaned on neglect and subsisted on a diet of scraps. He didn't always know how to behave or react when shown attention, but he always accepted it with tentative grace.

There was a rustle of fabric as her mother shrugged in her typically Gallic fashion. "Who are we to snub our noses at such an opportunity?" This was so like her mother, to see her daughter's blossoming courtship as an opportunity for advancement rather than a chance for her daughter to find her own happiness. Odette had always known her mother was far from a romantic; she never understood if the jadedness came from her own complicated romantic entanglements or playing role after role where she was the object of desire, though.

Perhaps Estelle Auclair believed romance was *only* for the stage.

"I think," her mother continued; "we should use Mr. Stratford's interest to our advantage. You've already charmed him and he so obviously finds you to his tastes from the way he looks at you. He's handsome enough, if somewhat peculiar. If you can tolerate this, then pursue him back. He doesn't seem like the type who would ever do you harm, though it is sometimes difficult to tell in the first blooms of attraction."

Odette looked up and frowned at her mother. "What are you saying?"

"What I'm saying is you have the buck in your trap…it's time to pull the snare." Her mother's voice was deadly calm and unnervingly even.

"I don't want to trap him," Odette replied, horrified. "Can't we just allow things to play out as they will? You said so yourself that he likes me—"

"A man like Stratford will dawdle for months, if not a year or more," she cut Odette off in a tone that brooked no comment. "We don't have the luxury of allowing him to slip away after dedicating all this time and effort. Though you possess an education to rival even the most high-born of ladies, very little will overcome your breeding," she spat the last like a curse, her French accent becoming more pronounced with her emotions. She had always known her mother's temper would burst forth full force if she allowed herself to slip fully into French.

Odette's mouth narrowed to a fine, taut line. Short of chasing off Mr. Stratford, she knew there was little she could do to stop her mother once she'd set her sights on something. This was the way things had always been: She claimed the role she wanted, she procured the protector upon whom she'd set her sights, and she imposed her will upon Odette with fierce determination.

Torn between wanting to spare Mr. Stratford from her mother's machinations and terrified of pushing away such a kind, interesting, earnest man, Odette was forced to silently succumb to her mother's wishes.

*****

As it turned out, her mother's plot began to include a great deal of poor chaperoning. She'd leave Odette and Mr. Stratford alone in a room when he came to call, or bow out and dare to let them go on an outing alone and unattended. Unfortunately for her mother, it seemed that she'd either miscalculated Mr. Stratford's honor or overestimated his ability to recognize exactly the opportunities as they presented themselves because his manners remained unchanged.

Odette had to stop herself from smiling as he'd continue a conversation as if they weren't alone, or when he made no move to compromise her or coax her into a situation or embrace that Odette didn't doubt any number of other men of the peerage would have taken advantage. He remained distant, if still attentive in his ways, and oblivious to the opportunities afforded him by her mother's questionable behavior. For her part, Odette refused to comply with her mother, and she, too, continued as if nothing had changed. However, if anything, she found herself more drawn to Mr. Stratford than before. The evidence of his honor and respect were more endearing and charming to Odette than any ode or words of flattery.

But a kiss from those mesmerizing lips of his might not have been entirely unwelcome.

Things continued on much in this manner for another two weeks; however, unfortunately for Odette, this peace was not to last.

She should have known her mother would grow impatient…she just didn't realize the lengths to which she would go to see her plan to fruition.

Her mother had been invited to a dinner party thrown by an obscure member of the royal family—some earl whose bloodline put him fourteenth or fifteenth in line for the throne. Odette had been invited by proxy and her mother, ever charming and able to get her wishes, was able to procure another space for Mr. Stratford to attend as their escort.

Though unaware of the plot simmering just beneath the surface, Odette had still been nervous about presenting the invitation to him. This would be an intimate party where he'd undoubtedly have to interact with nearly every guest.

His acceptance had surprised her, though the look she'd encountered in his sharp blue-green eyes told her he'd done so for her and only her.

And it made her positively tingly.

Odette practically floated as she entered the party on Mr. Stratford's arm. He looked immaculate and regal in his evening-wear; his lean frame was dashing and the endearing tilt of his lips when he saw her made her fragile heart flutter in excitement. At her mother's behest, she'd donned an ivory lace-trimmed gown with puffed sleeves and gold embroidery that shone when she moved in the candlelight. For once in her life she felt dainty and delicate on Mr. Stratford's steady, strong arm.

She felt more confident with him by her side.

It seemed that, separately, neither of them fared well in these social situations; together, however, they found a rhythm and a confidence that had previously eluded them. They made small talk, taking a pass of the room with a surety neither knew that they possessed. They'd even shared a few amusing, knowing looks when some other guests would make ignorant or inane comments. It would seem that they had come to share a sense of humor after all the time spent together.

Shortly before dinner was announced, Mr. Stratford was coaxed into a conversation with an acquaintance of his father's. Odette was content to observe the exchange, subtly admiring his profile and the perfection of his cheekbones, but she was interrupted by the hostess.

"Your mother has asked that I pull you away. She has need of you in the powder room," the older woman whispered.

Wondering what her mother could have done—perhaps lost a hair-pin or needed an adjustment to her skirts—Odette politely excused herself and left Mr. Stratford's side.

She did her best to tamp down her sense of excitement at his flick-er of regret when she took her leave.

Following the hostess's instructions, Odette exited the parlor and made her way down the hallway, locating the powder room with ease. She found her mother strategically adjusting a blond curl in the mirror a moment before she glanced up and caught Odette's reflection over her shoulder.

"You wanted to see me?" Odette asked, shutting the door behind her and noting that they were the only two in the room. Her mother gave her a cool smile, but didn't turn from the mirror.

"Yes; I wanted to see how your evening is going."

"Fine," Odette replied cautiously, unsure why she needed to be pulled away for such a question.

"And Mr. Stratford seems attentive—rather much more so than usual," her mother added.

"Neither of us knows many people here," Odette offered as an ex-planation.

Her mother finally turned and addressed her directly. "You've managed to captivate him, but he still doesn't seem much closer to offering for you." Odette wasn't sure if this was meant as a statement or an admonishment, so she said nothing in response. "I suppose some men simply move more slowly than others." Her mother glanced at the tiny clock set into the backside of the pendant dangling from the glittering chain at her neck. She looked striking in her deep mauve gown, which contrasted sharply with her porcelain features and honey-gold hair. "Come," she said, offering her arm to Odette; "we've been away far too long and it simply doesn't do to duck out on one's hosts."

Still confused by the situation, Odette accepted her mother's proffered arm and, together, they stepped out into the hallway and slowly began to make their way back to the party. It was all Odette could do not to drag her mother along behind her when she insisted upon a snail's pace.

"You know I've always done what I thought was best for you, Odette," her mother said suddenly, seeming more sincere than Odette had heard in a long while.

"Yes, *maman*," Odette replied softly, curious to see where this turn would lead.

"And everything I have foisted upon you was only so you would have more stability than I had at your age." Odette nodded mutely. Though she didn't always feel appreciated by her mother and she sometimes had difficulties accepting her methods, she couldn't deny that she'd benefitted from an enviable education and finishing; she'd been prepared for a life in Society and afforded opportunities of which her mother could never have dreamt. "Good."

They stopped in the middle of the hallway, halfway to the open door of the parlor filled with guests, its golden light slashing across the floor like a beacon. Her mother turned to face her and adjusted a lock of Odette's hair in a gesture that would have seemed motherly had it come from anyone else.

"I hope you never forget that all I do is for you," her mother said almost gently.

Odette opened her mouth to speak, but, in one swift movement, her mother reached around her, thrust open the door at Odette's back, and shoved her into darkness. Odette landed backward with a yelp against something hard and warm as the door slammed in her face.

Simon stumbled backward further into the pitch-dark room as something soft and fragrant and decidedly female-shaped collided with him. Momentarily blinded by a brief flash of light when the door was opened, he struggled to regain his footing and wound up collapsing haphazardly into a chair. He narrowly managed to gain his seat instead of tumbling to the floor in a heap. He gripped a pair of soft upper arms in his hands, a heavy curtain of skirts and a delightfully round bottom landed in his lap. The woman stiffened against him.

He knew in an instant exactly the woman he held in his arms.

He recognized her height, the feel of her skin, her delicate scent of clean powder and lilacs.

"Miss Leroy?" he inquired into the darkness.

"Mr. Stratford?" she breathed in a disoriented response.

"What the deuce is going on here?" he demanded, becoming more and more aware of the weight of her upon his lap, the way her curves nestled against him so perfectly.

"I—I don't, that is, I'm not sure..." she stuttered and stammered, grasping for a response, seemingly as taken aback as he by their sudden predicament.

"One minute I was being shown into the room by a servant, told a message had arrived from my family; the next, the door was shut behind me and I was thrust into darkness. I don't understand." Simon didn't care for surprises, nor did he enjoy situations where he felt lost.

Was there something he was missing?

Something he couldn't grasp?

Odette wriggled against him.

"Please, I know as little as you do. Let me up," she frantically breathed against him, the blackness filled with the sound of her rustling skirts as she attempted to stand. One of the layers tugged at his boot and he realized she was caught beneath his heel.

"Wait, let me—" He had to catch her and place her in his lap once more as she teetered precariously. Better to save her from smashing her pretty face upon the floor.

With some difficulty, he began to disentangle the layers of her lacy skirts from both their legs using touch and intuition alone. In doing so, he had to hold her flush to his body, pressing her chest against his so closely that he could feel the pounding of her heart beneath her ample breast. He struggled to remain composed beneath this onslaught of sensations; each of his other senses heightened since his sight had been stolen.

He was agonizingly aware of her short, rapid breaths against his cheek, the sweet exquisite scent of her flesh filling his nostrils, the cool softness of her silken stocking as he inadvertently brushed her calf with the back of his hand.

When she was finally free, he sat up and found that he was loath to release her.

Judging by the warmth he felt from her nearness, the gentle, sweet puffs of her breath, their faces were mere inches apart. How many times had he wondered what she would taste of? How many times had he watched those delectable lips of hers move as she spoke, and ponder what they would feel like against his?

Just as Simon began to incline his head to act upon those desires, the door to the room was flung open wide, blinding them both in a hellish onslaught of golden candlelight. They both flinched back from the glare, squinting against the illumination and struggling to focus their eyes.

"Odette!" cried her mother's unmistakable voice. Simon blinked several times before he was finally able to make out several barely discernible faces silhouetted by the backlighting. "*And Mister Stratford!*" Mademoiselle Auclair's hand flew to her neck in a gesture of shock and awe, the other began to fan her face as if a faint was imminent. Their host steadied her elbow while another male guest whom Simon didn't recognize chimed in.

"What is the meaning of this? An illicit tryst?" There was no mistaking the venomous glee in the man's voice.

It took Simon several moments to realize how the situation actually appeared. He turned his head to Miss Leroy, still in shock in his arms, swung across his lap, her skirts in disarray. As quickly as he could, he stood and helped her find her footing.

"That's not what transpired," he attempted to defend the scene, but he could already tell it was a losing battle. Miss Leroy, however, was either more adamant or less aware of this fact.

"Mr. Stratford has never had untoward attentions—this is all a misunderstanding. He was shut in this room awaiting a message. I was accompanying my mother back to the parlor and—"

"But Odette," her mother interrupted her, her large, beautiful eyes wide and doe-like as their host continued to support her arm; "you never came to meet me in the powder room. I stopped waiting for you and went back to the parlor alone, assuming you'd been held up by a conversation."

Odette's mouth snapped shut.

Simon was unable to read her expression, but her crystalline eyes grew wide and suspiciously bright.

"It would seem that she'd been waylaid by something else, indeed," chimed in the other nameless guest, wicked delight in every syllable.

Immediately, Simon, Miss Leroy, and her mother were shown into another sitting room where they could speak in private. They all knew that the closed door was only an illusion; there was likely at least one person lingering outside hoping to capture a juicy tidbit to feed to everyone like a scrap to ravenous wolves. Doubtless, the rest of the party had long since learned of the titillating scene that had been discovered when their host had offered to show off a rare book in his collection.

"This is entirely unacceptable, as I'm sure you're aware, Mr. Stratford," the older woman addressed him. "It is one thing to hold hands or steal a kiss or two, but *this*…" She seemed rather well-recovered; her color was much higher than it had been when there was more of an audience.

"I assure you, Mademoiselle Auclair, that the situation is not what it appeared to be," Simon tried to remain calm and sound reassuring, but the blood pounded nearly deafening in his ears.

"And if that is the case…*if* that is not the way it appeared… Well, if I have learned one thing from my time amongst your kind here in London, it's that they care little for the truth and far more for appearances." Her French accent became more pronounced as she continued, her tirade gaining speed, though never losing focus. "Do you think

one person here will believe that what we just witnessed was innocent?"

"But—" Miss Leroy attempted to interject, but she was swiftly cut
off.

"And what of her reputation? My daughter's name will be slan-
dered. Every ounce of meager respectability she has will lay in
tatters."

Simon risked a glance at Miss Leroy as her mother railed. He
briefly frowned when he saw a flicker of tears in her eyes before she
turned them down to her hands clenched so tightly before her.

How had this night gone so horribly awry?

"Then what would you suggest, Mademoiselle?" Simon asked her
mother, forestalling any further impassioned monologue she might
have spewed.

"Why, Monsieur Stratford, I would suggest you marry her."

*****

Several exhausting hours later, Odette and her mother finally returned
to their flat. Odette had remained stubbornly, painfully silent as her
mother had made their excuses to the rest of the party and then on the
carriage ride home. Now, as they were alone, all of the pain of her
mother's betrayal spilled over following her mother's bright statement
that, "That all went rather well."

"*Well?*" demanded Odette, raising her voice to her mother for perhaps the first time in her life. "You call that 'rather well?' You plotted
the whole thing; you shoved me into his arms without so much as a
'by your leave.' You entrapped him. You entrapped both of us."
Odette sobbed and swiped at the tears coursing down her cheeks,
staining her ivory gloves beyond all repair. She was tired of bottling
up the storm brewing deep inside her and she unleashed her anger and
pain in great gusts of emotion.

In the face of Odette's pain and tears, her mother simply crossed her hands before her and tilted her head.

"He didn't have to agree to marry you, but he did," she said matter-of-factly. "And you said so, yourself, that you cared for him. What is the problem?"

"Did you ever once bother to consider that I might desire a marriage born of love instead of entrapment? You've stolen that chance from me—from Mr. Stratford as well.

"Even if there had been a chance that we might one day love one another, you've unforgivably forced our hands. We'll never know for sure what might have been." Odette's chest heaved and ached.

Her mother scoffed. "Do stop being so fanciful, *ma fille cherie*; I thought you were past the point of fairy tales. No one truly marries for love, not if they want security."

"I refuse to believe that," she snapped at her mother, tearing off her ruined gloves and throwing them at the chaise; the result was less satisfying than she'd intended. "Just because you weren't able to hold onto your love doesn't mean love doesn't exist." The words struck her mother as if she'd been slapped across the face. Several tense moments of silence ensued; both women were wounded in ways they'd never believed the other would strike.

"You heard me," Odette panted, practically trembling with emotion; "I've always realized the truth of it. You loved my father—whoever he is—but you couldn't keep him for yourself. It is why you've always been so restless; you've moved on from one position to the next, one lover to the next, never willing to settle down despite the proposals and offers of protection. Just because it ended poorly for you doesn't mean love cannot work for someone else."

Odette stormed past her mother before she could reply.

Chapter Four

The next afternoon, Odette received a letter from Mr. Stratford. The writing was as straightforward and unpretentious as its author; his handwriting was neat and orderly, painstakingly legible. In it, he told her that he'd explained the engagement to his parents. Their response had been to procure a special license and, given the circumstances, to retreat to Bridleton, their estate in Kent, to prepare for the wedding in two weeks. After all, the official start to the Season had not yet begun, so they wouldn't be missing much in Town anyway.

The next part made the parchment tremble in her fingers. She and her mother were formally invited by the Earl and Countess of Aldborough to stay at the estate so they might have the wedding in Kent and their families could become better acquainted.

Odette had hardly seen and not spoken to her mother since their confrontation. She doubted she'd ever forgive her for her machinations and she knew her mother held fierce grudges; she'd likely not forgotten Odette's cruel words about love. This letter begged a reply she was unable to provide without her mother's approval, so there was no avoiding a conversation, no matter how much the thought made her stomach churn. She'd known her mother to be a woman who would stop at nothing to get what she wanted or what she felt she deserved, Odette just hadn't realized that those ambitions could extend to her own daughter, and to such an unfathomable depth.

She found her mother in her rooms, readying herself to rest before that night's performance. On the side table sat a delicate china cup Odette knew had contained warm honeyed water—a remedy her mother swore kept her voice in good condition after seemingly endless rehearsals and performances. She was dressed only in her pristine white shift and a rose-colored Oriental silk robe, preparing for her lie down when Odette entered. Though she was a master at masking her emotions and creating personas, there was no denying the ire that Odette recognized in her mother's delicate features.

"Yes?" her mother asked curtly, not pausing as she turned down her coverlet.

Odette swallowed back her bitterness. "A letter has arrived. From Mr. Stratford."

"Oh?" This, at last, stilled her mother's hands.

Odette walked over and handed the letter to her mother, who immediately scanned it once and then again for good measure.

"They are inviting us to Bridleton? To Kent?"

Odette nodded in reply. "It's a kind offer, given the circumstances. They would like us to have the ceremony at the estate."

Her mother gave a breathy laugh and returned the letter to Odette as she kicked off her slippers.

"Likely they're more concerned with saving some face in retreating to the country rather than provide you with an idyllic venue—especially after their foolish son allowed himself to be entrapped—"

"He is not foolish," Odette snapped, cutting off her mother.

She met Odette's eyes, but didn't scold her as she climbed into her gray-and-purple-striped bed. "You know I cannot attend; I'm in the middle of a show. I'll be damned if I step aside and let that idiot understudy, Ann, take my place," her mother groused as she tucked herself in atop a mountain of pillows to keep her head elevated almost at sitting height. "She hardly knows her lines, let alone her stage directions. She thinks her pretty young face makes up for a lack of talent—bah!" As always, the conversation was steered back to the theater.

"So, shall I send them our regrets?" The thought made Odette nauseous. She'd briefly allowed herself to be excited by the prospect of meeting Mr. Stratford's family, of seeing a different, more personal side of him. It didn't seem that that was meant to be—at least, not before the wedding night. The realization caused a nervous flutter in the pit of her stomach; excitement and anxiousness bubbling in equal measures. She couldn't very well travel to Kent without her mother, let alone be married without her. She was, as always, at the mercy of her mother's demanding schedule and lifestyle—even when it came to this, perhaps one of the most important events of her life.

"Of course not," her mother admonished, much to Odette's surprise. "We shan't give them any reason to reconsider. No. You must join them as soon as possible. Take Alyssa as chaperone," she added, speaking of their longtime maid.

"Won't you require her talents?" Odette asked, but her mother quite literally waved away her protest.

"I'll find someone else to fill in. Besides, you'll need her to look your best amongst the Stratfords. You will be the daughter-in-law of an earl, after all. Now, if you'll leave me, please; I'm behind in my resting."

With that, Odette was dismissed. She sat down at her writing desk, surprised at the unsteadiness of her fingers as she held her quill.

There was no turning back now.

Two days later, Odette sat in the forward-facing seat of the plush, well-spring Aldborough carriage, her snoring middle-aged maid slouched across from her. Odette was far too nervous to sleep and even the words on the pages in her hands were of no comfort to her. Instead, she could only watch the changing scenery as the city gave way to the countryside, and, eventually, the rolling hills and open sky of Kent.

Late summer seemed to settle in with much more ease here in the country. Birds darted happily through the wind and a thick cover of verdant leaves created a canopy over the road, reaching out from the branches of gnarled trees. The air felt undeniably cleaner, crisper than London. Life seemed more readily able to bloom and thrive without the suffocating buildings, the stink of the Thames, and the grimy coal smoke choking the air. The only other time she'd traveled had been when she was sent away for school North of London. This journey served only to underscore how little she knew, how much she had yet to see of the world.

They bounced along for what seemed to be interminable hours until they finally turned down a long drive. Odette had thought it was yet another narrow road, but the winding path soon became gravel and the trees began to march in orderly rows. She craned her neck to try to catch a glimpse of the house that awaited her. One window of the carriage proved fruitless, so she scooted over to the other side of the squab. Nothing. If the house was still so far away, then the Stratfords must truly be a wealthy family, indeed, to be able to afford such a long, well-manicured drive across so much land.

It was another quarter of an hour before Odette saw the first spire of the country house. Its shiny shingles winked at her in the afternoon sunlight, teasing her with a tiny glimpse. The path took another bend and she lost sight of it for a few moments until they turned again. This time, the estate came into full view, unhindered by trees.

It was magnificent, like an eclectic fairytale castle. Different architecture from the many decades—if not centuries—of the Aldborough Earldom made appearances throughout its structure, from the large square great hall, the white columns of the entrance, and rows upon rows of crystalline windows, to the tall gray spires and turrets with their archers' slits and undoubtedly superior vantage points. Rather than look mismatched and haphazard, the former earls had taken time to blend the architecture as much as possible, lending an air of love, fantasy, and great care to the building.

Odette was still struggling to keep count of all of the tall, sparkling windows as they pulled up the circular drive. As if on perfect cue, the wide front door opened, and out stepped several footmen in the Aldborough livery, followed by a black-garbed, silver-haired man who could be none other than the butler. She took as deep a breath as she could manage and focused on her gloved fingers clenched in her lap.

This was it.

She was about to meet the family who would become her in-laws. Her mother had made it abundantly clear that crying off the engagement was not an option to even be considered. She was to be stuck with these people, the Stratfords of Kent, whether they were kind or cruel, whether they looked down at their noses for her questionable birth or if they were open-minded enough to accept her, whether or not Mr. Stratford truly cared for her or resented her for the rest of their lives for having his hand forced.

So lost in thought was Odette that she didn't realize they'd glided to a stop until the carriage door was opened by a footman, flooding the interior in golden sunlight.

She took the proffered hand and stepped into her new life, for better or worse.

Simon allowed his mother to fuss over his cravat one last time before finally shooing her away. No matter how many times he reminded her that he was nearly eight-and-twenty years of age, she continued to peck and fluff like a mother hen. He'd long suffered her well-intentioned ministrations, but he longed for the day that it would no longer be proper for her to do so—even when it was just the family.

"Please, Mother," he sighed as he brushed her hands away from his coat. Again.

"This is a big moment," the countess fussed and plucked a bit of invisible lint from Simon's sleeve. A small crease had worked its way between her brows. His mother had always been a little overbearing, but she'd been set on her ear as soon as she'd learned of his betrothal to Miss Leroy.

She'd clapped her hands in joy, excited tears blurring her bright green eyes when he'd first told his parents in the privacy of the ice-blue family sitting room in Aldborough House. He hadn't relished having this conversation more than once, so he'd decided to settle with explaining the details to his mother and father, then sending along notes to his siblings at their respective homes to advise them of the pending nuptials, with details to follow. For his part, his father had seemed more than a little pleasantly surprised that his youngest son had made a match.

Their abundant joy, however, was shortly lived when confronted with the full story. Simon chose to leave out a few details—most notably his rather heavy suspicion that the whole incident had been carefully orchestrated—to avoid any blame being laid at Odette's feet. He'd spent all of a fraction of a second wondering if she'd been complicit in the scheme, but one look into her crystalline eyes had told him the truth: She was just as shocked and betrayed as he had been. And the last thing he needed to do was start her life in this family off by giving his opinionated parents and siblings a poor impression of her.

"But how—why?" his mother had stuttered, clutching her hands to her bosom. His father stood beside her, pressing his fingers into his eyes as if to stave off a blossoming headache. It was a gesture with which Simon was intimately familiar.

"Of my sons, you are the one I thought we had to worry about the least when it came to this," the earl had grumbled before raking back his silver hair and fixing Simon with a very piercing gaze. His father was not a cruel man, but he could demand the utmost respect with a simple glance. "How do you go from a book permanently in your hand to…to being discovered with an innocent in your lap at a dinner party? And by her mother, the Earl of Bane, and his guests, no less! Were it not for the witnesses, we might have been able to avoid all this and attempted to settle with the mother to satisfy the situation. You should have come to us before agreeing to anything."

Simon had shifted uncomfortably from foot to foot, feeling like a coltish youth once more. He'd never liked being viewed as a disappointment, and the scandal this would surely bring to the Stratford name (even if he did right by Odette in the eyes of Society) qualified as just that.

His mother had inhaled a shaky breath and placed a hand upon her husband's taut arm. "We must look on the bright side." She'd turned to Simon. "We never believed you'd wed, but now the issue has been taken into the hands of fate." The words hadn't been meant as a jab—his mother was well-meaning above all else, and never intentionally cruel—but Simon nonetheless felt the sting of being discounted. He'd spent his entire life being viewed as a few steps off of normal, and here was just another example of that. "Surely she is a nice enough girl to have attracted your attention; who are her people?"

Simon barely resisted the urge to flinch. He couldn't care one speck where Odette came from, but not all of Society could be so welcoming. He liked to think his parents were open-minded—especially when it came to their children—but he'd have been lying if he'd said he didn't fear the truth might just push them over the edge.

He'd taken a deep breath and surged forward.

The way his mother had dropped dejectedly onto the nearby chaise and his father had refused to meet his eyes were answering enough.

Not only had he embarrassed them by allowing himself to be caught in such a compromising situation, but he'd done so with an entirely unsuitable girl.

And now all of them were to live with the consequences.

"Leave the poor man alone, Mother," George's voice broke through Simon's spinning thoughts. "He's as white as death and your prodding and tugging at him aren't helping." He and Meredith had come down from London along with Simon and their parents, and intended to stay in residence through the wedding ceremony.

Only a few days in and Simon was already anxious and itchy from all of the attention. He sincerely hoped Miss Leroy didn't run screaming after she was shut away with his family. Bridleton was no tiny cottage, but it was still difficult to find peace when one had determined siblings.

Thank God for Meredith.

As an interloper herself, she was the best chance Simon had to gently integrate his future wife into the family and prove that not *all* of them were overbearing.

As if hearing his thoughts, Meredith offered him a reassuring smile. "I think he looks quite dashing; ready to meet his bride."

A band loosened around his chest—a pain he hadn't realized he'd been carrying. He was hardly a vain man, but to know he looked presentable for Miss Leroy first impression of his family was a great deal more reassuring than his mother's fluttering hands and constant adjustments to his person.

There was a silent, controlled flurry of activity as the entryway was filled with footmen and the butler. The crunch of gravel and clatter of carriage tack indicated Miss Leroy's conveyance had been spotted. Simon's heart redoubled in an unexpected way.

"This is it," his mother breathed, echoing the words throwing themselves against the walls of his skull.

There was a tug at his sleeve as the doors were opened into the golden afternoon light and Simon looked down to find Meredith's hand on his arm. She gave him a small, reassuring squeeze before they all followed the servants into the summer air.

Simon stood at the top of the stairs, flanked by his father on one side and George on the other, as Miss Leroy was helped down from the Aldborough carriage. After conveying Simon and his family to Kent, he'd had the carriage sent back to London for his betrothed and her belongings, not caring to have her travel all that way in a hired coach.

She shook the wrinkles from her blushing rose-colored traveling dress before looking up and tilting her head back to take in the soaring height of Bridleton's facade. Her hair—a unique shade of rich honey—had been plaited and pinned to her head, providing a sturdy perch for a small hat decorated with only a single silk peony. The wideness of her crystal eyes was adorable, but Simon somehow managed to prevent his lips from splitting into a grin. The thought of seeing her again after the unfortunate circumstances of their last encounter had caused him no small amount of anxiety. Now that she was there before him, in the flesh, all of his discomfort fled. He felt only a warm flood of relief through his veins, unexpectedly soothing and comforting.

He watched, unblinking, as she was greeted by the butler and ascended the steps to the front door. His heart thudded harder at every inch she grew nearer.

Unable to resist, Simon stepped forward and helped Odette climb the last steps. She seemed pleasantly surprised by the action and a warm flush crept across the apples of her cheeks.

"I trust your journey was pleasant?" he murmured and brought her gloved hand to his lips. He suddenly, inexplicably ached to feel her bare skin against his.

"Yes, thank you, Mr. Stratford," she replied gently.

"Simon," he interjected. "I believe we're well past the use of formalities at this point."

If anything, her blush intensified. "I appreciate your thoughtfulness at sending your carriage, Simon. It was by far the most comfortable journey I've ever experienced."

"I'm glad to hear it."

"And you shall call me Odette, of course." Her blush deepened and he found it infinitely charming.

Simon nodded in reply and turned to perform introductions only to find his family watching them with thinly-veiled interest.

Simon cleared his throat. "Mother, Father, George, Meredith, this is Miss Odette Leroy." He turned back to Odette, his mouth tilting in what he hoped was a reassuring manner when he felt her fingers tighten against his. "Miss Leroy, my parents, the Earl and Countess of Aldborough; my brother and his wife, the Viscount and Viscountess

Sommerfeld. My sister, Lily, and her husband, Jeremy, Baron Shefford, reside in a nearby estate and will be joining us for supper this evening."

Odette curtseyed appropriately and greeted each of them with just the right amount of deference and demureness.

The tautness of Simon's body relaxed some when his family greeted her warmly in return. Though his mother remained more distant, both his father and George bowed over her hand and shared welcoming words; Meredith stepped forward and took Odette's hand in hers.

"It is such a pleasure to meet you, my dear," she said, a genuine smile blooming and brightening her face, and then added sotto voce: "This family is so close-knit it'll be nice to have another outsider to keep me company."

George chuckled. "Don't scare the chit—we've all been nothing but the most welcoming." His brother turned his winning smile on Odette. "We don't all bite."

A bubble of laughter escaped the woman at Simon's side, but he knew her well enough at that point to recognize that it was more nervous than amused.

"Come, dear," his mother stepped forward, a strained smile on her lips, her movements stiffer than usual. "Surely you want to freshen up after your travels. I'll show you to your room, myself. Such a shame that your mother was unable to join us…"

There was a moment where Odette looked up at Simon and his heart stuttered. This woman would belong to him, would be solely his responsibility, would rely upon him in a matter of days. Sure, he'd comprehended the facts of the situation, but confronted right then with her eyes looking to him for reassurance, it was suddenly overwhelming…and exciting…and utterly terrifying.

Meredith smoothly stepped forward and slipped her arm through Odette's. "I'll join you," she whispered with a smile. "It can all be rather intimidating to be left with one's future mother-in-law after having just been introduced." She turned her eyes up to Simon and communicated silently: *I'll take care of her.*

Simon inclined his head slightly in gratitude before Meredith and Odette followed in his mother's wake.

A heavy breath he hadn't realized he'd been holding escaped from his lungs in one prolonged burst. He jumped when George clapped him hard on his shoulder.

"Well, you've survived the initial introductions," he grinned, enjoying this far more than Simon thought reasonable. Rather than respond, Simon began walking back into the house, his brother and father on either side of him as the butler and footmen followed behind. Odette's maid was supervising the unloading of their trunks and would then be shown to her room above stairs with the rest of the staff. "What say you, Father?" George asked, leaning on his cane as they moved.

Their sire grunted, seeming to weigh his words before speaking. "She's lovely and her manners appear quite polished."

"And?" George pressed, though Simon really wished he hadn't.

"And…we shall see how the next weeks play out. It's not as if there's much that can be done at this point. In inviting her here, we've accepted the match. The license has been procured. By all appearances, she seems respectable and demure—a rather pleasant surprise, if I may be so blunt."

They were talking around Simon when he stood right there between them. It was something he was used to, but this particular instance bothered him greatly because it was about Odette. *His* betrothed. Whatever the circumstances of their engagement, he had sought her out and begun courting her properly. It irked him that they would discuss her thusly as if he wasn't even there.

Fists clenched at his side, Simon lengthened his stride and sped off ahead of them toward the library in the far back corner of the manor house.

"Where are you off to?" George called after him.

Simon didn't bother to respond.

He needed to calm himself with order and peace.

Chapter Five

"I think the cream gloves should suit this dress," Alyssa tapped her chin thoughtfully, eyeing Odette up and down. It would seem that the lady's maid was taking her duties as de facto fashion enforcer in the absence of Odette's mother quite seriously.

The last hour had been spent with hot tongs in her hair and pins scraping her scalp as she was sculpted into something befitting an intimate supper in an earl's household. Her mother had insisted upon adding a few new items to Odette's wardrobe before she left. One of the theater's seamstresses had worked through the night to alter a new gown of her mother's to fit Odette; this was the gown she currently wore. Alyssa, who had a background in theater costuming before being drafted as her mother's maid, had been charged with continuing to finish several other dresses for Odette's time at Bridleton before the wedding. After that, her mother had assured her that the Stratfords would surely take her into their fold and shower her with any number of beautiful gowns and accessories.

For what it was, her mother had certainly chosen well. She'd always had an elegant eye for fashion and the gown Odette now wore was evidence of that. Cut snug against her bosom, the bust was trimmed in the finest, most delicate lace Odette had ever seen. The empire bodice was accentuated by a ribbon of the same pattern lace, tied at her back to trail down in a delicate tail. The petal pink was surprisingly virginal to have been ordered by her mother, but she didn't question it. It happened to make her skin appear dewy and delicate, and what Alyssa had managed to accomplish with her hair suited her quite nicely. Tiny pearls were affixed to her ears and a simple, elegant strand of the orbs hugged the curve of her throat.

The maid returned with the cream-colored satin gloves and, after slipping them on, Odette took one last look in the full-length mirror set in the corner of the spacious bed chamber.

The room she'd been given was situated in the center of the manor on the third floor of one of the newer sections of the building. The angle afforded by her window gave her a dreamy view of one of the corner towers dripping in ivy like a princess' castle. The pale lavender of the floral patterned walls and counterpane were delightfully feminine and richly appointed. She felt like an honored guest, indeed... even if Simon's mother had been less than exuberant in her welcome. Odette tried not to allow it to bother her—for all the countess knew, she had had a part in her son's entrapment in marriage. If she were in her place, then Odette knew some hesitation at welcoming such a woman would be the gentlest reaction she could muster. She would have to give her time, and she also needed time to get to know the Stratfords—the people who would become her new family.

The thought still sent her stomach flipping, even after days of having time to sink in. It had just been her and her mother for so long, the thought of having so many others close to her was nerve-wracking, but not unpleasant.

Viscountess Sommerfeld—Meredith—had made it clear that this was a very close family with uncommon warmth and a penchant for poking into one another's business. She'd assured Odette that it was, however, all done with the purest of love and the best of intentions. She had also told Odette to let her know if her husband, Simon's elder brother, ever overstepped and became unbearably annoying and she'd be sure to handle it. Their fierceness Odette witnessed in Meredith's eyes had made her grin and giggle. It was so nice to feel like she had someone on her side.

This knowledge bolstered her courage as she smoothed her skirts and stood up straighter to take one last assessment of her appearance. She practiced her smile with varying degrees of warmth, closed her eyes, took a bracing breath, and tipped her chin up. Her mother's words echoed in her head: It's all a play.

*****

Odette cursed herself for not considering that she'd need a guide to reach the dining room. Why, oh why hadn't she paid more attention when Meredith and the countess had shown her to her rooms?

Oh yes.

Because she'd been so nervous she'd practically been shaking in her serviceable traveling boots.

She released another groan of frustration when she turned a corner to find only another corridor lined with doorways instead of the staircase. The cobbled-together nature of the manor meant halls were connected at odd angles and levels, dead-ends were common, and you sometimes believed you had descended one story only to discover it had been an illusion.

"Was it two rights, three lefts, and one smaller flight of stairs?" Odette muttered to herself, trying to remain calm as the minutes ticked by. What an impression that would make upon Simon's family: She'd miss supper entirely and they'd find her corpse huddled in some far-flung corner weeks later. "No, no... One right, two lefts, then another right? Gah! Damn and blast!"

"I'd no idea you had such a mouth on you."

Odette shrieked and whipped around at the sound of a man's voice, terror lancing through her like lightning. Her shoulders slumped dramatically when she found only Simon standing a little ways behind her. "My goodness, Simon. It's only you," she breathed with a heavy sigh of relief.

"Don't worry," he said, cocking an eyebrow; "the family ghost resides in the South tower, not this wing."

She chuckled nervously, unable to quite tell to what degree he was joking with her. "R—Right. Well. As you can see, I'm terribly lost."

"I'd surmised as much when I found you wandering near the nursery." He approached her, gesturing to the door just ahead, and she noticed for the first time the state of his dress.

He'd removed the charcoal coat he'd worn to greet her, now dressed only in his shirtsleeves and dove gray waistcoat. His cravat was unwound and hung in loose loops around the strong column of his neck. Perhaps most interestingly, the fingers of his right hand and the once-pristine cuff of his sleeve were stained with dark, unmistakable blotches of ink. It would appear that he'd been working quite furiously in the hours since her arrival.

He halted less than an arm's distance away and she caught the distinct scent of warm parchment, leather, and beeswax; coupled with his heady, masculine scent, it was enticing in an unexpected way. A warm curl of something foreign unfurled low in her abdomen. Odette swallowed hard.

"N—Nursery?" she asked stupidly.

Simon inclined his head and then reached around her to open the door. Inside was a large, cheery room papered in daffodil yellow with three tiny beds for Stratford offspring, a larger bed for a nursemaid, a plush rug, tall cases brimming with books, chests for toys, and even tiny desks off in the far corner for lessons. Wide windows had been fitted with bars to keep children from tumbling out. Those windows allowed in ample sunlight and, when open like they were, a fresh, floral-scented breeze was carried in from the gardens below. An enormous fireplace also took up nearly one entire wall. She could likely easily stand inside of it with room to spare. The enormity of the mantle and stonework told even her untrained eyes that she'd meandered into one of the older areas of the manor. She strode into the room without thinking, taking in the cavernous space with its high, dark paneled ceiling.

"The space used to be the old earl's chambers. A wall used to separate the bedroom from a sitting room, but it was removed to create a space more suitable for a nursery," Simon explained as he stepped within the doorway.

Odette ran a gloved finger along the back of one of the miniature chairs for the child-sized desks. "Which one was yours?" she asked with an impulsive, mischievous smile.

His fascinating eyes locked onto her with boring intensity. "You've found it."

Odette looked back down at the tiny furniture. She could picture a younger Simon sitting there, so studious and serious beyond his years. It made her mouth tip in a wistful smile. When she glanced up again, she found Simon had strode further into the room…and she was suddenly very, very aware of how alone they were. In fact, they hadn't been this alone since that evening in the darkened room before they'd been discovered. She could still feel his arms around her, his firm body beneath hers, smell the light waft of the pomade he used. She swallowed again.

There was so much she wanted to say to him, so much they needed to discuss. And, even if they never got the chance, they'd still be wed, regardless, in less than two weeks.

"Simon...I..." He merely inclined his head to indicate he was listening. He didn't press her or urge her to finish, simply waiting in patient silence. "I want you to know I am sorry. How all of this happened...it...it wasn't fair to you."

His brows crinkled. "Is it not as equally unfair to you to have your hand forced?"

"Yes. I mean, no!" She sighed in frustration. "That is...I don't want you to believe I'd been forced."

"But you were."

"Technically yes." She nearly groaned in frustration. Her cheeks began to burn uncontrollably when next she spoke. "The timing of the betrothal was forced, but I've never felt forced to spend time with you." Simon simply stared at her; assessing, examining, considering. She steeled her resolve. "I quite enjoy it, actually. Spending time with you, that is. I only wish we'd been able to pursue this on our own time and terms."

He approached her then, standing more closely than even when they'd danced. She swore her heart stopped when he reached up, his hand hovering a breath's width from her cheek, so close she could feel its warmth, like when she stood too near to a fire—comforting and dangerous at the same time. His swirling blue-green eyes darted across her face, mesmerizing her with their ethereal intensity. His lips parted, but he only sighed and leaned forward, his lips barely grazing the top of her head. She felt him take a long, shaky inhalation before he spoke.

"I, as well, Odette. All of it."

Surprise and pleasure ebbed through her in equal measure. She tilted her head back to look up into his face. The intensity in his eyes was heart-stopping, so her eyes flitted to his sensuous lips. Her cheeks warmed again, the heat melting her coherent thoughts and painting her throat and chest a rosy pink.

"What are you thinking?" he whispered huskily, though there was no one else in the room other than his childhood memories.

"That no one has ever kissed me before," she replied *without* thinking. Her heartbeat of mortification was quickly quashed as his palm finally cupped her cheek, the pad of his thumb caressing her with infinite gentleness. Her eyes slid closed at the contact. How warm and careful he was. His other arm snaked around her waist and slowly, one-quarter-inch at a time, pulled her flush with him until every bit of them was connected. The hand holding her cheek gently tipped her head back and a fraction to the side. And suddenly, his lips were on hers. The touch began as light as a feather—almost too soft to feel— but the pressure increased with every pass of his lips over hers.

Just when she thought she might expire from breathless anticipation his lips finally fit against hers, a perfect seal, as if they'd been made for one another. The delicious caress made her knees weak and her heart stutter in her breast. Stars streaked behind her eyelids as the rest of the world melted away. Her hands clutched the sides of his waistcoat of their own volition, desperately needing to hold onto something to keep her body from floating away. She self-consciously began to return the caress, but his nudging kiss, the passing question of his tongue against the seam of her mouth, urged forth a sigh of surrender. Her lips parted and the kiss deepened further than Odette had ever imagined. His tongue tangled with her inexperienced one, showing it how to both give and take pleasure. And then, he stopped.

With a suddenness that left her reeling, Simon stepped back from their embrace, leaving the front of her entire body cold and chilled despite the warmth of the summer air drifting in through the open windows with their safety bars.

Simon's chest heaved, his eyes wild and uncertain as if he'd just witnessed something unbelievable.

In all, he looked exactly as Odette felt.

"Take a right out of this room, then two lefts, down the half flight of stairs, one right, and the main stairs will be straight ahead. The family dining room is the first door to your right off the great hall." With that, he spun on his heel and left the room in three brisk strides of his long legs, leaving Odette in the company of only her shaky breathing.

Simon didn't join Odette and the rest of his family for dinner.

In his absence, his family's efforts at making Odette feel more comfortable were well and above admirable. She was introduced to the only female Stratford sibling, Lily, and her husband, Jeremy, Baron Shefford. The juxtaposition of the two of them was striking. Where Lily was fair and petite, her husband was tall, broad, dark, and imposing. It wasn't difficult to imagine his deep chocolate eyes smoldering and his chiseled jaw sharp with determination. The baron was a formidable man with hands so large they could probably snap her in two. All her nerves fled, however, when she witnessed the careful way in which he handled his wife, his eyes fairly melting with adoration each time she touched his arm or leaned into his field of vision.

Odette had come to recognize a different, yet similarly palpable, affection shared by Simon's elder brother and his wife. Meredith and the viscount were likewise thoughtful in their attentions to one another. Each gentle touch of their hands or jolly quip between them made Odette sink more and more into a quagmire of guilt for what her mother had said about them. She had silently watched the couple for the several hours it took to chat and eat supper, and there wasn't a single speck of doubt in her mind that Sommerfeld would never, ever set aside his wife. If there was no issue from the union, then it was conceivable that they would still live a long and happy life together in their obvious love. And that meant…that meant Simon or his offspring would then inherit the earldom. *Her* children would inherit.

Rather than thrill or excite her as it would no doubt have any other woman—high-born or no—it filled Odette with an intense quiver of nerves and dread…and not just for herself.

If she'd learned one thing about Simon in the weeks since they had met, it was that he'd never had any ambitions other than to pursue his research. He was not a second-born son salivating over the possibility of inheriting a sturdy title and all the healthy land and wealth that went with it. He'd commented more than once how he prized his solitude and his work. Inheriting would surely hinder all of this if he wished to be a hands-on, dedicated lord. And she'd come to recognize that Simon did nothing to half-measure.

To Odette's delight, Lily and her husband had brought with them their two young sons, Vincent and Edward. She enjoyed children—especially since she'd missed out on much of her childhood being held backstage and monitored by other actresses—but she'd savored the brief times spent in the company of child workers in the theaters. The Balfour children had retired to the nursery early following the long carriage ride from Rosehall, so she had yet to meet them, but she certainly looked forward to it.

The thought of the nursery brought with it a flood of memories—both physical and emotional—of just what had transpired there only a short time before. Likely, she'd vacated the room only minutes before the Shefford boys had been brought in...how mortifying that would have been had they been happened upon. She felt her cheeks warm heartily.

Then again, she couldn't very well be more compromised than she already was; they were, after all, going to be wed in just under two weeks.

"Have you played pall mall before, Miss Leroy?" Sommerfeld leaned around his sister to meet her eyes down the length of the table.

Odette shook her head, trying to mask the fact that her head had wandered. "I'm afraid not." Her mother had not only insisted upon maintaining Odette's fragile, pale French complexion by limiting her time in the sun, but it was also far easier to keep tabs on one's daughter when she was confined to the same building in which one spent endless hours rehearsing and performing...

"Cards, then?" Meredith peeked her head around Baron Shefford's formidable chest as he silently polished off the last of his berry tart and clotted cream.

"Lord, no!" Sommerfeld groaned before Odette could reply, startling her with his vehemence. "I'm stepping in as champion in my brother's absence and refuse to allow anyone to trounce the poor girl within hours of meeting her...no matter how beautiful the swindler." He flashed his wife a devastating wink and turned back to Odette. "Don't worry," the viscount added in an awful stage whisper; "I'll not allow her to trick you into losing your pin money."

Odette tried to give him a cheerful smile of gratitude, but his stance served only to underscore the emptiness of the seat across the table from her. Either the family was used to Simon's unexplained absences or they didn't feel she needed to know the reason behind it, because nothing was said. Not a single comment was whispered as an excuse. Instead, the remainder of the Stratfords and their spouses stepped in to drag her from her quiet, uncomfortable shell and make her feel more at home and welcome than she'd thought possible in such a short amount of time. Still, the gaping hole in their party kept drawing her eyes against her will. It was difficult for Odette not to wonder if it had something to do with what had transpired in the nursery.

Could their kiss have been *that* off-putting?

She was finally successful in forcing a smile. "I should like to learn how to play pall mall," she chimed in.

"Splendid," Lily clapped her hands. Odette didn't miss the countess's flicker of a grimace at the sound, but she held her tongue short of scolding her daughter.

"Just don't put holes in the lawn," the earl groused good-naturedly.

"We shall play teams," Meredith chimed in.

"I'm more than happy to remain a passive spectator and enjoy the view," Sommerfeld answered and then turned to his brother-in-law beside Odette. "Right, Jem?"

The baron appeared about to agree with him but caught his wife's pleading emerald eyes and was instantly lost. The change was so sudden that Odette barely had a chance to stifle her smile.

"Teams isn't such an awful idea." Shefford's resonant voice quashed Sommerfeld's hopes.

The viscount rolled his eyes dramatically until he flinched with a grunt. If Odette wasn't mistaken, then he'd just been struck in the shin by a dainty woman's slipper.

"Don't act as if you're any less vulnerable to your own wife's whims," Lily scolded with a treacle-sweet smile, to which Meredith grinned knowingly. "The game was your idea, after all."

Odette's head fairly spun with the rapid-fire conversation flying like sparrows darting back and forth across the dining table. There was such a comfortability—such an ease—that was unfathomable to her. She had difficulty keeping up, let alone chime in with any regularity. She was content to sit back and watch, basking in the unmistakable familial affections borne of years together, but, my, was she exhausted by the end of the evening.

*****

Simon remained locked in his rooms until long after he was certain the rest of the household was asleep. And still, he sat in the overstuffed upholstered chair in his bed chamber.

The food deposited on a table by a helpful maid many hours prior had long since grown cold and congealed beneath its silver dome. It remained untouched and forgotten except for the lingering odor of cooked meat and vegetables.

The room had grown too dark to read, but that didn't stop his eyes from focusing solely on the fine print on the paper in his hands. Unusually, he didn't skim the page and lose himself amongst the numbers and letters. No. Simon's mind was unnervingly, steadfastly occupied by the kiss he and Odette had shared hours earlier in the nursery.

There, amongst the sunny wallpapering and the books and toys of his childhood, he'd experienced one of the most stirring kisses of his eight-and-twenty years. Her eager, untutored excitement stirred him deep into the marrow of his bones, made his skin tingle, caused his

hands to ache with the overwhelming urge to hold her. What had begun as relatively innocent contact quickly became consumed by a desire of which Simon hadn't known himself capable. So disconcerted
was he by the experience that he'd dashed away, pulse thrumming
deafeningly in his ears, and hidden like a coward in his rooms to do
what he did best: think.

The first quarter of an hour was spent attempting to calm his body;
slowing his breathing and willing away the pounding ache in his
groin.

The next hour was spent ruminating over every interaction between himself and Odette over the past several weeks.

There was simply no denying that he'd been drawn to her in a way
no woman had ever held his attention before. He was no stranger to
slaking his lust when the roar became impossible to ignore, though
those occasions were few and far between. But this...

This was different.

Odette was different.

He couldn't recall ever having wanted—nay, *needed*—a woman
with such sudden intensity as when he'd seen her in that pale pink
gown tailored to perfection to accentuate her graceful curves and generous, flawless bosom; when he'd gazed down into her doe-like crys-
tal-blue eyes and touched the petal-softness of her cheek; when he'd
tasted her...

God...when he'd *tasted* her...

He'd been lost.

And it terrified him.

If the kiss in the nursery had taught him anything, it was that
Odette was even more inexperienced than he might have believed—so
much for Rafe's suspicion that Odette had followed in her mother's
scandalous footsteps.

Of course, any lady might claim she'd never been kissed before out of a sense of propriety or to inflate a man's ego, but there was no pretending when it came to the act itself. A deep, primal part of his soul had roared to life when he'd tasted the truth of Odette's inexperience. It had shocked him to his core, sent tremors throughout his body, smothered every last rational thought buzzing in his brain.

It was unnerving how little he cared about anything else in the world when she'd begun to take his lead and kiss him back…

Simon jumped to his feet and began to pace from one corner of the rectangular room to the other, stopping only when he heard the crunch of parchment. At first confused, he glanced down to his hands gripping the sheets of text in a white-knuckled grip. Heaving a heavy sigh, he dropped the papers to the desk set beside one of the windows on the far wall and made several futile attempts at smoothing them against the sharp edge of the tabletop. He abandoned them after his efforts proved fruitless, choosing instead to stretch his arms high over his head, allowing the movement to free up each vertebra after his prolonged sedentary state. His gaze turned to the darkened window but caught only his own golden reflection limned in candlelight against the pitch blackness of the moonless night outside.

The wedding was a little less than two weeks away.

The date stood out in his mind with a very strange mixture of anxiety and…excitement?

It was confusing.

It set him off-kilter.

This was why a world of orderly words and numbers and logic was far preferable to this; at least that made sense to him.

And he decided right then that he had to find a way to move past whatever this was that had slowly ebbed into his consciousness and attempted to nudge aside his usual mental faculties.

He undid his cufflinks and blindly tossed them onto the desk as well before shoving up his ink-marked shirtsleeves.

Twelve days.

He had twelve days of bachelorhood and freedom before he undertook the responsibilities of a spouse and household.

Draping the length of his cravat across the back of the chair, he scrubbed the starch from his neck and froze.

Maybe all he needed to do was get Odette out of his system.

In only twelve days he'd be able to slake every last one of his urges without the least bit of guilt. It would be his right to hold his wife, to touch her, to claim her. And then, as it had for him any number of times over the years, his needs would slip back into their box and his mind would, once more, be able to focus on what was most important.

Until then, it was clear he needed to keep Odette at arm's length. Being too close to her made his sanity slip. Touching her made him burn. Kissing her wrecked him; leveled him like an inferno.

He hadn't counted on this reaction when he'd chatted with her at the theater all those weeks prior, and now it would seem he had no other options.

Though, as he contemplated Odette's sweet taste, her tentative exploration of his mouth and eager acceptance of his kiss, it might not be such a terrible thing.

Chapter Six

Odette was grateful for Meredith's offer to retrieve her at her chamber door so they could venture down and break their fast together; she felt the chances relatively high that she'd lose her way again and quite possibly encounter that family ghost at which Simon had hinted.

"Three years and I still get lost," Meredith had laughed at herself. "But at least I can finally get around to the most important of rooms when need be."

"I suppose you have a good enough reason to memorize the layout," Odette said as she admired the intricate carvings in the hallway's white crown molding high above their heads; "you'll be Lady Aldborough one day and all this will be yours." She immediately pulled her lips between her teeth, realizing how the flippant comment could be construed as speculative of the death of Sommerfeld's parents. Of Simon's parents.

What woman commented on the death of her in-laws before the marriage even took place?

If she was taken aback by the comment, then Meredith didn't show it. Instead, she slid her arm through Odette's as they continued down the center of the ruby-red runner. "I suppose that's almost worse—a lady gets lost in her own home, never to be seen again." Her laugh was airy and lighthearted enough that even Odette's mouth split in a smile. "For all my faculty with numbers and anatomy, I'm not the best at mazes." She proceeded to regale Odette with stories of the expansive hedge maze at Rosehall, Lily and Shefford's nearby estate, and how she had yet to complete it successfully despite several attempts. The stories were so amusing that Odette hardly realized they'd arrived in the breakfast room without her having paid attention to the last five or six changes in direction.

Blast.

The earl was seated, flipping through the paper his butler had already procured and ironed crisp and smooth. Meredith had told her the countess usually kept Town hours even when in the country, so she likely wouldn't be seen until afternoon and would break her fast in bed—as was the privilege of married ladies of the *ton*. Meredith was not a woman inclined to such leisure since she'd readily planned to meet early with Odette, who was still accustomed to waking early as she had when she'd been at school. Lily and her husband were clearly of the same ilk, as both were seated at the round, white-clothed table with food and cups before them. Neither Sommerfeld nor Simon was anywhere to be seen, and Odette had yet to inquire as to the whereabouts of Meredith's husband.

Both Shefford and the earl stood in greeting when they noticed Odette and Meredith's entrance, meeting them with welcoming smiles and wishing them good morning. The earl's silver hair was slicked back smartly; his impeccable charcoal-colored coat was paired with a honey-yellow waistcoat and crisp white cravat. Shefford was dressed similarly, but in much more muted tones that did nothing to disguise the impressive breadth of his shoulders. It took every last speck of Odette's comportment training not to fidget when she was the focus of so much attention, and especially when she stood next to Meredith's striking, red-haired beauty and across from Lily's ethereal delicate golden looks. Lily's delicately proportioned frame and Meredith's willowy grace made her feel inadequate, to be sure.

Physical appearances aside, she experienced a distinct discomfort at being in an unfamiliar dress. Alyssa had stayed up the better part of the night hemming the gown and correcting the seam allowances to fit Odette's more voluptuous curves. She'd done an admirable job, but it was uncomfortable, nonetheless, to be the object of so much attention when she didn't even have the shield of confidence provided by a familiar, favorite piece of clothing. This, of course, wasn't to say that the garment was not lovely. Her mother had sent a lavender morning gown with a gossamer overlay so light that it floated like dandelion down when she moved. The same fabric created elegant little cap sleeves and an ivory ribbon cinched her torso in just the right place to create the illusion of slimness. A matching ribbon held back her hair in a simple chignon appropriate for breakfast in the country. As soon as she'd been done dressing and witnessing all of Alyssa's hard work, she'd sent the maid to take the hours before luncheon to herself to rest until another outfit change was necessary. It was only their first day in the country and the poor woman had already been worked to the bone.

"Please," the earl spoke with a smile; "do help yourselves to anything. Tea or coffee?" He raised a hand to a waiting footman.

"Coffee, if you please." Odette practically sighed in relief. She'd inherited her mother's love of coffee and had been silently praying that the Aldboroughs would have some on hand; it wasn't served in all households.

What she saw when she approached the groaning sideboard, how-ever, nearly did make her melt into a puddle of gratitude. Piled high with rashers of bacon, sausages, eggs three ways, toast and no less than three types of jams and preserves, roasted potatoes, and even some sugar-glazed pastries, it was a food-lover's haven. The first meal of the day had always been Odette's favorite—probably because it was usually the most peaceful—but she'd learned to love and ap-preciate it more when away at school. Many of the other girls had foregone the meal entirely, opting for strange brews and a bite of dry toast instead—doing everything in their power to attain the silhouette they all so coveted. Every bite Odette took at the communal table felt judged and so, gradually, she'd forsaken her beloved meal and suf-fered the aches of an empty stomach until later in the day when it was easier to conceal the fact that she *enjoyed* the taste of food far more than she cared for the appearance of a pale waif that was all the rage. The same, unfortunately, couldn't be said about Odette's mother. Each time she returned to London during a break at school, her mother lamented Odette's bountiful curves, the plumpness of her hips, the fullness of her bosom. Slowly, Odette had been forced to taper off her eating at home as well, lest she receive a thorough nagging every minute her mother didn't spend rehearsing or performing.

Now, confronted by this mouthwatering bounty, Odette felt lost.

Did she indulge in being her authentic self in front of these people who were to be her new family? Or did she continue playing the part of proper society lady and pick at meager morsels without finding true satisfaction?

Odette cast a subtle glance in Lily's direction and her heart sank. There were only two slices of toast evenly coated in strawberry pre-serves, while Shefford's plate had clearly been piled obscenely high with some of everything on offer. Odette's stomach eked out a pitiful growl. How lovely it must be to be a large, hale, and hardy man.

She turned her attention back to the task at hand when Meredith passed her an ivory china plate decorated in delicate pink flowers and creeping green vines. Her hesitation allowed Meredith to proceed first. She watched her future sister-in-law add two spoons of eggs, a serving of sausage and a slice of toast to her plate. It was less than Odette's body craved, but it was still more than Lily had taken. She accepted it as permission to allow herself some grace and find a happy median. She couldn't outrun her mother's warnings, no matter how far away she was: "A round girl will make a fat wife; and Lord knows how that might turn out if there are children!"

Smothering the unkind voice, Odette spooned some coddled eggs onto her plate alongside a few slices of the delightfully crisp bacon, snatched a piece of toast—foregoing the enticing, gem-colored jams—and rushed back to take a seat at the large round table. Shefford took the liberty of assisting both she and Meredith with their chairs before returning to his wife's side. The earl resumed his seat as well now that the women were settled in.

A footman had filled a delicate china cup with rich black coffee for her and Odette could hardly wait to inhale the earthy, nutty scent once her napkin was draped across her lap.

"No George this morning, then?" the earl inquired over the bent edge of his paper. Odette's eyes turned toward Meredith over the edge of her cup.

"I'm afraid last night wasn't a good one." There was no mistaking the sadness clouding Meredith's indigo eyes. "Hours in a carriage will do that. He should be rested enough to join us in a few hours."

Odette's tongue fairly burned to ask what that meant, but her curiosity was saved when Lily spoke up.

"His leg?" She'd set down her toast, her doleful green eyes remarkably pained.

Odette felt Meredith glance in her direction, but she remained utterly still, hoping that they'd deem her close enough to family that the conversation would continue around her. She'd paid closer attention to the gossip surrounding the heir to the Aldborough earldom ever since Simon had come into her life, and she was no less immune to the curiosity surrounding his injury than most of Society. By many accounts, it had been a riding accident, but there was some speculation as to the truth of that excuse.

Meredith eventually nodded her head in response. "He's resting now and should be well enough recovered to join us later for our game of pall mall."

As if some deity had overheard their plans, the sky chose that moment to release a faint but steady sprinkle against the tall panes of glass lining the curved wall of the breakfast room.

The earl grunted in amusement and snapped his paper open once more. "It looks as if the lawn may live to see another day," he muttered with muted humor.

Odette tried not to allow her deflation to show on her face. She'd been looking forward to spending time out of doors—something she'd had little occasion to do in London, even less so with the opportunity to take in the fresh air of the country. The game would also have afforded a less formal setting to better get to know her new family…and (hopefully) her husband-to-be.

"The weather should clear and the lawn will dry in no time," Lily chimed in cheerfully stark contrast to the darkening skies outside. "The weather can be quite fickle in this part of the country."

Odette nodded as if she had any real knowledge of weather trends outside of London and the little corner of Essex where she'd attended boarding school. The extent of her travels led only far enough away for her mother to relinquish responsibility, but not far enough where Odette ever forgot the looming threat of a visit...if her mother ever took the time to leave the theater, that was.

"What do you do for entertainment, Miss Leroy?" Shefford inquired after he'd polished off yet another crisp link of savory sausage.

Odette replaced her cup of coffee on its saucer. "Oh, not a great deal. I read quite a bit."

A smile split his handsome features, softening his eyes and making him appear kinder, younger. "Now I understand the draw you've had on Simon. Never could get him interested in other activities once he'd discovered the written word.

"And what sorts of activities are those?"

Shefford inclined his head. "The usual sorts: hunting, fishing, shooting, riding. You don't ride, do you?"

She shook her head in reply. "I have never had the occasion to learn, unfortunately."

"Should you like to learn one day, you need only ask," Lily interjected with a grin. "Jeremy has always been an accomplished horseman—he taught me how to ride when I was a girl. We're working on improving the stock in the stables at Rosehall in the hopes of diversifying. The Shefford Barony has long been largely agrarian and heavily reliant upon sheep husbandry, but times are changing."

"Fascinating!" Odette replied sincerely. This was like a glimpse behind the curtain of a lord's estate, something to which she'd never thought to be privy. Not that she'd ever been particularly interested in the workings of such responsibilities, but it was a whole world outside of her limited realm of knowledge and experience. She'd likely have been fascinated if he'd wanted to discuss the correlation between crop yield and different types of fertilizer.

"We like to think so." Shefford beamed at his wife before turning back to Odette. "The stables here at Bridleton are quite notable and I've been angling to gain access to them by marrying into the Stratford family." The wink of his eye was undeniably charming.

The earl harrumphed from behind his newspaper, "If you think marrying my daughter is sufficiently endearing to allow access to Bridleton horses as breeding stock, then you've another thing coming."

"They jest," Meredith leaned in and whispered with a conspiratorial grin. "Shefford and his parents were longtime friends of the Stratfords. The earl is like a second father to him."

Odette gave her a grateful smile for the explanation. What must it be like to fall into such an easy rhythm with other people? To be comfortable enough to laugh and jest in such a manner? No veiled motives or barely concealed insults?

"George might have something to say about that," Shefford grinned.

"Oh?" The earl lowered his paper once more, but his tone was one more of interest than skepticism.

"He's decided he needs a project," Meredith spoke up. "Personally, I think it could be a very lucrative venture, indeed."

"Well," chuckled the earl; "with your faculty for numbers, my dear, it must be an interesting venture, indeed."

Odette sat back and soaked in the warmth of the banter surrounding her. As she sipped her coffee and nibbled on her eggs (which were delicious beyond all reason, by the way), she tried not to watch the ticking of the minute hand on the small clock set atop the nearby mantle. Minutes passed and still, there was no sign nor mention of Simon's absence.

In fact, Odette didn't see Simon for the better part of three more days.

Three days, she resided beneath the same roof, trapped indoors thanks to the unfortunately persistent drizzle that consistently threatened to become something more unpleasant, and still, she saw neither hide nor hair of the man whom she was to marry in just over one week.

While initially accepting of Simon's curious behavior, the Stratfords and Balfours appeared to gradually grow more uneasy with each passing day and every meal he didn't attend, seeming to have abandoned his future bride to the care of his family.

To their credit, they did their level best to continue to make sure Odette felt welcome and wanted—despite Simon's odd behavior.

She was regularly invited to play cards, though she now understood why Sommerfeld had refused to allow his wife to gamble in earnest; the woman's faculty with games and numbers was unparalleled. She was given a tour of the more notable rooms of Bridleton and eventually learned how to make her way to the library, where she was allowed free rein of anything that drew her fancy. She ate all of her meals with the family and came to know their different senses of humor. She was introduced to Lily and Shefford's sons, Vincent and Edward, and spent a few hours each day with the rest of the family as they played with the young boys, usually culminating in uproarious laughter. Nothing, however, filled the void left by Simon's absence. To say it felt odd to get to know her new family without the bridegroom in attendance—knowing he was, in fact, still under the same roof, but hidden away in some far-flung room—was an understatement.

She was wandering the halls following breakfast one morning, testing her slowly growing knowledge of the house and a bit of the grounds in between temperamental cloud showers, when she stumbled upon what appeared to be the family chambers. She might have passed the ivory ladies' sitting room and its mostly closed door had she not heard a sniffle from within. Odette froze in a moment of indecision—not wanting to tread where she didn't belong—but her decision was made for her when she heard a gentle sob of someone trying to conceal their pain.

Odette held her breath and pressed open the door and it swung on quiet hinges to reveal Meredith. She wore a white morning gown decorated in embroidered blue irises and lacey baby's breath and was curled up on a chaise, her red head in her hands providing a glowing centerpiece to the room.

"I—I'm so sorry for intruding, but are you alright?"

Meredith's head whipped up and she held a hopelessly crumpled handkerchief to her face. "Odette!" She took a shaky breath and tried to paste a wobbly smile on her lips. Sommerfeld's normally composed, confident wife being the one in such a state was more than a little surprising.

"Are you injured?" Odette asked, growing more concerned as she stepped further into the room. Meredith gave a minute shake of her head as she attempted to tuck a wayward red curl behind her ear.

"Here, let me…" She fished around to find the small pocket sewn into the layers of her morning dress. Filtering through the bits of ribbon she tended to use as bookmarks, she finally located a clean handkerchief and held it out to Meredith.

Her red-rimmed indigo eyes focused on Odette's hand for several seconds before accepting the handkerchief and setting aside her ruined one.

"Is the viscount—is he…?" Odette was unsure how to voice the question as a leaden weight settled in her stomach.

Meredith abruptly shook her head. "George is fine," she said with a shaky breath. "It's me."

Odette frowned, the weight settling even heavier than before. She dropped to the cushion beside Meredith. "Are you ill? Shall I call for a physician?" Any number of awful things began to dash this way and that inside of Odette's brain. Her blood chilled as she pictured wasting illnesses of various degrees of severity and then spiraled from there. She'd inherited very little from her mother, but a predilection toward melodrama was apparently one of them.

Meredith placed a stilling hand on her arm when Odette would have risen to dash over to the bell-pull near the door and call for assistance.

"Not ill. It's only...my courses arrived." Several fat tears fell from her eyes and speckled the skirts of her morning dress.

Odette sat back, confused. She'd never heard of a woman who cried when her monthly bleed arrived. As a matter of fact, she'd witnessed her mother cry tears of *joy* on more than one occasion when her own courses came. As far as Odette was concerned, it was part of being a female. It baffled her to be so upset about something part of the natural state of womanhood...but she had come to know Meredith as level-headed and intelligent; if she was upset, then there must be a good reason.

Sure enough, Meredith's perceptive nature recognized Odette's swirling thoughts. She swiped at her face and turned to face Odette more fully, offering her a gentle smile of patience.

"It means," she breathed shakily; "there will be no baby this month. Again."

Understanding struck Odette like a shock of icy water to the face.

Her mother's ugly words echoed in her head like locusts, ravenously gnawing away at the edges of her conscience. She gripped Meredth's hands in both of hers, a wave of protectiveness rising within her, though it was tinged with renewed anger that her mother could have spoken such hateful words.

How many months had Meredith cried like this? Had she weathered any of the vicious whispers of which Odette had only had a taste?

"Surely Sommerfeld isn't upset?" Odette exclaimed, aghast. She vowed then and there to take the man's cane and crack him over the head with it if he was the one who'd made his wife cry—no matter that he was nearly a foot taller than her and she'd likely end her marriage into the family before it began. No one deserved to be made to feel less for something out of their control.

"Of course not," Meredith squeezed Odette's hands in a gesture of appreciation. "To be sure, he'd be thrilled to start a family, but I...I am the one who is most upset. I feel as if I have failed."

Odette shook her head in denial. "The way your husband looks at you..." She considered all the loving glances, gentle touches, and tenderly teasing words she'd witnessed between them in the last week, alone. "You could grow a second head and Sommerfeld wouldn't find you lacking." It was a fumbling attempt, but it seemed to cheer Meredith up some; she chuckled and caught one last tear with the handkerchief. "He lights up when you walk into the room. Of course, I cannot understand exactly what you are experiencing, but I sympathize with feeling as if you come up short and how infinitely frustrating that can be; please don't allow it to consume you or define who you are."

Meredith gave a wet little laugh. "Aren't I supposed to be the one counseling and comforting you as you prepare to join this family?"

Odette squeezed her hands again. "I may be new here—new to a family such as this in general—but you've all gone to such great lengths to make me feel welcome. The least I can do is provide what little comfort, when and where I can."

"A great comfort." She enfolded Odette into a snug embrace. A pleasant warmth spread through Odette's chest, its gentle fingers curling around her heart and cradling it close. She felt like she had done something right, something good, something worthwhile. Even if Simon was too absorbed in his work to devote much time to her, at least this helped her feel a little more at home.

Meredith pulled back and swiped at her cheek one last time. Her eyes were slightly red from crying, but there was no denying just how lovely a woman Meredith was with her pale skin and charming smattering of freckles, her tilted indigo eyes with their cinnamon lashes.

"It might be overstepping," Meredith began; "but perhaps you'll allow me an opportunity to dole out a bit of advice now?"

"Of course!" Odette was taken aback, but she'd gladly grasp onto any small thread that might provide her with more confidence in this remarkable situation.

"I can see that you care for Simon."

Odette's cheeks began to burn. She hadn't expected quite such a blunt statement.

"You're far more forgiving with him than I would be in your place." Odette couldn't help her smile at the words, said with kindness rather than criticism. "Society—even most of his family—views his behavior as a bit unusual at times, and he can often seem distracted or rude, but I promise it is unintentional." Odette nodded. She'd learned as much about her betrothed in the weeks of their acquaintance, but it was nice to have confirmation from another source. "He is merely entirely dedicated body and soul to his work, which is truly commendable. There are very few second sons who would find something and follow through with half as much passion as he. You have been supremely patient thus far and, I do realize it's painful, but please continue to do so. He needs his own time to adjust, as well. That is, of course, not to say that you haven't endured as much change, but Simon…he deserves the grace he hasn't always been granted. You've been doing a stellar job of it thus far, but I don't want you to lose hope; your efforts are far from unnoticed. Might I suggest you ask him about his work when you have the chance? He will light up like you've never seen before."

The last made Odette's smile broaden. She'd caught glimpses of Simon's passion, but this was solid advice—something with which she could work. She made a mental note to learn what she could about Simon's research and make genuine inquiries. If it was important to him, then it would be important to her. She swore to take Meredith's advice to heart and make the most of their situation. They both had a great deal of adjusting to do, but Odette vowed to be strong.

Chapter Seven

Little did Odette know, her presence at Bridleton was, in fact, quite closely monitored by the man who would wed her in a matter of days. His work hadn't been the only reason for his seclusion. No. Simon was struggling to come to terms with the fact that his brief freedom was rapidly coming to an end. He would be a husband with new responsibilities, new living arrangements, and another person to remember to take into account.

While he'd initially begun his self-imposed exile in an effort to maintain his sanity until he could rightfully work Odette out of his system, it also allowed space for his mind to run rampant down each tangent it sniffed out.

Left alone to stew, he grew more and more frustrated at the fact that—for a man who was usually more observant than most—he didn't know how he'd allowed himself to be tricked into the arrangement. It wasn't that he regretted Odette, he simply regretted the circumstances.

His mind's next leap was annoyance at his family. Rather than sympathize with his situation, more than a couple of comments as to his good fortune had been made—how else could he have found a wife of his own? (Surely he would have failed miserably if left to his own devices.)

Simon's emotions were at war within his chest. His family insisted upon getting to know Odette; he struggled with resentment being aimed at a moving target. They made attempts to coerce him out of his rooms; he hid away and did his best to lose track of time.

George had banged into Simon's rooms that first rainy evening, making Simon instantly regret not having packed up his work and moved to another chamber with much more difficult access for some- one hampered by physical limitations. It wasn't precisely kind, but it was the truth of how he felt when confronted by his elder brother's glower.

"You're being quite selfish, you know." George limped into the room and towered over Simon where he remained seated at his desk. "You know I care about you, brother, and I've long accepted that you are the more observant, intelligent one of us two, but it is my turn to impart some blunt truth." George raised his eyebrow in an admirable approximation of their father until Simon set aside his quill and leaned back in his chair, begrudgingly waiting for his brother to con- tinue. "Your days of putting yourself first are over. Regardless of the circumstances of it, you're betrothed now. Not that you've been around to witness it, but we are all finding Miss Leroy rather charm- ing.

"Who knows? You may even find that you like her a great deal if you give her a chance—hell, you may even wind up enjoying wedded life."

A twinge of guilt pricked Simon's conscience, but he knew at the heart of it that no one truly understood him or his mind. They couldn't fathom just how or why his work was so important to him. They had never comprehended that he needed the orderly numbers and facts. These things made sense to him in the way the rest of the world didn't —the way his feelings for Odette tipped his existence on its ear in the most disconcerting way. These things helped to calm his frantic mind. They calmed him. Regardless of how it appeared to everyone else, Simon didn't merely want the escape into his work, he *needed* it. It kept him sane.

Now that he was going to wed Odette, he hoped that she might one day understand it…but there was no going back if she didn't. She'd been forgiving and kind up to that point, but Simon had learned on more than one occasion that even the most patient being could be tried by his habits. If Odette couldn't accept him as he truly was, then, well…it would not be all that different from the first twenty-seven years of his life. He was used to the loneliness. But George's words unearthed another of Simon's anxieties he'd done an admirable job of setting to the side: He wanted Odette. He wanted her with a fierceness that terrified him because it nearly trumped his need for the calm orderliness of his numbers.

Simon may have secluded himself in his rooms, taken his meals separate from the family and their beguiling guest, and staunchly refused to stray from his work, but that didn't mean that he'd forgotten Odette.

Far from it.

Indeed, his mind (and body) strayed to this knowledge more often than was conducive to productivity. He'd been able to gather together several more pages of research, but it was made more difficult by the fact that, following George's unwelcome interruption, he'd been forced to pick up and relocate to another part of the house lest someone else attempt to locate him and force him into being more sociable.

He'd determined that he couldn't trust himself around Odette until he could well and truly get her out of his system. As with his other preoccupations, this usually meant slaking his curiosity and moving on to focus once more on what was important. Unlike those other preoccupations, that meant wedding and (very promptly) bedding a woman. Until then, Simon was steadfast in his determination to spend whatever mental capacity he had remaining in his work. It wouldn't be wise to allow himself to be too near to Odette until he was free to act upon his desires. His brain, however, wandered of its own volition during those sparse hours he allowed himself to give into exhaustion and sleep.

His mind drifted back again and again to the kiss they'd shared—her first kiss, a baser part of him crowed in heretofore silent masculine pride. The way she tasted haunted his dreams, her light scent carried him off to sleep, the dreamy look in her crystalline eyes and the memory of her petal-soft skin made him wake hard and aching for release. He had to endure several minutes of deliberate breathing before his pulse would slow to a more normal pace.

He remained steadfastly silent until George gave up and left him alone.

As luck would have it, Simon's peace was disrupted the first sunny afternoon following the more pleasant turn in the weather. He'd just settled into his books and papers in an unused room in a far turret of Bridleton. It had, at one time, been used as a place to dry herbs and flowers from the manor's kitchen gardens for cooking and medicine. The wooden walls still held the ghostly aromas of clove and rosemary, lavender and other scents Simon couldn't quite place, though memories of them floated in the back of his consciousness.

Already absorbed in the figures before him, Simon hadn't heard his sister-in-law enter the room until she stood over him, hands on her hips, and spoke. "Did you really believe one of us wouldn't find you eventually?" Her tone was gentler than her words. Her approach was quite different than her husband's browbeating had been a couple of days prior. Bluster, Simon could handle…this gentler, more rational approach knocked upon his conscience and begged his attention.

Huffing a quick, resigned sigh, Simon slipped a strip of fabric into his book to mark his page and stood, as social graces demanded. "To be honest, I'd known it was inevitable…though I'd hoped to postpone it another few days."

Her cinnamon-colored brows knit together, more in concern than consternation. "But…why, Simon? I realize you're busy and how important your work is—really, I do;" and Simon believed her, he'd always felt Meredith understood him more than any other member of his family; "however, I have to say it's disappointing to see how little time you've spent with Miss Leroy." Simon's stomach sank with shame and he could no longer meet her gaze.

"You do like her, do you not?" Meredith asked. "You care for her?"

Simon's jaw clenched with the inexplicable desire to admit to just how much he did, but he settled for a single, terse nod. It would be far from appropriate to discuss with his brother's wife just how much he *liked* his future bride.

"I believe you do. And I also don't feel you should be expected to give up all of your endeavors now that you're to be married. But," she added sharply; "Miss Leroy deserves better. To her credit, she has yet to complain once, nor inquire after your absence." This last caused Simon's head to snap forward; Meredith's lips tilted in a smile and, for the first time, he noticed how red-rimmed her normally bright, indigo eyes were. "It's not for lack of curiosity, but out of respect. For you, I believe, sincerely."

Simon's heart skipped. "Now, are you going to join us all for a rousing game of pall mall this afternoon, or must I send George and Jeremy up here to drag you down to the lawn?"

Simon shook his head, the edge of his mouth tilting in the whisper of a smile. The truth of Odette's respect for his work and his eccentricities was an exhilarating realization, but it was also deeply unfamiliar.

Sensing his inner turmoil, Meredith stepped forward and placed a hand on his arm. Her voice was infinitely patient and soothing when next she spoke. "I realize just how overwhelming all this change is— especially when it's so unexpected. To share one's life with someone, even if you care for them, is a daunting prospect." Simon could only stare at the spot where her pale hand rested against the sleeve of his linen shirt. He hadn't bothered dressing in a coat, waistcoat, or cravat since he'd had no intention of interacting with another person that day. The gesture was incredibly sisterly and comforting in a foreign way. He'd always known his sister, Lily, cared for him, but she'd always been much closer to George than Simon. "My suggestion is you take the time before the wedding to get to know her better than you already do. You enjoyed her company before all of this, because we both know you wouldn't have spent as much time with her as you did." She patted his arm once before stepping back. "We're all going to take advantage of the break in the weather and spend some time out of doors. I insist that you join us in half an hour."

"Whose bloody idea was this anyway?" Sommerfeld cursed with a grumble. He leaned on his cane to rest his right leg. Odette tried not to stare, but she was infinitely curious about the leather and metal contraption he wore strapped to that limb. It was fascinating.

"I believe it was yours, my love," Meredith replied airily as she selected her mallet from the stack. She looked far better than she had in the family sitting room earlier that morning. She must have made good use of a cool compress because there was hardly a hint of tear-swollen eyes.

"Leave it to your impeccable memory to put me in my place." He rolled his eyes dramatically, but even Odette could sense the joke in his voice. He curved an arm around his wife's shoulders and pulled her close to press a lingering kiss to the side of her head.

A small smile curled her lips as she tested the weight of the mallet Shefford had handed her earlier. The little wickets had been set up by a couple of footmen before they'd tromped out to the expansive lawn. Some of the low points were still damp from the incessant drizzle, but, for the most part, the earth was dry enough for the game. As Lily explained it, the basic point was to knock one's ball through the metal arched wickets and be the first to reach the designated peg. There was some discussion of strategy and blocking and knocking an opponent's ball out of range, but Odette was far more concerned with not missing the ball and making an utter fool of herself as she fell on her rump.

The sun broke through the wispy clouds and the air felt instantly warmer and more welcoming. As much as she'd enjoyed exploring Bridleton these past few days—and could likely do so for many months and never learn the ins and outs of the expansive house—she was excited about spending time outdoors. She had yet to poke around much of the winding gardens she'd glimpsed outside of one of the corner turrets, or meander through the topiary and fountain arrangements. With just days left before the wedding, she hoped there would still be enough time to continue her investigations—in between wedding preparations, that is.

"Well." Sommerfeld shifted his weight from side to side as he surveyed their little group.

Shefford propped the weighted head of his mallet against his broad shoulder.

His wife nibbled the corner of her lip before looking back at her elder brother.

Odette caught Meredith's eye and there was a brief moment where her concern went unchecked before she pasted on a cheery smile.

Odette was no simpleton. She knew quite well they were all fretting over the fact that their group still had an odd number. Her fiancé had yet to make his appearance.

As each of the seconds ticked by like a deafening heartbeat, Odette tried not to focus on the glances filled with both concern and pity, the way her eyes began to burn, how her nose began to prickle. She willed herself not to cry. She'd taken such pride in her strength throughout all of this—her determination to refrain from being a demanding, insecure woman; to remain understanding and patient with Simon—but this afternoon was just about all she could take. Were she a bolder, more confident woman, she might have stomped throughout the manor, slamming open doors until she located her wayward betrothed.

But she wasn't.

And she didn't.

She closed her eyes once again, trying to use the warmth of the sun as it jumped out from behind another cloud to bolster her smile. She filled her lungs with the petrichor emanating from the earth around them and, although it went against her nature, she took a lesson from her mother: She injected her spine with steel and tapped her mallet on the soft grass beneath her feet before speaking with more cheer and conviction than she felt. "Shall we begin? I'm eager to watch and learn."

"Of course!" Lily jumped in brightly and proceeded to (none-too-subtly) nudge her husband into motion after it was agreed that the ladies would team against the gentlemen. "Normally, we would allow you to start off the game as our guest, but, seeing as how you'll be family in a matter of days, I'll begin and you can watch how we take our turns."

The game progressed through turns as Lily and then Meredith stood a specific way and knocked their painted balls across the grass with measured force. When Sommerfeld would have insisted Odette take her turn next, she declined with a shake of her head and deferred to both the gentlemen, claiming she needed more time to examine the proper form.

She became more relaxed as each took their turn and they all slid away from the awkwardness of Simon's absence. The ribbing between siblings and spouses was unbelievably warm and amusing; she'd had to mask a bubble of laughter when Lily quite irritatedly swatted her brother's sleeve after his ball knocked hers to the wayside.

"Your turn, Miss Leroy," Meredith said with a smile, yanking Odette's attention back to the task at hand. She eyed the orange-sized wooden orb nestled in the lawn before her and was suddenly, absurdly, unaccountably intimidated by the cerulean blue object. She swallowed past the lump in her throat, attempting to brush aside the knowledge that all eyes were on her once again. She puffed out a bracing breath and took up what she hoped was a sufficiently confident position.

"Your hands are all wrong."

Odette's head whipped up to find Simon striding toward her across the plush carpet of grass. So surprised and thrilled was she at his sudden appearance that she forgot all of her anxieties from before, all of her frustrations and embarrassment. He may have disappeared for several days, he may have been late, but he'd still shown up. Her eyes began to burn for an entirely different reason.

His long stride devoured the last several feet to where she stood, the mallet held limply in her numb fingers.

He'd bathed very recently, she pondered dumbly as she eyed his damp golden hair curling slightly at his temples, and freshly-shaven jawline. His starched cravat and dark coat, charcoal waistcoat and fitted breeches, and boots polished to an unholy shine were immaculate. And the man that filled them, even more so.

"Miss Leroy," he inclined his head and the deepness of his tone sent a barely suppressed shiver up and down her spine. "Odette," he spoke more softly for her ears only. This close, she could smell his soap, the clean, masculine scent of his skin.

His mouth twitched as if hesitant to see how welcoming she'd be to a smile, and she wished he would with every fiber of her being. She wished they were alone so she could run her thumb along his lower lip and help it along, to savor the softness she knew resided there.

"May I?" he asked gently as the pad of his thumb brushed the back of her hand. Odette all but dropped the handle of the mallet and leaped backward as if burned.

"Y—Yes, please do," she stammered, praying his siblings and their spouses were outside of earshot. The sight of his long, elegant fingers (now scrubbed pink and mostly clean of ink stains) entranced her.

"Your grip is too high," Simon explained and demonstrated the proper hand positioning before giving it a few experimental swings, the heavy mallet head gracefully skimming across the blades of grass. It seemed he did more than just dance with unexpected elegance.

"Come," he gestured to her, snapping her from her trance.

She stepped forward and accepted the proffered mallet shaft, then allowed him to properly position her hands. She tried to remain calm when the sensation of his fingers on hers brought back the memories of the way he'd touched her and held her. Kissed her.

He proceeded to stand behind her and show her how to swing the mallet so it connected with the ball. She felt the heat rolling off of the length of his body to caress her back. He stood improperly close with his arms wrapped around her, his head leaning mere inches from hers, but no one on the lawn said a word. In fact, their fellow competitors took great pains to allow the scene to play out as it would. Odette vacillated between gratitude and mortification. She could count the number of times he'd been this close to her on a single hand—less than that if she were truthful. And she looked forward to it occurring more often if she were honest.

They moved fluidly together, practicing several gentle test swings before Simon stepped back and allowed her to try her hand. The mallet connected with the ball with a satisfying click and rolled—if not even with—at least in the right direction of the other balls to remain in the game. Odette bounced with a little whoop of glee and found her betrothed watching her intently, his green eyes glittering with some unreadable expression.

She could get lost in those eyes. She could melt against the strong wall of his body. For all his faults, she couldn't help but be drawn to him.

Odette knew she should have been furious with him for his neglect of her since she arrived at Bridleton. She should have given in to her desires to storm through the manor and drag him out of hiding by his ear like a wayward lad. But all of that fled now that he stood before her. Her anxieties, if not banished entirely, were lightened by his presence. And, somehow, she knew he felt the same.

Separate, they were less than they were when they were together. Each provided an unexpected comfort to the other.

"Kind of you to join the land of the living, brother!" Sommerfeld called over to them, breaking the mysterious spell between Odette and Simon. "Take up a mallet and join in the game."

Simon turned and retrieved the final mallet and ball, dropping the goldenrod yellow orb to the grass, measuring his shot, and sending it sailing into the fray. Sommerfeld cursed as his crimson ball bounced into a puddle collected between the twining roots of an oak tree.

Odette had to stifle another snicker when Simon's satisfied eyes met hers and he swung his mallet over his shoulder in an unexpectedly jaunty gesture. There was a bashful tilt to his mouth.

"It's all angles," he said gently, by way of explanation.

Chapter Eight

The next several days passed in a blur with the countess spearheading final wedding preparations. One of the final items to handle before the big day was for Odette to endure what felt like interminable hours of fittings for her gown. Her mother had provided her measurements to a prominent London modiste and the gown had been shipped to Bridleton. Unfortunately for Odette, she had two sets of measurements: her real ones, and the ones her mother believed she should fit. This wasn't the first time her mother had ordered clothing for her with those optimistic measurements, but Odette silently thanked God that it would be the last. *Finally*, she'd be able to order her own gowns in a style and measurements that suited her best.

This, however, didn't solve the present and quite serious issue of her ill-fitting wedding gown.

While crafted from gorgeous gossamer shades of pink and pale rose, the scalloped neckline was indecently low on her ample bosom and the back simply refused to lace up no matter how tightly her stays were pulled; the beaded cap sleeves were cut far too tightly and were several inches away from sitting where they should; while the cut of an empire waist was normally flattering for most figures, there was nowhere near enough fabric to float around Odette's hips and it hugged her curves most unfortunately.

She felt—and looked—like a sausage bursting from its casing. She had to laugh to keep from crying.

Thankfully, as they had been throughout the rest of the planning process, both Lily and Meredith had been present for the disaster, offering consoling or reassuring words based on the particular moment and situation. There was no masking the pitying glimmers in their eyes at the sight of poor Odette in her gown.

Of course, the countess had also been there.

As Odette stood upon the seamstress's stool she'd set up in the privacy of the family parlor, the older woman eyed her from her seat on the sofa. And, though she had been nothing but polite and welcoming since Odette's arrival, she had a feeling her future mother-in-law found her coming up short.

She pasted on a brave smile as, following several moments of heavy silence, the countess suddenly stood and approached where Odette was frozen in place. She circled her once and then gently fingered the pink-tinted pearls and rosy glass beads decorating the low-hanging cap sleeve.

"Your mother's seamstress is talented with design…but her fitting abilities leave much to be desired," Simon's mother commented flatly. The bust line seemed to be particularly irksome to her; she was certain if her eyes could light a fire, the offending dress would have been reduced to ash twice over already.

Odette's cheeks burned uncontrollably. It felt wholly disloyal to her mother to lay the blame at her feet, but would it be better to do so than allow the countess to believe she'd hired an incompetent seamstress?

Before Odette could say anything, however, Lily spoke up. "It could be a beautiful gown, Mother," she said while smoothing the layers of fabric. "It is amazing how a proper fitting can make a dress feel like an entirely new garment."

The countess made a thoughtful sound in reply.

Meredith knelt before her and lifted the hem to check the seams. "Oh dear...she didn't leave enough room to let this out as much as we need," she sighed and worried her lower lip between her teeth.

"Well," the countess huffed. "This simply won't do!" Odette tried not to flinch. She'd been mentally preparing herself for days to be called out as unworthy as she was, in truth. What the countess said after calling over her modiste, however, made Odette's stomach flip. "We can't have this lovely girl feeling anything less than confident and beautiful on her wedding day."

Lily met Odette's eyes and the acceptance she read in her smile made Odette's vision blur. She turned back to the countess and the kindness she saw there was almost worse for her composure.

"What would you like, dear?" the older woman asked kindly, but not pityingly. "Should we attempt to alter this one or have a new one made?"

Odette swallowed past the lump in her throat. "S—Surely there isn't time to have a new gown made before the wedding."

"You would be surprised by what can be accomplished with enough money and the Stratford name," the countess replied with an airy laugh. "The choice is yours."

A choice.

When was the last time Odette had been given a choice? For that matter, had it ever happened? She'd had no say in her schooling, whether she was sent away from the only family she'd ever known, what she wore, what she ate, and now even who she was to marry...

And the countess was giving her this first choice of what could possibly, finally, be many throughout the rest of her life: She could choose what she wanted to wear on her wedding day.

"There are certain perks to marrying into this family," Meredith chimed in with a friendly smile.

Odette looked back down to her gown and immediately knew what she wanted.

"If we are able to refit this gown, then I should like to try it." The gown was truly beautiful—would be even more so once it fit properly—and she would accept it as a last gift from her mother. After this, she would be a woman who controlled her own life.

The countess gave a decisive nod and, with a flick of her fingers, the seamstress and her assistant flew in and immediately began their ministrations.

Odette's soul remained blissfully light and buoyant throughout the process, even when she was pricked with the occasional pin.

Two days before the wedding, Odette took advantage of a rare respite from the countess's strict list of "necessary" wedding preparations and slipped away to one of the quietest rooms she'd yet to encounter in Bridleton—at least, the only one she could reasonably make her way both to and from without losing her way.

The library was a tall, narrow room with towering leaded glass windows overlooking the vast expanse of ripe green fields. Books in earthen tones of all shapes and sizes filled the shelves to the ceiling. She couldn't imagine the effort it would take to dust the room from top to bottom; likely the poor servants had to start all over again just as they finished one go around.

The ceiling had been painted blue with puffy white clouds in a surprisingly realistic representation of the sky just outside those tall windows. If she laid just so on the chaise and the lighting was just right, she could almost imagine real swallows were darting to and fro above her head.

That afternoon, Odette planned to revel in the solitude she found in the library. She kicked off her slippers to lean back and pull her feet beneath her. Her mother likely would have had a coronary had she learned Odette behaved in such an informal way in the home of an earl, but Odette found she placed less and less weight in that opinion the longer she basked in the warm, accepting glow of the Stratfords. Besides, she was drained and exhausted from the preparations over the last several days. Who knew throwing together a hasty wedding could still create so much chaos?

She'd plucked a book of poetry from one of the numerous shelves and, while she made a great effort to read the words before her, her eyes began crossing and her vision blurred. It wasn't long until her head tipped to the side and she fell into a comfortable sleep in the warm rays of sunshine streaming through the windows, blanketing her in golden light.

Simon juggled the large stack of books in his arms as he strode down the stairs and back toward the library. It would have been vastly easier to have a servant replace the books, but he needed to grab a few more before he headed back up to his rooms; he had the library's layout memorized and it was simply quicker to do the task himself. He repeated the titles over and over again in his head as the other part of his brain argued for and against making a stop in the kitchens. He couldn't quite recall the last meal he'd taken.

In the two days that had passed since the pall mall game, he'd taken Meredith's words to heart and moved his research back to his rooms in a more accessible area of Bridleton. His family had made it very clear that he wouldn't be allowed to hide away. Several times, he'd been drafted into parlor games after supper, the ink still staining his fingers as he'd been dragged from upstairs after (mostly unintentionally) skipping the meal. It was the most tantalizing sort of torture to be that near to Odette, to hear the melody of her laughter and bear witness to her smile without being able to pull her fully into his arms and ravage her with his mouth and his body. Each time he was in her presence, it took his brain many hours to return to normal function. Rather than numbers and facts, his eyes saw only the perfect curve of her cheek, calculated the pleasing slope of her dainty nose, and pondered the softness of her skin. She was distracting. She drove him mad.

More than once, someone had flippantly accused him of bordering upon insanity with his intense obsessions with his various projects, but none of it compared to the looping images of Odette running through his mind like a ribbon with no discernible beginning or end in sight.

Simon did what he could with his work, diligently transcribing important text selections, referring and cross-referencing layer upon layer or mathematical writings; however, there was only so much he could accomplish when his mind—and his wayward body—longed, for the first time, to be elsewhere.

The door to the library was ajar, so it didn't take much effort for him to press it open the rest of the way with his back. He did nearly lose the small book off the top of the stack, but a fancy lurch kept it from tumbling to the floor. His eye on his destination across the long, narrow library kept him from realizing that he was not alone until he was nearly upon Odette.

He stuttered to a stop.

Draped across the comfortable chaise situated near the back window, she appeared to have dozed off while reading. Unable to resist, Simon tilted his head to read the title embossed upon the spine and a small smile tugged at the corner of his lips. Leave it to her to read some romantic poetry.

He placed his weighty stack of books on a nearby table, making sure they were piled sturdily enough that they wouldn't topple over, and turned back to her. His mother's continuous admonishment that staring was horribly uncouth echoed in the chambers of his skull, but it was impossible when Odette looked like that…besides, it wasn't as if Odette would know.

Her cheek was pillowed on a small decorative cushion a much younger Lily had embroidered with crooked flowers and absurdly fluffy lambs. Her hair appeared to have been tied back in a simple chignon and fastened with an ivory ribbon at one point, but several locks had come free to fall across her forehead and caress the curve of her cheek. One of her hands held the book open against her lap while the other rested palm-up beside her face, fingers curled as delicately as if she'd been positioned by a great painting master. For that matter, it appeared as if the entire scene had been so artfully cultivated just to torture Simon.

Limned in the most complimentary of golden lights, Odette fairly glowed. Her soft skin was now lustrous and her hair glittered; the individual strands of gold were picked out and shimmering in the sun. The delectable curve of her petal pink lips parted on a sleepy whisper of a sigh. The perfect swells of her bosom rose and fell with her gentle, even breaths; Simon's groin gave a powerful throb of need. His eyes drifted lower, taking in the flawless curve of her hip, the shapely ankles just barely revealed by the hem of her powder-blue morning dress trimmed in white lace flowers and rosettes. She was the personification of sweetness and innocence and all things good, his Odette. From the very moment they'd met, Simon had never been made to feel awkward or irritating; in fact, she seemed to have gone out of her way to accept him as he was. And, when she'd kissed him back, he was certain he'd tasted desire and not obligation.

All things considered, many men had far less to look forward to in their marriages than Simon did. Not that he'd ever truly given much thought at all to the possibility of his marriage, but seeing his future quite literally laid out before him was heady, and exciting, and terrifying in so many ways all at once. It overwhelmed him from the inside out, each emotion fighting for dominance, but, as he stood there watching Odette sleep so trustingly and peacefully, he felt only warmth and desire.

Simon allowed himself to study her for several more minutes before he turned and silently left the room, completely forgetting about the books he'd meant to retrieve.

Odette awoke a short while later feeling as if she'd missed something. She couldn't quite place her finger on it, but she didn't recall that stack of books on the nearby table before.

Chapter Nine

Simon had experienced more frequent urges to fidget since the commencement of the engagement than he had in the past ten years combined. What was it about this situation that made him squirm so?

"Do hold still, dear. Your cowlick just won't stay…"

Ah…there it was…

Before the past two weeks, it had been a blessedly long while since he'd been beneath his mother's well-meaning thumb for such a prolonged period. And, to top it off, she was extra attentive because today, of all days, he was getting married.

Not for the first time, Simon's stomach alternated between plummeting and soaring.

To once and for all be able to unabashedly enjoy Odette as his wife…now that was worth celebrating. (And, with any luck, he'd finally be able to focus on his work once more.)

Committing to being a partner, caretaker, provider, confidant, husband…that was terrifying to him. He'd spent so much of his life being forced to compromise bits of himself to fit into the mold set forth by his family and Society, and now, just as he was finding his stride and making headway in his ambitions, it was worrisome to consider how much more of him would need to be carved away to fit these new roles. It had nothing to do with Odette—that he wanted her and enjoyed being around her was never a question—and everything to do with Simon, himself.

What if he came up short?

What if he made Odette miserable?

"Are you well, dear? You look a tad green." His mother froze while adjusting his lapel for precisely the seventh time.

"Of course he is, he's getting married," chimed in George, who then followed it with a reflexive flinch, remembering a moment too late that his wife was not in the room to good-naturedly swat him for his ribbing.

"Don't act as if you haven't been deliriously happy these past few years," Jeremy added, cocking one dark brow. "I've half a mind to elbow you in the rib by proxy."

"Your elbows are far less bony than Meredith's, so I'll accept it."

As far as examples of wedded bliss went, Simon was certainly spoiled for choice. His parents were content; Jem's parents had been as well before the old baron's passing. Jeremy and Lily were like two halves of the same coin. George and Meredith were a shining example of how love can make you a better person—can help make you whole. What could he ever hope to offer Odette other than his name and a decently comfortable annual portion off of which to live? This would probably be enough for any number of women in England, but they were not Odette. She deserved these, and so very much more.

The incessant lurching of his nerves caused his stomach to roil uncomfortably. A weakness seeped into his joints and he fought the impossible urge to crawl out of his own skin.

Simon reached up and gently removed his mother's hands from his person. Her green eyes widened in response.

"Please, Mother. I require a moment." He needed to *breathe*.

She didn't want to let him go—that much was evident in her expression—but she responded with a reluctant nod and allowed him to step away. "I'll just go check on the ladies." She turned to go, but seemed to think better of it and caught Simon's hand once more. She stepped close and stood on her toes to kiss him on the cheek before whispering, "You'll always be my little boy. For what it's worth, these may not have been the most conventional of circumstances, but I don't doubt that Odette would still be a good match for you." Stunned immobile, Simon could only watch his mother as she slipped from the room.

"Brandy?" The earl approached Simon, Jem, and George with a crystal decanter and a full glass.

"Already? It's only—" George's protest died as Simon snatched the glass from his father and tossed it back, so numb with nerves that he hardly registered the burn.

Less than half an hour later, Simon stood at the front of Bridleton's great hall before the enormous, yawning stone hearth. The space seemed excessive for the meager size of the wedding party, but his mother had steadfastly demanded some pomp and circumstance for the occasion. She'd insisted that none of the parlors or sitting rooms would do and, Simon suspected, she'd had a change of heart and was determined not to make Odette feel as if they were not the least bit ashamed of the union. While appreciative of the gesture for Odette's sake, it still felt like an impracticality.

Aside from his close family, Jem's mother, and a smattering of nearby family friends, overly large flower arrangements of calla lilies, carnations, and roses punctuated by dripping vines of ivy filled the space. Most surprisingly, Blackwood had made the journey from

London to take up the role of best man when George had been nominated to walk Odette down the aisle and give her away by proxy. The countess had insisted that the pastor from Wrothsborough officiate despite the fact that the church pews were being refinished; the solution had been to have both the ceremony and wedding breakfast at Bridleton.

"Who knew we'd end up here when I coerced you into joining me at the theater, eh?" Blackwood leaned in and whispered behind Simon's shoulder. If he were a worse man and if the brandy hadn't done its job, then Simon might very well have jammed a well-placed heel into his friend's kneecap.

Just then, the room fell silent and the small congregation rose as one at the gesture of the priest. Simon's eyes hesitated, savoring the silent second as it was drawn out, before his gaze was pulled inexorably up the aisle between the sparse rows of chairs.

Lovely was too bland a word for the way she looked.

Beautiful was too common.

Angelic, too fanciful.

Breathtaking?

Yes.

That would aptly describe the way the sight of Odette froze the air in his lungs, stopped time, and made him want to remember her in this moment forever even if he expired from it.

He followed the motions and directions of the ceremony, but his mind floated elsewhere. This woman—this vision in diaphanous shades of petal pinks, pearls, and crystal clear eyes—drove him *beyond* the point of distraction.

If given half a chance, he knew she could push him into obsession.

When he held her ungloved fingers with his own, there was a shock of electricity.

When her voice agreeing to the vows caressed his ears, his heart flipped.

When Blackwood handed him the ring and he slid the band of gold, opals, and sapphires onto her finger, he actually had to fight back a chill of anticipation.

When the priest pronounced them man and wife and said they might seal the contract with a kiss, the words were barely on the air before Simon—savoring the widening of Odette's luminous eyes, the surprised parting of her full lips, the pale pink flush cresting her cheeks and the bridge of her pert little nose—pulled her close with an arm around her waist and the other palm pressed to the warm skin between her shoulder blades, and claimed her mouth in a kiss that could only be described as soul-searing.

The moment was only broken when George coughed into his fist.

Simon finally (more than a little reluctantly) pulled back and gazed down into his wife's—*his wife's*—glazed sapphire eyes with their dilated pupils and kiss-tinted lips. He didn't want to stop looking at her, savoring her, basking in the warmth of her sweet, shy smile. Despite his best efforts, she'd slipped into his life and already begun filling in the cracks and voids he hadn't even known existed, the missing pieces with which he'd coexisted for so long, he'd forgotten their location. All Simon knew as he sat beside her at the wedding breakfast surrounded by more floral arrangements and platter after platter of morsels, all he could think of was finally slaking the overwhelming desire for Odette. Of finally, irrevocably, claiming her has his, and his, alone.

The food in his mouth turned to dust, the drink lost all flavor, and he strongly suspected it would until he got this woman out of his system once and for all.

*****

Odette sat alone before the hearth of the inn at which they'd stopped for the night. She'd dismissed Alyssa for the evening and chose, instead, to plait her own hair by the warm licking light of the fire. As she stared into the glowing, popping logs, she was reminded of the way Simon had been watching her all day. His strange eyes were held rapt, focused on her every move, her every breath, since she saw him for the first time that morning waiting for her at the head of the makeshift aisle in Bridleton's great hall. She had been instantly blind to all the lovely flowers, the small gathering of guests in attendance, and she saw only Simon.

He had stood so straight and proud, but those eyes spoke of some dark promise she couldn't fathom, no matter how hard she tried. She'd been unable to stifle the chill of anticipation rushing up and down her spine and she knew Viscount Sommerfeld had felt it where he held her arm. He'd glanced down at her curiously, his green eyes slightly widened in question, but Odette refused to allow him for even one second to entertain the belief that her shiver had been born of hesitation. She'd tightened her grip on his steadying arm and practically tugged the man into motion to march down the aisle toward her husband.

Her husband!

Odette tied off her plait and stared down at the gold ring on her finger. An opal cabochon was flanked on either side by triangular-cut deep blue sapphires. It was unique and unusual. And she loved everything about it. Of course, she would have been happy with a simple band–or even no ring at all—but the surprise of it had been as equally thrilling as the piece itself. She hadn't been able to take her eyes off the piece. Never in her dreams had she contemplated owning such a beautiful, expensive piece of jewelry. Then again, never had she thought she'd marry a man such as Simon.

The thud of boots echoed up the hallway, growing louder with each step before finally halting just outside her door.

Odette's heart began to race, increasing its speed more with every second of silence. Simon had earlier quit the room under the guise of offering her privacy to change from her traveling dress in peace and to have a quick word with the innkeeper.

The entire carriage ride to the inn had been silent, neither quite seeming to know how to fill the silence. He sat beside her on the comfortable forward-facing cushion, but not once did his knee so much as brush against hers.

Forced to find her own entertainment, she'd enjoyed the shifting scenery, watched as they drove over the rolling hills and the outskirts of villages, beneath the shady canopies afforded by copses of trees... but she had also caught Simon watching her intently on far more than one occasion. He'd opened his mouth as if to say something or shifted in his seat as if to move closer, but none of it ever came to fruition. Instead, she'd passed the time fiddling with her skirts and twisting a spare scrap of ribbon around her fingers while he tapped his thumb against his knee and pretended to read the book in his lap—she knew it was pretending because even she had memorized the first paragraph by the time they arrived at their destination.

The Silver Hind was a popular travelers' inn on a well-ridden route along the coast between Kent and London, and it catered to well-off clientele in search of comfortable beds and quality food. Prior to the wedding ceremony, the earl had offered to send them on a honeymoon trip but Simon had resisted, saying he couldn't possibly leave his work at such a crucial point. A compromise was attempted when the seaside was suggested—it was far enough to give them privacy, but not so far that Simon wouldn't be able to lug along his trunks—it was decided that they'd stop there for the night on their way back to Town. They were foregoing a traditional honeymoon trip to, instead, take the time to set up their own house. It all seemed rather appropriate given the fact that there was nothing really traditional about any aspect of their relationship.

Yanked back to the present, Odette watched as the door handle finally began to turn and, in just those seconds, everything her mother had told her about her wedding night came flooding back with as much force as the disintegration of a dam. To her mortification, she was privy to the general mechanics of the act in which she'd now be expected to participate. Her mother, being the consummate professional she was, then insisted upon educating her further…because it was integral to playing any role to go above and beyond. Odette had been enlightened as to how men liked to be touched, how they enjoyed it when women told them how wonderful they were, how some of them liked to feel in control, how a man might expect her to do things with her hands and her mouth—

All of it fled just as quickly when Simon's head and shoulders appeared around the door. She decided in that moment that her eyes met his and his lips tilted into a small, charmingly unsure smile, that she would give herself to him without shame. She wouldn't allow her mother's extensive lesson to overpower her or make her nervous on what was to be the very first night spent in this man's arms.

"Are you well?" he asked.

"Quite," she croaked. Despite her best intentions, it was difficult not to be keenly aware that she was sitting before the fire in nothing but a thin white nightshift. Mostly modest, there were bands of lace inset in the sleeves and at the hem, lending little glimpses of pale skin when she moved. It was simultaneously virginal and seductive—another of her mother's orchestrations.

"Is there anything else you need this evening?" Simon inquired, still only partially in the room.

She smiled bravely and shook her head.

There was another heartbeat's hesitation before Simon stepped all the way into the room and pressed the door closed behind him. There was a resounding click as he twisted the heavy key in the lock without looking away from her. They remained there in a silence broken only by the light popping of the logs in the hearth until he finally pushed himself away and began unknotting his cravat with deft fingers. The long strip of fabric was then draped over the other wooden chair in the room. His dark coat soon followed, as did his gray waistcoat. Her eyes were riveted on the notch at the base of his throat revealed by his gaping collar. Every inch of her skin began to tingle.

Really, how could such an innocuous piece of flesh create such a reaction?

Her toes curled beneath the hem of her nightshift and she fought the urge to wiggle in her seat. A flush crept across her cheeks and the warmth spreading throughout her had nothing to do with the fire and everything to do with the embers burning in his blue-green eyes. So consumed was she by his neck that she didn't realize just how close he was to her.

"Are you nervous?" His deep voice broke the spell. She tilted her head back to look all the way up into his face. She shook her head and his mouth tilted again in reply. "Do not lie." The words weren't unkind, but she still hesitated when he held out his hand to her. She accepted it and he gently pulled her to her feet. "Do not ever feel as if you need to lie to me. About anything. No matter how small." He lowered his forehead to hers. "I took all of you today when we said our vows." Odette's stomach fluttered uncontrollably. The heat spread further and a liquid warmth pooled at the juncture of her thighs where she felt suddenly, unfamiliarly swollen and wet.

Her lips parted, but no sound came forth—what was she to say to something so honest? So raw?

She was saved from having to reply when Simon's nose touched hers, grazing it from side to side, his mouth lowering incrementally. They'd kissed before—a few times, she was proud to say—but this was different. There was an undercurrent of anticipation of something more, something greater than she could ever hope to imagine. Something wild. Something the girls at school whispered about with feigned confidence, and the women of the theater smiled knowingly. His arms slipped around her waist, pulling her body flush with the lean strength of his a moment before their lips finally met.

If she'd believed their previous kisses to be passionate, then she'd been sorely mistaken. This mating of their mouths, the caress of their tongues and desperate clicking of teeth were so much more exciting, more volatile with promise than she'd ever believed possible. Her hands fisted in the fine fabric of his shirt and her knuckles were singed by the heat of his skin beneath the thin barrier. The sensation of every inch of his front held against hers was heady, indeed. One of his large hands slid down her back to cup the curve of her rear, pressing her lower body even more fully to his. She felt the unmistakable hardness of his arousal against the contrasting softness of her abdomen and silently cursed her mother—she had certainly downplayed this part of the male anatomy…though Odette supposed it was for the best. She might have been terrified had she truly known the size of what she might expect.

She gasped in delighted surprise when Simon broke their kiss and swept her into his arms, holding her high against his chest as if her weight was no more significant than a stack of his beloved books. He held her just as carefully, reverently, as he strode over to the bed and laid her down with infinite gentleness.

The bed was large—larger than Odette had expected from a travelers' inn—but she wasn't going to complain, not when she knew she'd be sharing it with Simon's large body. He braced his palms in the feather-stuffed pillows on either side of her head, gazing down at her intensely and intently as if peering into her very soul. She swore he could hear the rapid pounding of her poor heart and she briefly wondered if the organ might give out. Her nipples were becoming almost unbearably sensitive to the rubbing of the fabric of her nightshift, the hem of which had ridden up past her knees…though she couldn't find it in her to care.

"Do you know what to expect?" Simon breathed. There was a very faint tremor to his normally cool and collected tone. It was as intoxicating as a liberal amount of fine wine to realize that this situation had shaken him so. Perhaps he wasn't as unmoved by her as she'd once thought.

Odette could only nod mutely once before Simon placed one more deep, searing kiss on her lips. A small groan emanated from a bottomless well in his chest, but he pulled back all too soon, his hair slipping from her fingers.

When had her hands knotted themselves in the soft, short hair at the nape of his neck?

He leaned back and began to tug his shirt from his black breeches, her eyes watched his jerky motions with rapt attention and then widened at the lean expanse of smooth, sculpted skin revealed when he tugged the garment off over his head. He dropped the shirt in an uncharacteristically negligent manner and gazed down at her, his eyes never leaving hers as he began to undo the falls of his breeches.

Odette's cheeks flared more with every inch of him he revealed, the trail of coarse, dark blond hair leading from his navel to disappear beneath the fabric of his breeches and smallclothes, the thick ridge of his arousal barely disguised and held in check beneath his clothing. She only realized she was holding her breath when his fingers stalled. Her eyes flicked up to his face, where she already found him watching her.

"I should slow down," Simon whispered hoarsely to himself. Odette's brows knit together in confusion and she opened her mouth to tell him to continue—she didn't think her nerves could take the onslaught and anticipation for much longer—but he knelt with one knee between her thighs and pressed a kiss to her forehead.

"Y—You don't want—"

"Oh, I want…very much…" Simon settled himself atop her, his forearms bracketing her head as he placed feather-light kisses to her cheeks, her brows, her chin, her jaw, the hammering pulse in her throat. "I simply want your pleasure more." His words were hot puffs of air on her neck.

Her heart stopped.

She felt the gentle tugs of his nimble fingers as he undid the small bows securing the front of her nightshift. He pressed an open-mouthed kiss at every inch of skin revealed by his languorous ministrations.

"I crave it." His voice was a deep rumble she felt in her every nerve. Her entire body fairly vibrated with heightened awareness.

Her breath caught raggedly when he palmed and then cupped her breast through the gaping fabric of her nightshift, gently capturing her erect nipple at the vee of two fingers. He emitted an approving purr and, for the first time, Odette was thankful for her body.

If this man enjoyed it, then surely there must be something of which to be proud.

If she could cause the tremor in his voice, the subtle hitch in his breath, then she was far more powerful than she'd ever imagined.

One of Simon's long fingers hooked beneath the edge of her gown and he tugged aside in an agonizingly slow motion. A shaky sigh escaped his parted lips when the pink, tightly puckered bud of her nipple was finally revealed. By all accounts, she should have been embarrassed, but she was overwhelmed with the pleasure of his palm on her, then his lips as he kissed and laved the tight bud with his tongue. Her fingers flew to his hair, unsure if she was holding him there or trying to push him away to find relief from the delicious torture. He massaged her other breast as he lavished attention upon the first, worshiping it with his tongue and teeth; his hard thigh worked higher between her legs until it was pressed firmly against the moist juncture of her thighs. She could no more stop the undulating of her pelvis than she could her shaky gasps for air.

As he pressed kiss after open-mouthed kiss to the sensitive undersides of her now bare breasts, his hand trailed down between them to drag the hem of her nightshift up and over her head. He reared back to sit on his heels and the garment fell unnoticed from his fingers as his starving eyes roved over her. Drank her in. Memorized her. The swirling blue-green irises were nearly swallowed by his dilated pupils. A muscle in his angular jaw worked repeatedly, hollowing out his cheeks beneath his perfect cheekbones; his nostrils flared.

"Odette," he croaked.

Though agonizing, she held perfectly still, allowing him to take his time to devour the sight of her ivory skin. His eyes danced over the arch of her collarbone, the heavy swells of her breasts with their aching, raspberry-red nipples begging for his attention, the curves of her hips and the gentle slope of her abdomen, the thatch of pale, dewy curls between her legs, the shapes of her thighs, calves and ankles.

Every inch of her was on fire from his gaze. She tingled. She burned in the most delightful way. His eyes flew to her face. She couldn't name the emotion she saw there, perhaps because it was a maelstrom of many of them warring for dominance. It was strange and powerful. It was thrilling.

As if afraid she might dissolve into mist if he moved too quickly or touched her too firmly, one finger made a whisper of a trail up from her hip bone, across her ribs, scaling the slope of her breasts, the pulse in her throat, and the curve of her cheek. He cupped her there and met her eyes.

"What you do to me…" his voice trailed off as if in pain.

Before she could overthink it, however, he covered her body with his. The sensation of his hard chest with its dusting of coarse hair against her sensitive, naked breasts was shocking. He kissed her deeply, sipping and savoring every drop of desire he was creating within her. A groan of satisfaction reverberated from his chest through hers when his fingers discovered the moisture coating the petals of her sex. Once again, she should have felt mortified or shamed, but how could she when he was so pleased with her? He spread the liquid heat with his fingertips, gently toying with and caressing her in a place she'd never been touched before. And it was glorious. He traced the seam of her sex, plucking and swirling, as her legs fell wide for his ministrations. He settled both legs between her thighs, spreading her open and vulnerable with his knees, as another finger joined the fray. Together, his brilliant, nimble fingers, caressed and teased, dipping lower to press at her entrance and ever so slightly press inside. She gasped at the intrusion, but more out of surprise than pain.

"So tight," he murmured against her lips. "So sweet." He nipped her lower lip. "And all mine."

She shivered at the possessiveness in his tone, but it quickly dissolved into a cry of unexpected pleasure when he discovered a particularly sensitive spot at the crux of her sex. He dedicated himself to finding a pressure and rhythm that drove her wild, listening and learning from her sighs and gasps, her mewling whimpers of pleasure as electric darts of it flew through her limbs from that point of contact. She trembled and shook, unable to stop herself from climbing higher to a dangerous peak no matter how she clung to him. The only thing tethering her to the world was Simon's body atop hers, his hands and mouth on her. He must have sensed a change in her frantic breathing, the way she clutched at his shoulders with her nails, because he didn't stop. He didn't slow. He maintained his steady teasing and growled, "Come for me," a moment before sucking the tip of her breast deep in his mouth.

Odette's mother had once been gifted a gorgeous porcelain figurine from one of her sweeter admirers. The sculpture had been of a woman posing with a fan, coyly peering over its lacy edge. Odette had believed her one of the most beautiful things she'd ever seen. She'd spent months admiring the figurine on her mother's makeup desk until one day her seven-year-old self had been able to refrain from touching it no longer. She'd scurried up the tufted stool and stretched her plump little arms to reach the figurine. She'd held it reverently, only intending to examine the pretty pleats of her pale pink gown and the rose-red tint of her lips. She'd startled when her mother had unexpectedly reentered the room and she'd teetered dangerously atop the stool. Odette had been safe, but the figurine had tumbled from her tiny hands to shatter into a hundred minuscule pieces. An arm skittered across the floor, the pretty dress crumbled to dust and pieces so fine there was no hope of repair.

This was precisely how Odette felt the moment her climax claimed her.

Her body seized up, her lips parting in a silent scream, her back arching her breasts into Simon, as she drowned in pleasure. She broke apart into more pieces than that figurine, and she knew she'd be like-wise changed beyond recognition. There was no going back to the woman she had been, not when Simon had taught her such joy exist-ed. Not when he'd given her the gift of such knowledge.

Her whole body trembled right down to her soul as he continued his onslaught of her senses. So far gone was she in her rapture that she didn't realize he'd yanked his breeches down to free his member. It pulsed hotly against her inner thigh when his hand once more slid lower to her clenching entrance. This time, his fingers probed more deeply, stretching and filling her as she ground herself against him. He curled his fingers inside of her, hooking them to find just the right spot and rubbing her and teasing her from the inside-out. She writhed beneath him, silently begging for more things she could not name, until the pressure mounted once more. She didn't know what he was doing, but she never, ever wanted him to stop. When his thumb joined in the dance, rolling the pearl he'd discovered earlier, Odette lost all sense of self. She was nothing more than a bundle of nerves and gelatinous pleasure as what little was remaining of her blew away on the wind of another climax without ever having been allowed to re-cover from the first.

Simon held her while she sobbed and trembled. He pressed kisses to her face and chest as he slowly coaxed her down from where she floated in the clouds, his fingers gradually stilled. The only sound in the room was their mingled panting breaths.

"Oh—oh my…" Odette would later kick herself for the inane comment, but it was truly the only thought her brain could form.

"Indeed," Simon breathed in an approximation of a chuckle.

She gradually noticed that his body was still taut with carefully checked need, the thick column of his sex was resting heavily against her. She risked a glance down to see its broad flushed head and his hand still situated between her legs. Really, it was absurd to blush at that moment, but she did, nonetheless.

All nerves melted away once more when Simon kissed her sweetly, longingly. His fingers slid from her slick, swollen sex and she felt oddly bereft. When he placed one of his fingers between his lips to taste the dew, she lost all further capacity for thought.

"So sweet." His husky tone set off a chill of anticipation through every one of her vertebrae.

She knew there was more. She didn't know how she'd survive it, but she did know there was more to come.

Simon reached between them once more and rubbed his member through the slick petals of her sex, eliciting a gasp of surprise and then trembling pleasure. He positioned himself once more at her entrance and met her hazy gaze. The muscles in his neck stood taut and a fine sheen of sweat covered his brow, plastering his blond hair to his skull. Whatever it cost him, he'd been determined to see to her needs first, to give her blinding joy before he sought his own.

"Tell me if I hurt you," he breathed. She nodded, not quite sure what he was asking. Until he began to press forward.

His pace was slow and steady, relentless and patient. She squirmed and clutched the firm, arching plane of his back. He continued well past the point where she believed there surely could be no more of him.

"Simon!" she gasped his name. She'd doubtless be split in two if this continued.

He froze immediately, those uncanny eyes of his focusing on hers. The lines bracketing his mouth were painfully taut; the familiar line creased the skin between his brows. He appeared to be in agony as he held himself in check, but she knew deep inside her soul that he would still stop entirely if she asked him to. She had no reason not to trust him. And this seemed to be one of the worst, most awkward moments to stop.

She wrapped her arms around his neck and pulled his face down to hers, initiating a kiss for the first time. She relaxed as he kissed her back and they took turns tasting and nipping. Her thighs dropped to the sides to create a wider cradle for Simon's pelvis. One deep thrust of his hips and he was home; he breached her last weak defense and was seated to the hilt.

It was his turn to gasp as he screwed his eyes shut and laid his forehead on hers, their noses grazing as he started to move. He began slowly, infinitely careful and gentle. When a moan was torn from her lips, however, something snapped. Gone was Simon's cultivated self-control, an animal was released from deep within. As much as she'd appreciated his care earlier, she savored this side of him. She hadn't known her husband all that long, but she knew this wasn't a side of himself he let anyone see.

He reared back to his knees and changed the angle of his thrusts. Watching him above her, witnessing the flexing of his beautiful, lean body as he worked her toward another pinnacle was almost too much for Odette. She twisted her fists in the sheets in a helpless effort to ground herself, to not lose control too soon. Without missing a beat, Simon snatched up one of the pillows before it fell to the ground, knocked wayward by their rhythmic movements. He so easily lifted her with one hand and shoved it beneath her hips. His palms held her thighs open wide and he watched the place where their bodies met like a starved man eyeing his first meal. He was so thick, so deep. His gruff sounds of pleasure, the rasp of his voice as he mindlessly told her how good she felt, how much he loved her body, the erotic sound of their wet flesh gliding and colliding nearly shoved her over the edge. She had to bite her knuckle to keep from screaming when Simon coated his thumb in her slickness and caressed that magical bud. He seemed to be enjoying the sounds she made, the way her body clenched involuntarily around his member because his head fell back in a guttural groan. His body never stopped moving, grinding against hers, stroking her higher and higher.

"Come again, Odette," he panted. "Come again for me. I *need* you to come—"

Odette shattered.

She came apart for what felt like forever and was only dimly aware when Simon followed behind. The muscles of his abdomen clenched and his hips moved jerkily as he swelled and throbbed deep within her, filling her with liquid heat, a roar of pleasure ripped from his chest.

This time, Odette could only think in wonderment, *Oh…*

Chapter Ten

Oh no…

Simon lay awake later that same night, staring into the flickering orange-tinted dimness. He pondered the pulsing shadows dancing across the beams of the low ceiling, the lines and angles as they disappeared and reappeared when another flare of fire bloomed in the hearth. Hours had passed since he'd returned to the room to find his wife looking virginal and pristine as she prepared herself for bed. For *his* bed. It had taken every fiber of willpower in his being to not immediately fall upon her like a voracious beast. Even as he'd done his best to hold himself in check, he knew he'd probably been bolder, rougher than an innocent required…but Odette hadn't seemed to mind. In fact, she seemed only too glad to take everything he had to offer and still be hungry for more.

He'd slaked his immediate desire for his wife twice over now and already his body stirred for more…

As if sensing the turn of his thoughts, Odette curled more tightly against his side, snuggling herself closer to the warmth of his body. Her cheek lay on his chest above his heart, her arm curled loosely around his waist and her soft, shapely thigh thrown over his. The neat plait in her blond hair had long since come loose and the faintly floral-scented blond locks were spread around them like the spiraling fan of the Fibonacci sequence.

Even above the scent of their lovemaking and passion-induced sweat, Simon savored that sweet hint of something all Odette. His nose was already as attuned to it as his ears were to her sighs and laughter, as his eyes were to the way her expression softened and her eyes glazed when she neared her climax. He hadn't a pocket watch on hand, but he hazarded a guess that they'd been married for less than twelve hours…and already he was more absorbed in her than he'd been before.

This night was supposed to be the culmination of his undercurrent of obsession with this woman. This night was supposed to be his cure, not an escalation.

Simon had a habit of hyper-fixating on tasks and other things that interested him. This was part of the reason his work so consumed him —more so than many of his peers. If something intrigued him, his mind wouldn't let go until he'd examined it from top to bottom, inside and out, dismantled it and then rebuilt it, earned an in-depth knowledge of the subject, and squirreled away his newfound knowledge in the library cubbies of his mind.

Most of his all-consuming preoccupations passed once he satisfied his curiosity; the nagging of his mind would quiet once he'd assuaged his need for knowledge and exploration, and he'd then be allowed to return to his usual routine.

The freedom of finally taking Odette to bed was supposed to have quieted his mind and his body; it was supposed to have exhausted the insatiable desire he had to touch her, to be near her, to taste her and feel her… It was supposed to have allowed him to move on and focus once more on his work. But this…

Curiously, this evening had the opposite effect upon him.

For the first time in his life, Simon was spending the night in bed with a woman, rather than satisfying his natural urges and moving on. He'd been so confident in his usual routine that he'd even reserved another much smaller room across the hall. It wasn't that uncommon for married couples of the *ton* to maintain separate bedchambers, so the innkeeper hadn't so much as batted an eye at Simon's request for additional accommodations.

All thoughts of the empty room immediately fled his mind when he saw Odette sitting before the hearth. All of his sterile intentions were instantly dead in the air.

Simon closed his eyes and filled his lungs with a long, deliberate breath. He held the air inside for one, two…five seconds and then expelled it. Odette's head sank in minuscule increments as his chest slowly collapsed, now empty save for the thick desire still sitting leaden in his core where it demanded attention and craved *everything*.

Simon's usual routine was to run through his mental lists as a way to relax and lull himself to sleep. Now, all he wanted to do was bury himself in Odette, to lose his carefully cultivated peace and order as he brought her to another all-consuming climax.

This wasn't good.

Not at all.

This night had only whetted his appetite for Odette.

His wife made a little coo in her sleep, the soft pillows of her breasts pressed against his ribs, and Simon lost his battle with his self-control.

Desire pooled in his groin once more as his fingers trailed across the lush curve of Odette's hip and pressed a kiss to the top of her head. His fingers tightened as she nuzzled more closely. She wore a dreamy tilt to her lips when she tilted her head back and her eyes slit open, the lids still heavy with sleep.

This was the point of honeymoon trips, wasn't it? To take every opportunity to learn and explore and *enjoy* one's new spouse?

Simon rolled Odette so she lay over him like the world's most succulent, tempting blanket. He tangled his fingers in her hair and pulled her mouth down to his.

It was only logical…

Simon had elected to stay at the inn two more nights than they'd planned. Odette had barely registered the passage of time because she hadn't bothered to leave the room.

Or dress.

(Her husband had made it *very* clear that he'd simply remove any item of clothing she managed to don, so it was hardly worth even the smallest bit of effort.)

The door remained bolted against any interruptions or servants. Wood for the fire was left outside the door, along with other necessities. Simon had even ordered their meals left on a tray to be retrieved by a mostly-naked Simon when the hallway was deserted once more. Together, they'd shared the pies and stews, wine, freshly baked bread, and even some pastries the innkeeper's wife had baked herself. Simon saw to her every need, so much so that she didn't even see Alyssa at all until they all departed days after their initial intended date. Nor did she see the sea…which had been the point of taking their brief honeymoon detour to the coast.

Odette had blushed at the raised eyebrows with which Alyssa had greeted her; she was even more embarrassed by the realization that it would no doubt get back to her mother just how little anyone had seen of the new Mr. and Mrs. Stratford since the wedding day. But one look into Simon's face and everything else melted away. How could there be shame in enjoying the time spent with one's new husband?

Odette climbed into the Aldborough carriage and Simon followed shortly thereafter, waiting until she settled her skirts before, this time, taking up the rear-facing cushion.

"We should reach London by nightfall," he said as he situated himself and laid his books out beside him on the seat before rapping on the roof twice and they jerked into motion.

"Will we be going to your flat?" Odette asked though she felt more than a little silly at not having considered their actual destination before—aside from the metropolis of London, of course. Now that she thought about it, however, she was quite intrigued about seeing where Simon lived and worked.

"No," he said flatly. "It was one in a building with suites bachelor's rooms and it is unsuitable to bring one's wife. Women, in general, are not allowed."

"Oh."

"The flat was vacated and emptied this past week." They rocked along for another minute before he added, "I do hope they followed my explicit instructions on packing up my work, otherwise it'll be a bloody nightmare to set to rights," beneath his breath. He turned his attention out the window.

When he failed to elaborate further regarding their living arrangements, Odette asked, "So where shall we be staying, then?"

Simon turned back to her, his eyes slightly wide as if he hadn't realized she didn't know—or if he thought he'd already told her, but the
conversation had taken place only in his mind. "Why, we'll reside at
Aldborough House until we can pick new accommodations – no one
is in residence at the moment anyway and my parents will allow us
privacy and remain at Bridleton until we are well situated. My father's
solicitor has already prepared a list of four rental properties for us to
tour tomorrow."

Her own home.

The realization that she was to be the lady of her own household—
in charge of herself for the first time in her life—had occurred to her
like a faint undertow. Now, however, it was reality. She could choose
her own furnishings, dress how she wished, arrange her own meals,
break her fast with any food she fancied! No one would be looking
over her shoulder to question her. She felt bubbly, giddy like the next
good bounce of the carriage would send her floating up to the heav-
ens.

Then again, no one would be there to help catch her if she stumbled.

Odette's stomach felt a little less buoyant.

A woman gave up a great deal when she married; she laid her life
and her future in her husband's hands. There was something to be said
about the faith a husband had to have in his wife, too, though. Even if
her mother had an unorthodox lifestyle, Odette had had it drilled into
her when away at boarding school that a woman was responsible for
running the day-to-day. She managed a multitude of infinitesimal
tasks men often never saw and even more often took for granted. She
would handle household accounts, plan their social calendar, take up
her new place in Society as a respectable matron, and generally make
her husband's family proud. She was now Mrs. Odette *Stratford*.

Odette snuck a glance at her husband, but he'd already laid one book open in his lap and held another one in his hands, his blue-green eyes darting back and forth between the pages. He'd already moved on to other mental occupations, while Odette's thoughts danced and spun.

She was grateful that their new household wouldn't be too large—fewer things for her at which to fail or get wrong.

As part of the marriage arrangement, Simon had told her his annual portion as a second son and, while they would not be supremely wealthy, it was far more money than Odette had ever dreamed would come to her life without working herself to the bone.

As for their social calendar, she strongly suspected (rather, she *knew*) Simon would be quite content never having to go out into Society. For her part, she'd likely feel much the same. As comfortable as she'd become around Simon and his family, she wasn't ignorant enough to believe that the rest of the *ton* would be nearly as welcoming as her new in-laws. It still wasn't widely known that she was Mademoiselle Stella (née Estelle) Auclair's daughter, but it would inevitably be brought to light that she did not come from "good stock", as they said. (She didn't even know who her father was, for goodness' sake!) Truly, the Stratfords had done more than their share in welcoming her and she knew the support of the Earl and Countess of Aldborough, Viscount and Viscountess Sommerfeld, as well as Baron and Baroness Shefford, was going to go a long way toward gaining her entrée into certain circles, but, set that aside, and she was still only the illegitimate daughter of a French actress. Educate her, dress her up, marry her off to a man whose pedigree dated back centuries, and she was still going to be that girl beneath it all.

Odette's nerves set in and she stewed in them all the way to Aldborough House.

*****

The London home of the Earl of Aldborough was a stunning building
hewn of white stone, soaring columns, and several stories of glinting,
evenly-spaced clear glass windows. The butler and housekeeper
greeted Simon and Odette when they arrived. Both appeared to have
been a part of the household for a significant length of time, given
their advanced years and their keen knowledge of Simon's habits.

"Your belongings have been moved to your old room and un-
packed, Mr. Stratford," said the apple-cheeked housekeeper. Mean-
while, the white-haired butler nodded to a pair of footmen as they met
Alyssa and began unloading the trunks from the roof of the carriage.
"I've taken the liberty of having Lady Lily's former room prepared for
Mrs. Stratford." Odette had been addressed thusly less than a handful
of times at that point, and hearing it on the lips of someone she'd just
met sent her heart skipping.

"Thank you, Mrs. Lang," Simon replied, already leading the way
further into the house.

As the housekeeper's words sank in, Odette tried not to overana-
lyze how she and Simon would no longer be sharing a bed chamber.
Perhaps he was acting out of respect for his parents' household;
maybe he was simply going along with the living arrangements common with her new social class—surely it was through no malice of the
housekeeper, judging by the kind twinkle in her gray eyes as she curtseyed in greeting.

Odette followed her husband further into the large, open foyer with
its black and white tiling, wide curving staircase spiraling in an elegant curve to the upper floors. Larger-than-life portraits of Aldborough ancestors graced the walls alongside majestic landscapes in
thick, gilded frames. Having spent two weeks at Bridleton, she should
have expected nothing less than this stunning opulence...but it was

another thing to be confronted with it. How different this small portion of the population lived from the majority of Londoners.

"Mr. and Mrs. Stratford." The butler's voice stopped Simon's retreat further into the house. Both of them turned on their heels to see the older man holding a silver tray with a thin, cream-colored envelope. "This arrived for you this morning."

Odette's brows knit together. Who would be writing to her? Who would be writing to them? Was it possible that the news of their marriage and return to Town had spread so quickly?

When her frozen feet did not move, Simon strode back over to the butler and accepted the letter, returning to her side. The wax seal was crimson red and unmarked. Simon used the thin letter knife the butler had so conveniently provided, slit the paper open, and, together, they found a thin, unfamiliar script bearing an utterly unbelievable message.

"A house?" Odette squeaked after having read through it twice. She still had to wait for confirmation from her husband to believe her eyes.

"It would appear that way," Simon's forehead furrowed, the lines between his brows deepening significantly. "And it's unsigned." He pressed his fingers to the bare space which should have held a mark and then turned it over, but it bore no additional marks.

Odette plucked the letter from Simon's hands to read it again. And again.

Three lines were scrawled there on the fine parchment.

Three lines set their future off on an unbelievable trajectory.

Three lines meant they no longer had to spend a large portion setting up their own household and paying toward rent.

A townhouse on St. James's Square had been purchased for them and placed in their names. Paid for in full. The address was one they couldn't have dreamed of affording on their own.

And they had no idea who'd gifted this to them.

"Is this some sort of farce?"

"Who delivered this, Manley?" Simon asked the butler, disbelief evident in the lilt of his voice.

"A hired courier, Mr. Stratford. He wore no livery and no card was left."

Odette handed the letter back to Simon, who did as she had and skimmed it twice more. "This is implausible," she whispered.

"Incredible. Mind-boggling. Inconceivable," Simon, seeming to be experiencing a similar confusion, murmured more incredulous adjectives before his voice trailed off.

She looked up into Simon's bewildered face. "Your parents—"

"They would have said something in person, or at least used my father's seal. Your mother?"

"Could never have afforded such a thing," Odette replied with a shake of her head. They stared at one another for several heartbeats, clearly both wondering the same thing but unsure how to voice it: *Could this be a cruel joke?*

"I'll send a note to my father's solicitor in the morning. He can make some inquiries."

Chapter Eleven

It was truly a benefit to the Aldborough Earldom to have such an expeditious and efficient solicitor.

It wasn't much past noon the following day before Simon and Odette stood in the parlor of the townhouse at the address on St. James's Square contained in the letter. As far as anyone had been able to discern, the note hadn't been a hoax; there was even a deed placed in Simon's name to prove it. According to the solicitor's office who'd held it until the earl's men of business tracked it down, the title was his, free and clear. They immediately handed over the deed, the key to the home, and various documentation related to the purchase. Despite extensive combing for clues, none of it provided information as to the identity of their benefactor. The home had been purchased through a tertiary solicitor whose records were kept tightly sealed.

There remained no leads, though his father's solicitor had promised to continue to investigate. He was, however, careful to underscore the fact that there were no guarantees. "This is a remarkable gift—a good fortune for any second son," the solicitor had said. Simon knew the last wasn't intended to be a slight, more a comment of incredulity. It was a sentiment he was well used to. "My advice? Accept the property. It's a boon for any newlywed couple."

Simon glanced over at Odette, admiring the way she turned in a slow circle, her head tilted back as she appraised the soaring height of the ceilings with their thick crown molding.

Theirs.

This house was theirs.

Simon held the large cold key in his hand. It was just the two of them in the townhouse. It was unfurnished but comfortable, appeared well-built, and was in a highly desirable area. It was also better than anything he could have ever hoped to offer his wife. He may not have been the most conventional man, but he did still have some pride and it was dinged by the realization that he never could have provided Odette with what this anonymous giver had.

There wasn't much wealth in scholarly endeavors.

As he silently followed Odette from room to room, appreciating her quiet gasps of surprise and delight, watching the way she admired the details of an ornate hearth mantle or the convenience of a window seat in one of the four bedchambers, drinking in the tilt of her head and the delicate curve of her cheek, the way her dress floated along her delectable curves.

It had taken every ounce of willpower he possessed to refrain from seeking out her bed the previous night, their first in London. The situation—knowing she was just on the other side of a single wall—was a true test of his mental fortitude and Herculean physical restraint. He had repeatedly told himself that their stay at the inn had been astoundingly pleasurable, but now was the time to return to his work and scholarly applications.

The first step in his list had been accomplished; the next was to dedicate himself to his work. His deadline waited for no one and nothing—not even an unanticipated wedding. There had already been a small stack of letters waiting on his desk, brought over from his rooms to Aldborough House when his belongings had been transferred there. Sir Nigel had already been waiting for a reply for several days, so Simon had settled for staying up the prior night and rededicating himself to his project, doing his best to ignore his intrusive thoughts of Odette only feet away in another room.

With quite literally nothing else around them upon which to focus his mind, Simon could only watch Odette's movements, the graceful sway of her hips as she moved throughout the townhouse.

He was so enthralled with the tilt of her lips that he hardly heard her ask, "Your face is so serious; what has consumed your mind so?"

He took an opportunity to cast a broad sweep throughout the room into which he'd followed Odette—some sort of private sitting room, he supposed—before meeting her eyes. "I'm wondering what you think of all of this."

"It's so much more than I ever wanted or could have dreamed of," she replied airily and made her way toward him from across the narrow room. His blood began to sing as if her every movement called to his very essence. "But how can we accept such a gift?"

"The solicitor indicated nothing is preventing us from moving in immediately. This property legally belongs to us and there are papers to prove it."

"Us?" The angle of her smile was something his brother, George, would have described as coy, he was sure, but Simon wasn't given to such observations. And he sincerely doubted Odette had a coy bone in her body, especially not when it came to him. One thing he appreciated the most about their time together was the lack of artifice from their very first interaction.

"Of course, us," he responded, his eyes riveted on her lips. "This will be our home. Together."

Odette's hand trailed down his sleeve until her fingers laced with his. "I like that thought very much." There was a flicker of something in her eyes, something he couldn't read. So he waited in silence for her to continue. "I wonder, though, if I might at least ask my mother if she has any idea as to the identity of our mysterious benefactor. I know your father's solicitor is looking into it and I know she couldn't have been the one to purchase this house, but I believe it would go a long way to assuaging my concerns if I at least ask her."

Simon didn't have much warmth toward the woman who had birthed his wife. Though he and Odette still had yet to expressly discuss it, he was firm in his belief that the French actress had played her role of a lifetime arranging the compromising situation in which he and Odette had found themselves. Then again, he supposed he did have her to thank for the past several days of finally having Odette in his arms...

"If that is what you wish to do, then by all means."

His response must have been the right one because her fingers squeezed his in gratitude and she rose on her toes to press a kiss to his cheek. He couldn't help but inhale deeply of her delicious scent. His groin stirred with a fierceness that was almost crippling.

He couldn't help it; he held onto Odette's fingers when she would have stepped back.

Simon brought her hand up and pressed a kiss to the delicate skin on the inside of her wrist. Her delectable lips parted ever so slightly, even more so when the next caress landed upon the sensitive skin on the inside of her elbow. He tugged her closer still and wrapped an arm around her waist.

"What are you doing?" she breathed, gazing up at him with wide, innocent eyes that aroused him to no end.

"Kissing my wife." He followed through with his statement by pressing his lips on the soft skin of her collarbone and then the slope of her neck.

"Well, that much is clear," she tried to laugh airily, but the tremor in her tone gave her away. "I mean, why are you doing this here?"

"Why shouldn't I?" he retorted. This was so unlike him. She made him reckless. She made him wild. He needed a steady supply of Odette if he was going to retain any shred of sanity. Sleeping without her the prior night had been torture. Spending the morning in her presence had been a tease. And now he had her alone and all to himself, and he couldn't resist.

"What if someone comes in?"

"Well, then they'd be trespassing, wouldn't they?" He gestured around them with a tilt of his head. "Until we're informed other-wise—which seems highly unlikely at this point—this home belongs to us. And, as we have yet to hire any staff, we are more alone than most people in London. Anyone who might interrupt us is trespassing and will be forcibly removed;" he placed a kiss on her temple; "or run through with a sword for their untimely interruption."

Simon claimed Odette's mouth, kissing her deeply, tracing the seam of her lips with his tongue until she opened for him. An uncon-scious groan of approval rumbled through his chest like thunder heralding a tempest. She was so responsive, so eager… He loved how she felt against him, how soft and warm her body was, the way she moved and smiled, every sigh and breathless gasp with which she awarded him. Of their own volition, his palms cupped her rear, kneading it as he pressed her fully to his rolling hips and thickening arousal. She clutched his lapels in her tiny hands, hanging onto him as if he were her anchor in a storm when she stretched up on the tips of her toes.

His brain slowed and narrowed its focus onto just the two of them in that sunny room with its honey-blond wood floors and bare walls, tall windows and white crown molding.

He began maneuvering them to the nearest wall, which just so happened to be closest to the hearth with its carved marble columns and ornate mantle, a judgmental lion's head as its centerpiece. He caught her when the heel of her slipper became snagged in the hem of her pink dress and, rather than simply set her to rights and continue, he bent and hiked Odette into his arms. She made a little yelp of surprise as he hitched his arms beneath her supple thighs and wrapped her legs around his hips, but she melted rather quickly once again and wound her arms around his neck, meeting his ravenous kisses with her own. She eked out a little squeak of surprise when her back met the wall, but it only urged Simon on as he used it for leverage to press them together more closely.

She tasted like the late-summer berries she'd had with luncheon, but she made him feel as if he'd drunk a whole bottle of brandy. She was sweet and intoxicating, she slowed his world and his whirling mind to the crawl of molasses. His throbbing cock strained for the heat of her core. Despite his best efforts, he'd thought of little else these past eighteen hours other than having her back in his arms. Beneath him. On top of him. Here, pinned between his body and the wall, thighs spread wide and wet just for him, her heart racing in anticipation of the joy he could give her.

Reaching between them, Simon's fingers sifted through the layers of her skirts until he found the lace of her garters and reached higher to locate the slit in her drawers. The flesh he found was already dewey with her desire. She practically purred against his lips when he caressed the petals of her sex, swirling and drawing the infinity symbol, omega, and the Sigma notation again and again as she mewled in the most delicious of ways, her slickness coating his fingers like the most succulent, forbidden honey. His mouth salivated with the mere thought of tasting her, but it would have to wait. His body could handle no further delays.

Simultaneously, he bent his head to partake of her delectable décolletage and rip open the falls of his breeches. He nearly groaned like a randy youth when he was finally able to take his cock in his hand and rub it through the moisture with which her body had awarded him. If he failed her in all else, at least Simon knew he could give Odette this; he knew he could fulfill this need and bring her incandescent physical pleasure.

Her thighs hugged him more tightly and Simon took that as his cue to allow himself to slide home. His breath was ripped from his chest as he was enveloped in her tight, wet heat. Her flesh stretching to accommodate his girth, the way her inner walls sucked him more deeply until he was buried to the hilt, caused his sanity to slip.

Nothing in his life had ever felt so right as when his body was joined with Odette's.

It was part of what terrified him.

He cupped the lush curves of her bottom to tilt her hips, canting her pelvis to meet his deep thrusts. What began as tender quickly turned into something far more frenzied and fueled by overpowering need. Every pull of her slick muscles against his cock, every soft cry of Odette's incredulous joy when their bodies met again, and again, and again worked Simon higher. He wanted to fill her with his seed; he basked in the knowledge that she would forever be his, alone.

The combination of her scent and her taste drove him beyond all reason. Her narrow sheath fluttered around him and he knew she was already close. His own crisis began with a tingle in the base of his spine. He pressed himself closer, grinding his pelvis against her in a way that created just the right friction exactly where he knew she craved it the most.

His chest swelled watching Odette throw her head back in abandon, as she cried out and clutched his shoulders for purchase—not because she was afraid he would drop her, but because she wanted everything he had to give her. She gladly accepted it all.

His teeth grazed her sweat-slicked throat, savoring the salty tang as it mixed with the decadent flavor of her flesh.

"Simon!"

"That's it," he growled, continuing his relentless onslaught of her senses. "Let go."

All at once, Simon felt every one of Odette's muscles tense, her nails bit into the skin at the nape of his neck, and she gave a keening cry as her crisis finally broke over her. He rode wave after clenching wave of her orgasm, the strong, rhythmic throb yanking him closer to the edge. She was still trembling around him when he drove himself again and again to the hilt, holding his body as far within her as he could while his climax swelled and crashed with the pounding rush of a tide.

Gradually, Simon floated back down into his body to the sensation of Odette's fingers lightly scraping his scalp. He took a languid inhalation of her scent and held it for several heartbeats before releasing it. Slowly, he helped Odette lower her legs and stand, then they set about putting themselves to rights. He watched as she shook out her skirts and found that he loved knowing he had been the one to put the color in her cheeks. She caught his eye and the shy smile he received was enough to make his heart skip a beat.

He had to find a way to refocus himself.

He had to.

He had worked far too hard for far too long to allow it all to fall apart this close to the end of his first real project. He'd spent years cultivating professional connections and relationships…and even *he* knew how damaging it would be to his reputation if he stumbled now. He'd come up short many times and in many areas deemed important to Society, but this…this was something to which he'd dedicated his life. To lose it meant everything would have been for nothing. All the years of research and work would go to waste—of corresponding with others in his field and getting them to take him seriously as opposed to only viewing him as a spoiled son of an earl who might be fickle in his interests and unworthy of their time. He may have proven his intelligence many times over, but abandoning it all now for this inexplicable obsession he had for this woman…was not an option.

The thoughts still consumed his mind when he accompanied his wife in the carriage to the West End flat she'd once shared with her mother. Odette had said there were typically no performances scheduled that day of the week, so her mother would likely be located there.

Sure enough, Mademoiselle Auclair was in residence, though it took her nearly an hour to prepare herself to receive her daughter and new son-in-law. While they waited, Simon busied himself by working through some mathematical problems in his head, trying to recall where he'd placed one of the books he required, and allowing his eyes to skim over the room.

He'd called upon Odette several times during their stunted courtship, so he had been in this room on several occasions. It was

small, but comfortable. The dark furniture with its red-patterned up-
holstery was of uncommon quality. Vases filled with large arrangements of flowers sat on the mantle as well as each end table. No art
was hung on the walls, but the intricately-patterned silk wall papering
was a focal point unto itself. The room was opulence of the cultivated
kind, where wealth was spent and displayed very intentionally to
make the greatest visual impact upon visitors. It was all yet another
part Odette's mother was playing, he thought wryly.

Simon glanced over at his wife beside him. Dressed in her blush-
pink gown, she was like a breath of fresh air when compared to the
false wealth and cloying facade of the room around them. There was
no doubting Mademoiselle Auclair was a popular actress and sought-
after in social circles as a woman known for her looks and her interesting history, but this was all tenuous. What must it have been like to
grow up in this place—or within that woman's shadow, for that matter? It was remarkable to Simon that a woman such as the one who
finally breezed into the room had given birth to the kind being who
his wife had become.

"*Ma fille cherie!*" Mademoiselle Auclair spoke loudly, dramatically, as if the very room was a stage and her voice was required to carry
some distance. Simon supposed the whole world was a long line of
performances for a woman such as her. "And now a married woman
glowing with joy!" She held her arms open wide to Odette. For her
part, his wife was wide-eyed with indecision, as if she was unused to
such a show from her mother. After another moment's hesitation, Simon watched as she walked into her mother's arms, accepting the
French custom of three kisses on her cheeks. It made his skin itch, but
Simon allowed Odette's mother to do the same to him.

"To what do I owe the honor of this visit? And on what should be
your honeymoon trip, no less!" She smoothed her ruby-red skirts cut

to the highest fashion and trimmed in black lace. The bodice of her gown was scooped almost indecently low and was clearly intended to display her bosom and impossibly narrow waist to their fullest advantage. Not for the first time, Simon looked back and forth from mother to daughter and appreciated just how fortunate it was that Odette had somehow managed to become her own woman despite the powerful force and personality of the woman who gave her life. A less imaginative person might call Odette a watered-down version of her mother; she was shorter, less defined, her hair and eyes less remarkable, she even wore a more muted shade of rose…but Simon knew the truth. Odette was her own person. And every time she didn't berate him for his wandering mind or look at him askance for an off-topic comment he made, his heart filled and swelled just a little bit more.

"That is part of the reason we dropped by," Odette began as she unclasped the pink satin reticule looped around her wrist. "We returned to London and this was waiting for us. I wondered if you might be able to shed some light as to the sender's identity." She held the folded parchment out to her mother, whose eyes skimmed over the nondescript wax seal with practiced assessment and began unfolding the note.

"I am happy to look, of course, but I don't know why you might think—" The words abruptly died and, in the months since he'd first met her, Mademoiselle Auclair was speechless. Her wide, bright blue eyes skimmed the words again and again. Still, she remained silent, her full lips parting as she mouthed the words.

"Someone has gifted us with a house," Odette spoke up when it became clear her mother would not. "The Earl and Countess of Aldborough, though wonderful, generous people, were not the ones who gave us this gift. There is no one else we can think of who might have done such a thing."

Mademoiselle Auclair merely shook her perfectly coiffured head, her eyes widening to a shocking degree.

"Your daughter is of the mind that perhaps we should not accept such an overly generous gift–"

"*Non!*" Mademoiselle Auclair's head whipped up, startling both Simon and Odette with her immediate adamancy. "You cannot decline a gift such as this."

"That is what the earl's solicitor said," Odette replied with a frown knitting her elegant brows.

"You cannot risk offending the giver."

"We cannot risk offending a party whom we do not know?" Simon tilted his head quizzically. There was something in the way Mademoiselle Auclair didn't meet his eyes.

"Regardless of the giver's identity, this is a gift too generous to turn down." Mademoiselle Auclair took her daughter's hand in hers, her knuckles whitening. "To have a house such as this, a future such as the one you have secured, is beyond what I could have realistically hoped for you, my child. This is a security and constancy I never knew." She turned her eyes back to Simon. "And your Mr. Stratford has already shown to be more upstanding than most men of my acquaintance." Simon didn't place much stock in his ability to read people, but he almost believed he witnessed a glimmer of apology in the actress's bright eyes. She turned back to Odette. "My advice is to forget about the who and the why, and simply be appreciative that the sun has chosen to smile upon you and your new marriage." She slipped the folded note into Simon's hand.

Chapter Twelve

One distinct benefit of starting new and having very little to their names meant Simon and Odette were able to move into their new home with speed and efficiency. Simon's parents had given them a wedding present of a rather substantial sum of money, which went a long way toward beginning the furnishing of the house and hiring the most necessary members of a small staff.

After a brief discussion, they began with the largest bed chamber along with the most public and necessary rooms: the front parlor, a desk and seating for the study, and necessities for the kitchens. It would be foolish of them to live outside of their means and fully furnish the large townhouse and fill it with staff the two of them hardly anticipated needing.

With his parents' permission and the blessing of the butler and housekeeper at Aldborough House, they'd borrowed a few of the seasoned maids and footmen to help set up the household and train their future staff. A novice cook was soon hired on a trial basis upon the

recommendation of Aldborough's longtime cook. They didn't anticipate hosting many meals and they had to keep in mind all the while
that Simon's income was structured. They could certainly make do
with a cook who was untried in preparing grand, ostentatious meals.

Simon was quite pleased with the home's large study. There was
plenty of shelving for his books, with room to grow. There were tall
windows to allow in ample lighting. With the addition of a large desk
they found on the floor at a local furniture maker's shop and a tolera-
bly comfortable chair, Simon was prepared to resume his work.

And he did just that at every opportunity.

Much to Odette's silent dismay, their lives returned to some semblance of what had taken place at Bridleton before their wedding. Simon disappeared into the study for countless hours at a time; mean-
while, Odette busied herself with locating items and pieces that
brought her joy and, she felt, represented her personality to bring life
into their new home. She'd selected new ivory papering for the walls
of the parlor to compliment the hunter-green chaise and sofa she had
selected with Simon's minimal input. A new rug was next and, after
days of searching, she chose one with a lovely romantic floral pattern
that reminded her of the climbing ivy on the tower back at Bridleton.
She was quietly very pleased with her work and the thoughtfulness
she put into every decision.

Though they'd selected only one bed and mattress and Odette had
hoped so sincerely (and silently) that she and Simon might return to
the closeness they'd achieved back at the inn on the first days of their
marriage, it was not to be. She was unsure where Simon slept, but the
three nights since they'd moved in she'd remained alone in the large
four-poster bed with its new pale blue coverlet and plush pillows.

A little bit of her heart chipped away and disappeared each time it
happened.

She knew Simon well enough at that point to optimistically believe he wasn't actively avoiding her, and she'd learned that she needed to be patient with him. They were still learning one another's habits and customs. But she couldn't help but long to get closer to him more quickly.

For the most part, she was left to her own devices during the day. She wandered the empty rooms, made lists of items each room would require to become habitable, and then sat down to prioritize those lists. After that, when she became overwhelmingly bored, she would alphabetize those lists. She read. She would have written, but she had no friends with whom to correspond. She didn't feel like striking up a correspondence with the few girls who hadn't treated her poorly at school—whatever would she say, anyway?

Warmest greetings, Prudence! I don't know if you recall, but you once offered me a sweet from the tin your mother sent to you after I helped you with your French elocution. How are things? By the way, I've managed to quite literally fall into a marriage with the second son of the Earl of Aldborough! Can you imagine? I am quite smitten with him, though I see him less hours in a day than fingers I have on one hand...

Yes. That would go over well.

Still unfamiliar with their new corner of London and having no companions upon whom to call, she had to settle for keeping her own company. She became quite adept at holding two sides of a conversation within the confines of her own head.

Though she did her best to ignore it, a heavy fog of melancholy began to seep into her breast. It settled dark and heavy within her, though she refused to allow it to stain the rest of her life. She pasted a smile upon her face and soldiered on.

*****

There was a delay in the delivery of the dining room table and chairs Odette had ordered, so she was taking dinner in her room one afternoon.

Alone.

Again.

She'd encountered Simon on her way back to the bedroom earlier that day, bumping into him as they'd both rounded the same corner coming from opposite directions. Her heart had fluttered in that exciting way it did whenever she saw her husband. Just a glance at him brought back the flood of memories from their stay at the inn…the first time they'd been in this very house…she couldn't even enter that parlor without her body humming with awareness. And when he looked at her with those swirling blue-green eyes of his, her knees grew weak.

"Simon! I hadn't expected to find you up here," she blurted out, then silently berated her for the inanity of the comment.

His face was as cool and collected as a mask as he held up a small leather-bound notebook. "I needed to retrieve this," he replied evenly. "If you'll excuse me, Odette." He had inclined his head and skirted around her with a wide berth as if afraid she might latch onto his arm like a leech and prevent him from returning to his work.

Odette replayed that awkward interaction over and over again in her mind as she picked at her meal. Try as she might, it was growing more difficult for her to look past the blatantly deliberate way in which he did his best to avoid her in favor of his work. Meredith had warned her; she'd seen colors of it before their wedding. Odette had believed herself prepared to be married to a man who had a deeper, more intimate bond with his work than any other human connection, but it was another thing to live it.

If only she could have some concept of what was so fascinating to him…

Odette dropped her fork with a clatter.

Simon had come to this room earlier to retrieve that notebook.

She knew she was a reasonably intelligent woman—she had earned decently-high marks in maths back in school—but she doubted she'd be able to comprehend much, if any, of Simon's work…but that didn't mean she couldn't try. If she grasped even one percent of what enthralled him, then it was at least a toe-hold in his world and it afforded her an opportunity where she might show him how much she did care about him and everything that made him the man he was.

Odette glanced around the room, but it remained a relatively impersonal space. Furniture had begun to arrive, but it was still only the barest necessities; not to mention, Simon had yet to spend a single night there. Her eyes caught on the dressing room door. Simon *did* have a couple of trunks still tucked away. He refused to hire a valet and the maid had yet to tackle the task, so there they sat tucked away. Odette had stubbed her toe on one the other day, so she was well aware of how heavy the trunks were.

She dropped her napkin on the small table and headed to the dressing room. There, in the corner, were two large rectangular trunks set side-by-side. She recognized them as the ones having made the journey with them from Bridleton to Aldborough House, and then here to their new Townhouse. She spent a minute biting her lower lip in indecision before her curiosity won out. She dropped to her knees, unlatched the first trunk, and lifted the heavy lid.

The contents smelled of warm parchment, thick layers of ink, leather, and Simon. Her heart squeezed at the onslaught to her senses. Organized in thick stacks bound together with twine and ribbon were hundreds upon hundreds of sheets of parchment covered in Simon's

neat, confident script. She skimmed the top pages of a few of the
stacks, but they contained a complex code of shorthand notes indeci-
pherable to her. Another stack held drafts of what appeared to be an
essay. She didn't know precisely what she was looking for, but this
wasn't it—she couldn't comprehend any of it, let alone form enough
coherent thoughts to have a conversation about it.

Another stack appeared to be chronological correspondence with
several of his colleagues. She had only one side of the conversation,
so it didn't make all that much sense to her. From what she deci-
phered, however, Simon appeared to be rather well-respected in this
field for a man of his age. One man in particular, Sir Nigel Wright,
seemed more than a little thrilled to be co-authoring a piece with him
—something about using non-numerical signs in mathematical equations. Odette wasn't ashamed to admit that she didn't understand a
lick of it, but she was still supremely proud of her husband. The way
his mind worked baffled her, but it was beautiful in its unique bril-
liance.

Carefully, she replaced the papers just as she'd found them and
closed the lid. She shuffled over on her knees and opened the second
trunk. This one was filled to the brim with neatly stacked brown
leather-bound journals, each was closed with its string wrapped and
tucked around it to cinch it closed. There was even a small gap where
Simon had removed the journal she'd seen him with earlier that day.
She picked up the nearest one and unwound the string. Like the sheets
of parchment in the first trunk, the pages of the notebook were filled
with Simon's writing. Less neat than the full pages in the other trunk,
the first several pages were filled with a diagram with arrows she did
not recognize. Another page held symbols and scrawls that quickly
morphed into another symbol. She spotted a few Greek letters she
recognized, but not much else. She nearly closed the notebook and

moved on to the next when she spotted something different about the following page. There were no symbols or numbers. She sat more fully on her heels to read.

G has decided to hide my books. Again. I am a man of seventeen and still my elder brother knows precisely how to torture me—

Odette gasped and shut the notebook with a smack. The work had turned into a very private journal. It was a representation of the way Simon's mind functioned–complex thoughts interspersed with brief glimpses of personal thoughts and observations.

She knew what she *should* do: lock away the notebook and forget she ever saw it.

Her eyes turned back to the journal in her lap.

What she *wanted* to do was continue reading and learn more about what went on in Simon's head.

She chewed her lip, huffed a sigh of resignation, and reopened the journal to the page her finger had (rather conveniently) saved.

What she read wound up breaking her heart. The words penned approximately one decade earlier struck her as sharply as a physical blow.

G claims he does so only out of concern for my social well-being, but what he cannot seem to grasp is that I have no desire to be of the world in which he has found so much fulfillment. He repeatedly mentions how I used to follow him and J around when we were all lads, but that was under a misguided boyish desire for acceptance. They were so much older than I, and I had yet to discover the unwavering acceptance of my books.

I shall undoubtedly be mocked for this, but to hide my books is tantamount to torture. I am missing a limb. I am foundering. My mind is no more steady than a finch in a gale. I am unmoored in a confusing world which I do not understand and does not understand me—

Odette set aside that notebook and retrieved another, flipping through pages until she found a journal entry from a year before the first.

R suffered another bloodied nose, though it was quite insignificant when compared to the beating that insufferable boor, M, received. Another split lip for me and ink intentionally spilled across my schoolwork; at least I managed to save the bulk of it this time. My mind has latched onto a new equation and it fills my every waking moment. I lie in bed at night and stare at the cracked plaster, watching the numbers dance and spin for me like the gears on a clock. I do not always realize when someone is speaking to me, or where I am walking, or if I am unintentionally offensive.

R continues to insist that I join him in his pugilism studies, but bruised knuckles are not for me. He insists it'll be better for protecting myself than my fencing practice, but I argue that a sword is mightier than a fist. I smile as I hold this quill and ponder the words of The Bard, for perhaps I really am holding the mightiest weapon of all—

She fished out another journal.

Journal after journal revealed to her a man who was every bit as lonely as she had been for the majority of her life.

She'd always known he was brilliant, but she hadn't realized the depth of the misunderstanding with which he'd been forced to contend. Each page her eyes devoured afforded her an insight into a great intellectual torrent and torment, whether or not he realized it fully.

He seemed to struggle with change—having found it more than a little distressing to manage when his dorm was moved halfway into the term after a horrible leak from the roof developed and made the space uninhabitable. He'd coped by throwing himself so deeply into his work that the new environment melted away.

Much like he'd done since their betrothal when his entire life had been uprooted...

Odette continued to flip through the notebooks. She sat on the ground, propping herself up against the gaping trunk and settling in to learn more about the man she'd married.

She cried fat, silent tears when she realized just how he'd been bullied by his classmates—even through University. She was grateful when she discovered the entries after Meredith came into his life and showed him more acceptance and understanding than most of his blood family had. She very much appreciated how George had matured throughout the years; she'd seen firsthand that their brotherhood was much improved from the early years of the journals, but she still would've liked to have boxed the younger viscount's ears a time or two.

The journal entries halted about a month before she and Simon had met, taken over by unbroken chains of notes and calculations. Odette was disappointed that she wouldn't have an insight into how he felt about their marriage or what he was currently experiencing, but it was probably for the best. She'd invaded his privacy far, far more than she should have. She could admit to herself that she felt only a little bit guilty about it, however, because now she felt like she understood him. She'd gained more insight into him in the past couple of hours of silent reading than they'd had in any actual conversation. Even if he couldn't express himself outwardly, it was clear he felt an enormous depth of emotion, felt the weight of obligation and then of the possibility of coming up short.

Odette made the decision right then and there to make sure Simon felt secure and accepted. She would mold their marriage into a safe place for him and she hoped, in turn, he would open up to her and let her in in his way.

Now, with a goal in mind, her heart felt lighter than it had in days.

Chapter Thirteen

Odette began her efforts the very next day after spending the night lying alone and staring into the darkness, her mind turning all she'd learned over and over again. She decided to start with small gestures to show Simon that she wasn't going anywhere; that he could be safe with who he was around her. She would need to make adjustments, herself, but she was confident that she cared enough for Simon that she could at least do her best to put in the necessary effort.

She recalled her promise to Meredith and, when Simon surprised her by joining her for tea that afternoon, she took the first step and inquired after his research.

"How goes your work?"

Simon's brows rose, clearly indicating she'd caught him off-guard; his cup was paused halfway to his lips. "Fine, thank you." He averted his eyes and finally took a sip of his tea. "It's not something I'll bore you with—"

"No!" His eyes flew back to her face and she was briefly mesmerized by them. "That is…your work doesn't bore me."

Simon emitted a self-deprecating huff. "I know that isn't true."

"Simon. I wouldn't ask if I didn't genuinely care." Several seconds of indecisive silence ticked by until Odette set down her cup and moved to sit beside her husband on the sofa. "Please. Tell me."

Simon's mouth formed a tense line as he tried to decide whether or not to launch into an explanation.

Odette leaned forward to impress upon him her sincerity. "I know it's mathematics, but I have no grasp of your project. I should like to know. If it's important to you, then it's important to me. That is what marriage is."

Simon's eyes widened before looking away.

"These branches of mathematics are called geometry and algebra," he began; "specifically non-Euclidean geometry." Odette waited patiently for him to continue. As if realizing that she wasn't going to interrupt him, Simon quickly leaned forward and set his cup on the table. "Imagine, if you will, a circle drawn on a piece of paper. It is flat, but still, certain mathematical rules apply." Odette nodded, she'd paid attention enough to understand circumference, radius, and diameter. Her heart sped up when Simon took her hand in his, palm side up, and drew a circle on the tender skin there. She fought not to shiver at the gentle contact. "Now, imagine a sphere—still a circle in the second dimension of a piece of paper, but, in reality, a three-dimensional object, like you and I." He cupped his hand over hers as if, together, they cradled an imaginary ball. "My research partner and I are working on developing certain theorems to explain how the various planes meet and separate…"

She listened raptly as he explained how various coordinates were calculated when planes were not flat, the variations between ideas called Elliptic Geometry and Hyperbolic Geometry with their positive and negative curvature, and how those ideas differed from the ancient idea developed by a brilliant, long-deceased Greek man. On and on he went, and, far from being bored, Odette was transfixed. Of course, she understood very little of what he said, but he managed to make it fascinating. His long, elegant fingers used her hands to demonstrate the difference between a triangle drawn on a plane and one drawn on the surface of, say, a ball. A few of the drawings she'd come across in his journals began to make sense, but she was easily resigned to the fact that full comprehension would forever remain outside of her reach.

She asked a handful of questions and was thoroughly impressed with how Simon managed to (for the most part, at least) slow his racing mind and words to a pace she could better follow. He came alive with the golden light of his passion; he and his intelligence shown so brilliantly Odette had a difficult time understanding how everyone wasn't blinded by it all.

"And you plan on submitting a paper to a journal?" The reaction Simon gave her made her heart flip. He beamed and his eyes glowed with excitement.

"We intend to submit it for publication. The hope is it will bring attention to my work and also gain me entrance into the London Mathematical Society," his words were swift and joyous, tumbling from his lips like an eager child's. "This work could greatly advance the knowledge and understanding of algebra and geometry; it could bring England notoriety in the field, on par with Germany and France. Do you see?" He held her hands tightly in his and she gripped him right back, his passion utterly captivating. "This work could be revolutionary."

Meredith had been right. Watching Simon discuss his work generated an infectious excitement, an unbridled joy she had not witnessed from him before.

"This is amazing, Simon. Truly, it is." She grinned up at his dear face and felt herself fall for him a little more. "I'm so proud of you."

His smile suddenly faltered, the light in his eyes flickered. She worried he might pull away and retreat back to his office, shutting her out once more, but, instead, he leaned forward. Simon slipped a gentle hand behind the nape of her neck to pull her closer and pressed his lips to her forehead in a slow, sweetly tender kiss. Odette's eyes fluttered closed and she basked in the warmth of this tender contact, filled her lungs with his scent, savored the moment. She'd done something right, and, more than that, she felt more connected to her husband.

Odette spent the rest of the day reading in a warm patch of sunlight. Rarely had she had the opportunity to enjoy such peace. At school, there had been an overabundance of girls creating distractions or schoolwork which took precedence over reading for pleasure. Even at home, her mother had constantly toted her around on one errand or another, or she'd been deposited in the theater. If anyone believed a private moment could be had there, then they had clearly never tried to find a quiet corner when everyone else around you was running and calling, wrestling with set pieces or costumes, whistling for attention above the bustle. Even her time spent at Bridleton had been relatively busy with all the wedding preparations. Now, truly having her own space—without anyone yanking her to and fro—for the very first time, was novel, indeed. However, Odette wasn't naive enough to believe that this would always be her life.

She didn't doubt that word of their hasty marriage and their return to London had made its rounds through Society, but it was almost pleasant to postpone having to face reality for the time being. They were spared from social obligations while people waited the appropriate amount of time for their honeymoon period to pass before they indulged in their curiosities by calling upon them at their home or extending invitations to the new Mr. and Mrs. Stratford.

When Simon didn't appear for supper that evening, Odette made sure to request that a tray be brought to him. She would have much rather dined with her husband, but she had a new understanding and appreciation for his passion and the importance of his work. She could share his attention, even if it sometimes felt like she was competing against an intangible rival for it.

She experienced a little nudge of guilt; she supposed it was not all that fair.

He'd loved his work long before they'd married…and not once had he indicated that he felt anything akin to that for her.

And, now that she'd snooped through his private journals (and painstakingly replaced them in perfect order in the trunk), she had a new respect for just how much Simon *needed* the order and escape of his numbers, the challenge to his mind.

Odette eased into this solitary routine for the next two days. She maintained an optimistic speck of hope that she'd see her husband each day and, when he did not appear, she'd slip down to the kitchens for a little bit of human interaction, usually under the guise of requesting they set a tray for Simon to eat in his study. She found she liked their new maid, Mary, quite well and, though she sometimes poked Odette's scalp with hairpins and often burned the toast when she assisted the cook, the girl was eager to learn and seemed extremely grateful for the position in a household as quiet and informal as theirs.

The Aldborough servants had completed their temporary tenure and returned to their usual duties back at the home of the earl and countess, leaving behind an organized household, a maid, their new cook, and a butler. The staff were all relatively untried, but everyone seemed to get on well enough, and Odette was secretly grateful that she didn't have more experienced staff to judge her for her slip-ups as she, too, learned the ins and outs of their new life.

Tired of taking tea alone, Odette had even eschewed custom and sat at the rough kitchen table just to enjoy a bit of noise and chatter while Mary and Cook prepared tea or supper. The maid continued to refuse to join her—it seemed to offend her sense of propriety to do so, even in her inexperience—though she seemed to like having an audience for her amusing stories starring her large family with her six brothers and sisters. She was also rather adept at ignoring the disapproving stares of the cook as she continued to chatter on and on.

Odette had concluded her supper in the kitchens one evening, determined to finish the last page in a chapter of her book before she left the warm closeness for the rest of the empty house, when the maid returned carting with her the same tray she'd brought up to Simon sometime earlier.

"Has Mr. Stratford finished his supper, then?" Odette asked absently, her eyes still skimming over the words before her.

"Untouched, as usual," Mary sighed as she set the tray on the table. There was a clatter in the larder where the cook had decided to undertake some reorganization.

Odette frowned and looked up. She hadn't expected that answer.

Peering at the tray, Odette could, indeed, see that nothing had been eaten. The thin slices of beef were untouched beside the small roasted potatoes and carrots, slices of warm bread lay cold and stale. Even the delicious berry pie remained in perfect condition. The latter half of the maid's statement sank in.

"As usual?"

Mary's eyes widened as if only just realizing to whom she spoke and the informality of the statement. "I–I only mean that Mr. Stratford hasn't taken much of anything from any of the trays I've brought to him today." She wrinkled her pert little nose; "Or yesterday, for that matter."

"He hasn't eaten?"

"Nothing substantial, anyway." The girl tilted her shoulder and set about tidying up. "I might attribute it to the cooking if you complained, Ma'am." She was cheeky, but she was right.

"'Tisn't anything wrong with ma cookin'," the cook chimed in, her thick Northern accent echoed out of the larder.

"I did ask him if there was aught he might prefer, but he didn't look up and just shook his head with a hand in the air and dismissed me." The maid flitted her hand in an imitation of Simon's earlier gesture.

Odette watched as the food was removed and the plate and silverware were cleaned. She chewed on her lip and her indecision in equal measure. She wasn't Simon's mother; she didn't want to nag him about eating. She also didn't want to disturb his work. Perhaps most of all, she didn't want a husband who wasted away because he was too consumed by his occupation to remember to eat.

She was still ruminating over the situation as she lay in bed that evening. The lights had been doused and she was alone in the bed chamber.

As usual.

As she stared at the shadows on the ceiling, she couldn't stop thinking about Simon continuing to labor below stairs. She knew his work was important and, with the impending deadline, he needed everything to be perfect, but that was no excuse to forget to take care of himself.

Odette heaved a sigh and tossed away the coverlet with a huff. She stomped over to the chair and threw on her dressing gown, punching her arms through the sleeves.

Of course it was the woman who had to be the sensible one…

She was careful to be quiet enough not to rouse their staff as she lit a candle and strode down the hallway to the stairs. Sure enough, the door to the study was closed, a faint strip of golden light creeping out from beneath the heavy wooden barrier. Odette pivoted and headed toward the back stairs which led to the kitchens.

She'd spent enough time down there lately to know where most things were kept. She easily located a plate and poked around the cool, dark larder until she found some bread, hard cheese, and a couple of apples. Carefully setting aside her candle on the table so it didn't tip, she selected one of the clean knives and set about slicing the food and arranging it on the plate. She stood back with her hands on her hips and examined her handiwork. The spread would win no culinary prizes for either presentation or quality, but it would do in a pinch.

She took up the candle and balanced the plate in her other hand, stepping carefully through the darkness until she found herself outside the study once more. It took some juggling and several tries, but she was able to balance everything and open the door.

Simon sat hunched over his desk like some ancient warlock manifesting a mystical spell. So enthralled was he with his work that he didn't so much as lift his head when she entered. The room was dim and the hearth had gone cold, but his desk was lit by candelabras ablaze with several candles each. His lean form and broad shoulders were aglow with all of the golden light illuminating the sheaves upon sheaves of parchment laid out before him. No less than three books were open on the desk as well, their pages revealing secrets only he could comprehend and separate and reform into something amazing.

"Simon," Odette began softly as she walked into the room. He held up several ink-stained fingers to indicate he was mid-thought as he continued to scribble with his quill. Odette waited.

And waited.

"Simon," she finally repeated herself. This time, she received no response. She was close enough she could see the dark shadows of fatigue beneath his eyes, the tracks his fingers had made through his dark gold hair, the slight hollowness beneath the stubble of his already-lean cheeks that made his remarkable cheekbones even more prominent.

She extinguished her candle and stuck it in an empty arm of one of the candelabras. She continued to hold the plate and spent several minutes contemplating her next move before her impatience and annoyance won out and she set it right in the middle of the desk.

"I told you, Mary, I am not hungry," he grumbled in irritation and finally tore his eyes from the numbers before him. "Odette?" His tone changed as abruptly as his expression, telling her he had no idea to whom he'd held up his hand for silence. It was a bit comforting that she seemed to rank lower on his list of annoyances.

"I heard you hadn't eaten today, and possibly yesterday as well," she said, suddenly more meek now that she was confronted by those eyes and expressive brows. She gestured at the plate. "I couldn't sleep knowing you had gone without food for so long."

He tilted his head and stared up at her, unblinking, as if trying to translate her words—her concern—into something he could understand and accept.

*****

"You must eat, Simon," Odette insisted, the passion in her voice evident even without her having to yell. It stopped Simon's quill midword. He looked up to find her passion flashing with the candlelight in her sapphire eyes. Her lush lips were pulled in a taut line of seriousness and her arms were crossed over her bosom. At first glance, she was about as intimidating as a wet kitten, but Simon knew her better than that. His wife was fiercer than she was given credit for.

If she wasn't, then she wouldn't have survived in her mother's world for long.

He dropped his quill back in the ink pot and rolled his wrist, noting his ink-stained cuticles and the smudges creeping up the skin of his forearm exposed beneath his rolled shirt sleeve. A fist-sized spot between his shoulder blades ached and his back screamed in protest. How many hours had he sat there without moving? He tested his neck with a roll and managed not to flinch too badly when it cracked. Somehow, these lengthy sessions had been easier on his body five years prior. He supposed sleeping at his desk or draped awkwardly across the too-short sofa did not help matters...

Odette nudged a plate closer to him—or as close as she could without disrupting his work.

"Eat. Please." Her eyes pleaded with him to obey and, as was usually the case when confronted with his wife, he was relatively helpless to resist. It was part of the reason he'd stayed away. He couldn't focus when she was this close. He couldn't think when he caught her faint floral scent in the air. When they touched, he lost all sense of time and place. Nothing else mattered.

As wonderful as it was, he couldn't live like that and still accomplish his goals. Until he figured out a way to balance his needs and desires for his wife with his passions and obligations, Simon knew he had to do what he could to separate these halves of himself. He reasoned that a hard line between these parts of him—a well-constructed delineation—was the best way for him to move on with his life.

What he now saw before him was one of the things that had concerned him about marrying. He had another person to take into account. No matter what worked for him, it was no longer about just him. He might be fine with his finite amount of sustenance and sleep as long as he had his numbers and equations to keep him fed, but that didn't mean someone else wouldn't worry. And it would appear that he'd caused his wife more than a little bit of concern. His stomach sank straight through the floor of the study. It had never been his intention to cause his wife any pain or anxiety, but, in simply trying to achieve his goals and live his life as he had these past several years, he'd done exactly that. To put it plainly, it wasn't fair to her. Guilt began prodding away at his conscience, relentlessly poking at him and needling his resolve in the most uncomfortable, inconvenient of manners.

Simon gazed up at Odette from his seat at his desk. She leaned the delectable curve of her hip against the edge, her soft wrapper tucked around her body like a maddening shield, her arms crossed beneath her breasts in a way that was more inviting than it was a gesture of frustration, and warding off his attentions. The way she looked down at him, a mixture of gentle concern and admonishment, the tilt of her head, the long plait of her hair and its virginal satin ribbon…that last bit proved to be his final undoing.

He was suddenly ravenous…and not for the small plate of food Odette had so sweetly created and carried up from the kitchens.

He scooted the legs of his chair back several inches to create more space between himself and the desktop. His fingers trailed up the outside of Odette's thigh to curl around the swell of her hip; as if with a mind of its own, his thumb caressed the tender flesh where her thigh met her pelvis.

His heartbeat became deafening when she released a little gasp of surprise as he slid her against the edge of the desk and pressed her to sit more fully on the surface. She allowed him to guide her bare feet to the leather-upholstered arms on either side of his hips. He caressed the gentle curves of her feet peeking from beneath the lace-trimmed edge of her nightrail, ran a finger along the ticklish arches, rubbed the slope of her ankles and languorously massaged the flesh of her calves, all the while inching her hemline higher and higher. His knuckles kneaded the tendons behind her knee and he couldn't resist placing an open-mouthed kiss on the pale skin he'd exposed. Her lips parted on a silent gasp.

He inhaled deeply, reveling in the sweet, soft scent of her flesh, the heady aroma of her sudden arousal. His groin throbbed. His mouth began to water.

"Simon—what are you—"

"You are the only sustenance I require," he murmured before ducking his head beneath the hem of her night dress, kissing her *there*.

Chapter Fourteen

Odette's hands instantly flew to Simon's mussed hair, her fingers knotting in the short locks as she squealed in shock and then quickly began to melt. What began as a push quickly morphed into a pull as she instinctively fought to bring his lips and tongue closer. She wanted to take more and give him more at the same time. Simon, determined to make his feast last as long as possible, resisted against her frantic tugs and the undulations of her hips. He focused all of his attention on the delicious, dewey folds of her sex; nuzzling and licking and tasting and nipping, inhaling deeply of her delicate, freshly-washed scent. His lips and tongue were everywhere except for where he knew she needed him most. He never wanted to come up for air. He could bury himself in this glorious place surrounded by Odette's petal-soft thighs and breathy sighs and gasps, and die a content man.

She leaned back onto her elbows atop the stacks of parchment and books laid out on his desk, one hand still burrowed in his hair, its nails flexing against his scalp. Nudging himself closer still, Simon tugged her legs to his shoulders to hook her knees just there and wrapped his hands around her hips. The vibration of his moan of delight echoed through her sensitive flesh, eliciting an open-mouthed gasp of delight. Finally, he rolled her pearl between his lips, flicking it in a relentless rhythm and then laving it was the flat of his tongue. Her hips jerked against him, her breathing morphed into sobs of delight. His grip on her hips tightened as her movements became more desperate.

He needed to taste her when she came.

He needed this more than he needed food or drink.

She would sustain him.

Odette was his harbor in this world and she was all he required to survive.

"Simon!" she cried to the ceiling as he looked up the hills and valleys of her body spread out before him. Only him. The pink flush of her throat, the tantalizing glimpse of her teeth biting her full lower lip.

It was all for him.

His tongue stroked her in long, firm glides, exploring every fold and secret place. When his tongue speared into her entrance, invading her and tasting her in the most scandalous of ways, she shattered.

Her body went rigid, her other hand flying once more to his head as her thighs clenched around his skull to muffle his ears as she rode wave after wave of her climax and he drank deeply of her passion.

Gradually, Odette's sobs melted into gentle tremors. Simon slowed his ministrations, gentling them in increments until he finally placed open-mouthed kisses on her inner thighs and sat back to pull his wife's sated, pliant body into his lap.

She purred and nuzzled herself against his throat. "I wanted only to bring you supper," she finally said sleepily.

"But you brought me something so much better," he replied and stroked her virginal plait, wrapping the end around his fingers.

Odette's palm found his cheek and turned his head so his lips met hers. He kissed her deeply; the thought of her tasting herself on his tongue was more erotic than he would have thought possible. Another wave of desire shot straight to his groin, pressing insistently against Odette's bottom. The glazed look in her crystalline eyes and the pink cresting her cheeks nearly shattered his resolve.

"Simon, um, don't you need to...?"

He shook his head and pressed his forehead to hers, content just to breathe in her nearness. This hadn't been about slaking his lust, but about giving his patient wife the pleasure she so rightly deserved. Tasting her glorious release had been reward enough for him.

"Well," Odette daintily cleared her throat; "in that case..." She leaned to the side and plucked something off the desk. "You still need to eat." There was simply no resisting the charming curve of her lips as she held a cube of cheese to his mouth. He blew an amused sound from his nose and obligingly parted his lips to accept her offering and he chewed the salty, creamy morsel. His stomach clenched and released a pitiful growl. Maybe it *had* been too long since he'd paused for a meal.

The only evidence that she'd heard it was the confident arch of her brow as she selected a thin slice of apple from the plate and slid it past his lips. He couldn't resist nipping the pad of her thumb as she fed him the next bite of cheese.

"Have you always been like this?" she asked softly, uncertainty coloring her words.

"How?"

"So busy with your work that you forget to eat for days at a time?" A small line of worry knit her brow.

"Sometimes," he answered and accepted a bite of crusty bread. "When I'm lost in my work, the rest of the world falls away." He didn't know how to describe the all-consuming obsession he experienced when there was a particularly promising development; how the sounds and distractions of the outside world amounted to little more than the falling of sand in an hourglass. He felt no hunger or thirst. When his mind was occupied thusly, there existed nothing else except the numbers before him.

That was, until he'd met Odette.

Even shut away in his office, he'd occasionally hear her slippers pad past the door and he'd freeze, a puddle of ink accumulating unnoticed in the middle of a sentence he'd been penning. He'd catch a hint of her laughter or the lilt of her voice in another room and he'd be yanked from his reverie, so attuned was he to her that he couldn't help but latch onto the sound. Nothing had occupied him or consumed him as fully as his work until he'd met her. And it still terrified him.

"You feel no hunger?" she tilted her head in question and he shook his head in reply.

"Nothing else matters but the problem before me." *And you*, he added silently, more than a little unnerved with how quickly that sprang to his mind.

She selected another bite of food from the plate and frowned in consideration of his words. "I can't say that I've ever been so absorbed with something that I forget to eat for days at a time," she finally said and he caught the proffered cheese between his teeth.

"I cannot explain it," he replied after chewing and swallowing. "I simply don't." His mind had always been obsessive in that way. When something intrigued or fascinated him, there was no letting go of it. His brain simply would not allow it. He knew it had caused his mother no small amount of worry, just as it had earned him quite a bit of ridicule back at Eton and University.

Where the other boys and young men had simply viewed school as a means to an end—they were getting their compulsory education so their parents would leave them alone to pursue more interesting pastimes—Simon had seen it as a new world of opportunity. He could expand his starving mind and explore whatever topics caught his fancy. He hadn't anticipated his classmates to take such an interest in his odd behavior, nor had he expected to earn so much contempt for his single minded desire to succeed. Thank god for Blackwood. As a lad, the young lord had taken more than his fair share of pummelings (and subsequent punishments) in his inexplicable efforts to save Simon from his tormentors.

Things had become somewhat easier for Simon as an adult, but now words were the weapons of choice among the *ton*. And he knew no good name—no matter how weighty it might be—would save Odette from them entirely.

Desperately in need of a change in subject, Simon plucked the next piece of cheese from Odette's fingers before she could feed it to him and moved it toward her mouth instead.

"I couldn't," she shook her head in denial. "The food is for you."

"You can, and you will," he insisted. "I know how you enjoy this cheese," he added when she wouldn't part her lips for him. He witnessed the indecision flit across her face and knew instantly what had caused it.

It was a common misconception that he didn't care to know or examine the thoughts and feelings of those around him. On the contrary, he cared, perhaps, too much about the opinions and feelings of those select few whom he kept in his small circle. He faulted himself greatly whenever he happened to miss something of import. Even he, with his predilection toward preoccupation with his work, had caught on quite early to how controlling Odette's mother had been…the disapproving glances and comments whenever Odette would partake in a sweet or enjoy a delicious meal a dash too much. And Simon had been on the receiving end of enough similar comments and stares that he knew how unpleasant an existence it was. He vowed to make this space in their marriage a safe one. Odette had gone to great lengths to ensure Simon never felt the odd duck or less than he was around her, and he would be damned if he did anything less for her.

"I want to watch you enjoy it," he murmured and those lips parted to admit the morsel of cheese. As anticipated, Odette's eyes slid closed and she savored the bite. Simon barely suppressed a chill of delight from the sight. He had to clear his throat before he could speak again. "What was it like? To grow up in the theater?" he asked and popped a bite of apple in his mouth, chewing around the sweet, tart meat. Odette lifted one nonchalant shoulder.

"I have nothing against which to compare it. I know it was highly irregular and often difficult, but parts of it could be quite fun." A smile flitted across her lips as she recalled some pleasant memory and he felt his mouth mirroring hers.

"Such as?" He chewed thoughtfully on some bread and waited for her to elaborate.

"It wasn't until I was sent off to school that I realized I was both more and less free than many of the other girls." He felt her watching as he sandwiched a piece of cheese in a folded slice of bread and took a bite; her smile warmed even further. "I learned every corner of the theater and kept less restrictive hours. I didn't have many friends my own age, but everyone was kind so long as I didn't get in the way. I remember when Garret was hired as a stagehand. I loved watching him climb into the rafters and work the pulleys—he was nimble like a little spider."

"Garret?"

Odette nodded. "Garret Frost. He played the leading male role in the performance where you and I first met. He's come a long way from where he once was."

A small prick of jealousy irked Simon, but he set it aside as best he could. Instead, Simon tucked a curl behind Odette's ear and tilted her chin to look up into his face. She was so bloody beautiful it was painful.

"As have you," he murmured. The slight change in her breathing signaled her realization of his intent as he leaned forward and pressed his lips to hers.

Odette awoke later than usual the following morning, having spent more time in Simon's study than she'd intended the night before. As she dressed for the day, her cheeks gradually warmed from the memories of all they'd done; her skin tingled in all the places he'd kissed her. Her heart skipped a beat when she found Simon's mark near her left nipple. When she walked, the chafe his stubble left behind on her inner thighs was a scandalous reminder of all he'd taught her.

By the time she'd left him to his work in the wee hours of the morning, she'd managed to convince him to finish his plate of food and she could well and truly rest better knowing he wasn't inadvertently starving himself. They'd very contentedly nibbled and chatted, kissed and touched one another for hours.

She'd learned more about Simon's childhood in Kent and he'd surprised her with his earnest interest in her time away at school. Both of them had suffered no small degree of teasing, but it seemed, Odette felt, to have made the two of them better for it, in a way. Not that she'd ever willingly go back and relive the experience, but she felt it had afforded her a small measure of patience and understanding when it came to her husband, and it made Simon less quick to judge her and

where she came from. In all, she felt closer to him for it and it made
her every step light and bubbly. That was, until she heard a shout from
the first floor, seemingly echoing up from the back of the house.

Odette's steps faltered and she froze, at first unsure if she could
trust her ears. Could it have been a stablehand in the mews? Someone
in the alley? She had almost convinced herself that the clatter of metal
was the jangle of tack when another shout echoed up through the
floor.

Her heart leapt into her throat as she gathered the skirts of her ice-
blue morning gown in her numb fingers and dashed down the hall.
She nearly tripped down the stairs and her slippers skidded on the polished floor as she rounded the corner and headed toward the back of
the Townhouse. If she wasn't mistaken, the sounds were coming from
the as-yet-unused formal dining room. The long, narrow room with its
floor-to-ceiling windows overlooked the small walled-in back garden.
She and Simon had purchased a table for informal dining in another
room, but had yet to consider making a purchase of a larger table for
this room—neither of them was quite inclined to host a big enough
gathering to warrant the purchase. In the meantime, the room had sat
clean and vacant.

The heavy double-door was ajar and Odette shoved her weight
against it, her heart pounding in her breast, and she was greeted by the
most curious of sights.

Simon and another man were advancing and retreating in turn,
flashing silver blades slicing the air between them glinting in the
warm morning light. The other man's graying hair was worn in a low
queue at the nape of his neck; while he'd removed his coat and cravat,
he'd remained garbed in his black breeches and waistcoat. Simon, on
the other hand, captivated Odette with his grace and agility…his
body. Her husband had tossed aside his shirt entirely, bared from the

waist up in a dizzying display of lean masculine muscle gleaming with a fine sheen of sweat from his exertion. The bicep of his arm bent behind his bare back held her rapt until Simon advanced upon his opponent. Every rhythmic slice and jab of the blade fired off similarly elegant combinations of muscles everywhere from his rounded shoulders to the slim definition of his chest and abdomen, the bunching and flexing of his back and shoulder blades. He'd mentioned several times that he fenced, and she'd bore witness to his grace on the dance floor, but it was something else completely to watch Simon in action.

And still something else to witness him doing it shirtless.

"Point and match!" Simon shouted triumphantly as he tapped the tip of his rapier against his opponent's chest. He raked a lock of his blonde hair from his sweat-slicked face and the men gestured and bowed to one another in a movement of amicable sportsmanship.

Odette couldn't help herself from breaking out into excited applause. Her heart hammered against her ribs for an entirely new reason as the men met her eyes, startled to realize they had an audience. Simon raised a brow and executed a courtly bow in her direction. She noticed for the first time the blunt tips on their narrow-bladed weapons to dull any blows and prevent serious injury. She didn't doubt that contact might still hurt, but at least there was effort to prevent any real bloodshed.

"Brilliant!" she gushed and strode into the room, her eyes only for Simon. His color was high and his chest was heaving from his deep, powerful breaths; there was a pleased lilt to his lips that was so rare she cherished it. He was not a boastful man, but it was clear he'd enjoyed having her witness his win. He took her hand in his and pressed his lips to her middle knuckle.

"Master Monroe, may I present my wife, Mrs. Odette Stratford?"

The other man bowed deeply with a flourish of his rapier. "The pleasure is all mine, Mrs. Stratford."

"Have you been training together long?" she asked as Simon collected his shirt and, much to Odette's disappointment, tugged it over his head. The other man took up his coat and previously discarded cravat.

"Since Mr. Stratford was at Eton," he replied, and Odette recalled how one of Simon's journal entries indicated he'd taken up swordplay and preferred its brand of physical exertion over pugilism.

"I didn't mean to intrude, but it was quite a fascinating display," she couldn't help but offer another compliment. She was inordinately pleased by the bashful expression flitting across her husband's face before he turned his head and mopped his brow with a cloth.

"Honored, Mrs. Stratford," the fencing master inclined his head and pulled his watch from the pocket of his coat. "If you'll excuse me, I am to meet my next pupil shortly. Excellent work today, Mr. Stratford, as always."

"Will we meet at the same time next week?"

"Certainly; though I will reiterate that it may be time for you to begin training with someone better able to keep up with your agility." Master Monroe leaned in and winked at Odette. "He may have become more agile over the last fifteen years, but I, on the other hand, am a man past middling age at this point."

"Nonsense," Odette replied with a smile. The fencing master may have been near fifty years of age, but he seemed more hale and hardy than some men half his age. He had the lean figure and grace of someone who had spent many years honing his physical craft and perfecting his art. She didn't doubt that Simon's ability to best the fencing master had less to do with age than skill and practice. Her husband seemed to do nothing in half-measure.

"It is the truth," the man replied, shaking the wrinkles from his coat before slipping it on. "Mr. Stratford has been outpacing me for years. For all his faculty with books, he's equally talented with a rapier. But he's nothing if not loyal—won't overthrow me for a sparring partner less long in the tooth."

Odette turned her warm smile on her husband. His dedication and unwavering loyalty were some of the things she found most enchanting and endearing about him. She also recognized Simon's tendency to stay within his sphere of comfort—much easier to stay with a fencing master who had trained and challenged him for many years than seek out another who might not be so amiable.

"There's something to be said for loyalty," Odette said fondly with a tilt of her head.

"Indeed, there is." The master clapped his hands and smiled, deep lines carving into the outer edges of his eyes. "If you'll excuse me, I must be off. It was a pleasure to meet you Mrs. Stratford."

"Likewise, Master Monroe."

The smart clip of retreating boots followed the fencing master down the hall as he saw himself from the Townhouse, leaving just the two of them in the empty dining room filled with warm morning light. It took everything in Odette's power to not stare openly at the swath of glistening flesh revealed by Simon's gaping shirt collar. She cleared her throat as delicately as possible.

"I was about to break my fast; will you join me?"

Her heart sank at the reflexive half shake of his head, the hair several shades darker for the sweat from his exertion. When he opened his mouth to speak, however, he seemed just as surprised by the words as she.

"You know, I think I will." His swirling eyes met hers, the brows above them arched in a quizzical display.

Odette's lips bloomed into a smile. "Wonderful!"

"Allow me to freshen up and I'll join you presently." Simon, still seeming confused by his own acquiescence, gathered his things and retreated from the room. His brow was knit into a mixture of consternation and confusion as he attempted to puzzle out what had just happened.

For her part, Odette latched onto the small grain of hope. First, she and Simon had shared a pleasant evening in his study, trading morsels of food and companionable conversation—not to mention an unspeakably erotic encounter—and now he'd agreed to break his fast in her presence without any coercion. She'd count that as a tally in her "win" column of this marriage.

She practically floated from the room.

Chapter Fifteen

Much to Simon's surprise, he and Odette settled into a new routine. With each passing day, he wondered if he'd gone about his intense need to be with Odette all wrong.

What if it hadn't been as straightforward as claiming her and getting her out of his system like a simple slaking of carnality and baser urges?

What if keeping her close—having her in consistent, small doses—actually served to keep his mind more focused because it wasn't being torn in too many directions at the same time?

Odette had joined him during his late night work on several occasions, most often when she was aware that he had been working for too many consecutive hours without a break or sustenance. In theory, it should have been annoying, distracting, or even mildly inconvenient. In reality, however, it was surprisingly pleasant to realize he didn't have to be alone. There was something simply satisfying about having her in the same room; it helped to quell his fractured thoughts and comfort his racing brain.

Rather than interrupt him, she often read while reclining on the sofa near the hearth, always clothed comfortably in her nightshift and wrapper, her dainty bare toes peeking out from beneath the lacy hems. She'd brought with her several books of poetry she enjoyed and even made the silent effort to read an essay by Sir Nigel. Other nights, it seemed she saved her correspondence so she could craft her replies during their late-night sessions. More than once, she'd even helped him locate a book or particular note misplaced amongst his stacks of work. She was calm and patient when his mind worked so frantically that his skin fairly buzzed with it.

And she brought him food.

Odette had worked some sort of spell upon him. She managed to find a way to distract and redirect him enough that he didn't realize he'd finished the plates she so carefully fixed for him until she was removing them from his desk and out of the way of his work.

She knew him.

He might not be the most perceptive man, but he recognized when the effort someone put in was above and beyond the norm. Never before had someone taken such an interest in him as a person, and with such honest, earnest intention. Odette with her silent and supportive presence made Simon more seen and heard than he'd ever felt in his life.

She didn't mind when he rambled to himself, repeating phrases and numbers and sequences as a way to think through a problem. She didn't mock him or grow annoyed if he became so lost in a thought that he stared off into the air for an hour at a time.

He'd never experienced such peace.

Another week passed in this pleasant fashion until the letters and invitations began to arrive. Gone was the safety and silence of their solitary little world. The *ton* had waited its requisite period before in-filtrating their household with sealed envelopes and calling cards. It began slowly at first and then picked up its pace as soon as Society concluded that it was now appropriate to call upon the newlyweds. And Simon knew the newly-minted Mrs. Stratford was an object of interest to their prying eyes and nosy ways.

Of course, he found his wife fascinating and enthralling...he also wasn't unkind enough to take the stance that she wouldn't be deemed a new gem in the trove of the elite; however, he was pragmatic enough to recognize that a great deal of the interest likely stemmed from the fact that she was *his* wife.

He might have been called aloof and he may have taken little inter-est in many social niceties, but he was far from deaf to the nasty whispers and tittered comments about the "odd Stratford son." He had been painfully aware for longer than he cared to admit that he was misunderstood amongst the *ton*; it stood to reason the inundation of invitations and callers was likely owed a great deal to the fact that So-ciety wanted to see what woman would be foolish enough to attach herself to the socially-inept, odd Mr. Simon Stratford. The nature of their abrupt engagement and quick wedding was enough to set the tongues to wagging; the identity of the bridegroom simply added more kindling to the gossip. Give the *ton* a nugget of salacious gossip and they'd drool over it. Give them interesting characters in the play and they'd run rabid.

The last thing he wanted to subject Odette to were the cruel words and whispers of Society and, with every letter that arrived, his need to protect her grew larger in his breast. He was long used to their actions and acidic words, the sidelong glances and smirks, but the last thing he wanted was for his wife to endure them. He told her as much one evening as she sat on the sofa in his study, sorting through a stack of cards and invitations by the light of the candles on the small table before her.

Simon's quill had sat dry in his hand for some time at that point, unused and forgotten. Despite Odette's best efforts to remain unobtrusive, he couldn't take his eyes off of her. He despaired of getting any work done that evening, settling only for watching her crystalline eyes as they scanned every line, every word offered up as enticement to join this woman for tea or accept a certain invitation to a musicale hosted by another. And to bring her husband along.

"You don't have to accept every invitation we receive," Simon finally said as he set aside his quill. She was so lovely when she glanced up at him that it made his heart ache.

"I know that, Simon," she replied with a smile. "I don't intend to accept a majority of these; it's simply astonishing to see who has sent them." She flipped through the stack until she came to an envelope once sealed with a black daub of wax. "The Countess of Heppelwaite has invited us to dinner. And this one," she added, plucking an embossed card from another stack; "is from the Duchess of Moreton. A *duchess*!"

Simon's mouth thinned into a grim line. "I'm sure there are one or two in there from earnest individuals, but a great many are simply curiosity-seekers."

Her elegant brows came together and she was silent for several moments. "Am I a curiosity, then?" she asked softly.

"Not you." His reply was so gentle she might have missed it had she not been watching him. The room was so quiet they could both hear the ticking of the clock upon the mantle.

There was a rustle as Odette leaned forward and set aside the papers she'd held in her lap. "Surely you don't believe this many invitations stem from some...cruel desire to make a mockery of you—of our marriage?"

Simon had to avert his eyes. It was the truth. Whether Odette believed it or not, he had spent nearly thirty years as the butt of jokes, the recipient of cruel words and comments. He'd built up a thick hide because of it, but the last thing he wanted was for his wife to have to do the same. Society was savage and he wanted to do everything in his power to protect her from it; he didn't want this marriage to change her any more than necessary. To allow it to happen would be the verist of injustices and likely dilute some of the things he adored most about her.

"Oh, Simon," she sighed, not unkindly. If anything, he could hear her heart in her voice. There was a pause where she mulled over her next words before speaking. "The last thing I want is to discount your experiences or make you feel as if I do not believe you...but we cannot hide away from the world." He watched as she tucked her legs beneath her. "Perhaps we can start small and invite your sister and Meredith? They can help me filter through these invitations, and I promise not to accept any on both of our behalf before consulting with you. Is that acceptable?"

Simon sighed.

As much as he wished to protect Odette, he knew he couldn't keep her shut away like a princess in a tower. It would be easy for him to cut Society out of his life, but his wife deserved more from her existence. She should have beautiful gowns and jewels, to be appreciated for her sweet heart and infectious smile. He knew, if given the chance, she would be as adored outside of these walls as she was within them.

Because he had...come to adore his wife, that was.

And denying her the opportunity to experience the world and find her place outside of her mother's shadow was not something he could completely bring himself to do.

"Is that agreeable?" she asked hopefully.

He inclined his head in acquiescence and then pushed himself back from the desk. Holding out his hand, he silently beckoned her into his arms.

Lily and Meredith, along with the countess, had eagerly accepted the invitation to see Simon and Odette's new home on St. James's Square. The laughter and gay chatter of the women echoed through the unfurnished rooms as they were led on a tour. It wasn't long before Odette was whisked away on a shopping trip to decorate and furnish several more rooms, along with adding to her wardrobe before the Season was fully underway and modistes were overwhelmed with orders.

Hours of peaceful silence passed during which Simon was able to work uninterrupted. But several times he'd caught himself staring at Odette's unoccupied place on the sofa. The correspondence had been cleared away and the pillows replaced and fluffed by their maid, but Simon still caught the echo of her scent, his ears still yearned for the sound of her voice, and his eyes craved the sight of her.

This was a rather unfortunate development.

Frustrated, Simon shoved away from his desk. As he stretched his back and worked a cramp from his hand, his stomach emitted a powerful growl.

And that was another unfortunate development.

It seemed his body had grown used to Odette's incessant insistence upon regular sustenance. And he knew it wouldn't let up until he satisfied the craving.

He could easily have yanked on the bell-pull near the door, but it felt quite good to stretch his long legs after hours of sitting. Rather than summon the maid, he decided to make a foray to the kitchens himself and see what he could scrounge up. He and his siblings had spent a great deal of their youth pilfering treats and snacks from the pantries at Bridleton and Aldborough House, so he had sufficient confidence that he would be able to do the same here in his own home. At least now there was no one to chastise him; he couldn't very well get in trouble for eating his own food, now could he?

It didn't take him long to locate what he sought—he had only to follow the scent of herbs and smoke, the nutty undertone of browned sugar. He found their maid, Mary, humming to herself as she stirred a heavy pot hanging from an iron hook above the crackling hearth. The cook was busy kneading dough—perhaps for the bread they'd enjoy with supper. The temperature in the room was at least ten degrees warmer than the rest of the house, but the maid, especially, seemed nonplussed as she flitted around the basement room to follow Cook's orders, her hair tied back in threadbare a kerchief. The back door to the alley had been propped open to allow some of the heat to escape.

Suddenly, the maid turned and jumped, pressing a hand to her chest. The cook spun around, snatching up a nearby knife and wielding her knife like the weapon it was.

"Mr. Stratford! You gave me such a fright!" Mary fanned her flushed face and wiped her hands on her apron. The cook slumped in visible relief before resuming her task. "Did you ring?" She glanced over at the collection of bells on the wall as if one might tell her she'd missed its chime.

Simon shook his head. "My apologies." He suddenly felt more obtrusive than a horse in the kitchen. "I was merely seeking out something to eat."

"Oh. Oh!" The young woman perked up as she processed what he'd said.

"Supper won't be ready for some time yet, but I believe there is some cold roast chicken from luncheon, grapes, a little of Mrs. Stratford's favorite cheese," the cook replied helpfully as she covered the ball of dough with a towel and wiped her hands on the broad apron at her waist.

"Sounds lovely," Simon replied and Mary jumped to prepare a plate for him, seeming thrilled to have more to do than watch the stew simmer for the next few hours. She began to chatter happily as she moved from the pantry to the cupboard, slicing from the block of cheese, laying out the grapes on the plate. In just those couple of minutes, he learned that the maid couldn't eat grapes because they made her cheeks itch and her grandmother had kept an onerous cow who hated being milked, but happened to produce a cheese the quality of which was unmatched. She was also rather adept at ignoring Cook's unsubtle glances. It wasn't until she was halfway through a story about a spilled bucket caused by an indelicate sneeze that she seemed to catch herself and remember to whom she spoke. She had the good grace to blush.

"My apologies, Mr. Stratford. I'm sure you don't wish to hear all of this—I quite forgot for a moment that I wasn't speaking to Mrs. Stratford."

"It's no trouble," Simon replied honestly. The one-sided conversation had been superfluous, but it was actually quite pleasant to learn something about the maid. It humanized her to him, gave him a connection to her as more than just an employee. He'd been born into privilege and, along with his tendency to dismiss anyone and anything not directly related to his interests in that moment, it was tragically easy to forget that servants were people too. "Although I'd believed my wife and I to be of somewhat differing appearances. I shall endeavor to stand up straighter."

Mary giggled. "I beg your pardon; I meant only that I'm used to her visits here to the kitchen for meals. She gave me leave to speak freely and I'm afraid my mouth has taken that and run."

The cook scoffed, not unkindly.

"My wife takes her meals here in the kitchens?"

"Mostly," the maid replied with a lift of one shoulder. "I realize it's highly irregular, but we both enjoy the company."

"Do you," Simon replied thoughtfully, not really expecting a response. His eyes focused on a dark knot in the scrubbed wood table in the center of the long, narrow room. How lonely must Odette have been if she'd sought out the company of the maid? How many meals had he forced her to dine alone? He didn't need a brilliant head for numbers to realize it was far too many.

"Shall I bring this to the breakfast room for you, sir? Or your study?" the maid asked, holding his now full plate in her hands.

"Thank you, no." Simon pulled out the simple wooden chair at the table. "I think I'll eat here, if you don't mind." If Odette could spend her meals here, then he could do the same.

"Of course!" the maid leapt to serve him after half a second's confusion. "I'll just fetch you something to wash it all down."

There in that warm kitchen of his home surrounded by the gentle sounds of cooking and cleaning, that meal wound up being one of the more pleasant ones Simon had ever experienced. It felt like home. The only thing missing had been Odette.

Simon's wife returned a few hours later looking happy, but exhausted. His heart throbbed when she fairly glowed with joy as he stepped from his study to watch her unload her parcels. His mother, Lily, and

Meredith had continued on their way once they safely delivered her and her purchases at their home. Observing Odette excitedly sift through her parcels and chatter delightedly made Simon feel buoyant and effervescent. When she caught his eye and her heart-shaped face split into an unabashed grin, when she glowed at him, his abdomen clenched and his knees actually felt weak.

"Simon!" she laughed joyfully. "I have something for you." Odette proceeded to sort through a stack of wrapped parcels until she located the correct one. The butler gathered up a large stack of the other packages and set about delivering them to their proper rooms per Odette's instructions. Alone in the entryway, Odette's demeanor turned more bashful. "Here," she whispered, holding out the parcel to him. He accepted the offering and carefully unwound the twine and found inside a thick packet of rich parchment, creamy in both color and texture. "I thought you might use it for the final draft of your paper." She twisted her fingers together, so like a child looking for approval as she glanced up at him from beneath her gilded lashes. "It's silly, I know, but—"

She was cut off when Simon wrapped an arm about the curve of her waist and tugged her close, immediately covering her mouth with his for a deep, claiming kiss.

This woman.

His wife.

She was *everything*.

Chapter Sixteen

One week later, Simon stood before the full-length mirror in the dressing room he shared with Odette. There was the occasional murmur and rustle as she dressed in the bedchamber with the assistance of their maid.

It had been quite pleasant to not have to don his formal black-and-white evening wear for so many weeks, but that time appeared to have come to an end. Odette had, with his acquiescence, accepted their first formal invitation as a married couple. The ball was one of the first of the Season and was held by the Earl and Countess of Haverford, long-time acquaintances of Simon's parents. Meredith and George had also accepted an invitation; Lily and Jem had declined, as expected—there were too many people for Lily's comfort, and she didn't have the best memories of the Haverford events. It would undoubtedly be quite the crush and, Simon hoped, this meant a great deal of the attention would be off of them. It would certainly be easier to disappear in a crowd of this size than, say, a quaint dinner party.

He exhaled a deep breath and rapped twice on the door to the bed-chamber. There was one final rustle of skirts before Odette bid him to enter. He noticed a stray thread on the cuff of his coat just as he opened the door and he was preoccupied with it as he stepped through the doorway, not immediately noticing his wife standing in the center of the room. The soft click of the maid ducking from the room pulled his attention upward and he froze.

From one thudding heartbeat to the next, Simon came to the shock-ing realization that he very much wanted to stay home that evening… and not to work on his research.

Odette had mentioned that she'd be wearing a gown for which she'd been fitted on her shopping excursion a little more than one week prior. And Simon took great note, indeed.

The gown was mauve—at least, he believed that was the name for the color caught somewhere between dusty rose and purple—trimmed in subtle lace of a similar color and cinched just beneath her ample bosom with a dark pink satin sash. The swath of pale flesh at her col-larbone and shoulders, the delectable amount of décolletage displayed was tantalizing and elegant with a hint of daring. This was a woman comfortable in her own skin. A woman who knew her worth. A woman who could drive a man mad with wanting.

Simon's mouth watered with the need to taste the curve of her throat, to nibble the sensitive flesh just beneath her ear revealed by the upswept style of curls and small plaits piled at the back of her head. His fingers tingled with the overwhelming desire to strip her of the elbow-length ivory gloves, to remove piece after piece of her clothing until she wore only the amethyst necklace and matching earrings.

Odette offered him a shy smile. "Do I look presentable?"

It took Simon a moment to realize his mouth hung agape. "Yes. Quite." He stood up straighter, prouder, and offered Odette his arm.

"I'm so thrilled you decided to attend!" Meredith laughed and handed Odette a cup of punch. The overcrowded room was sweltering, but even the lukewarm drink provided some relief. Odette tried not to cringe at the overly-sweetened concoction.

"I am, as well," she replied before handing her empty cup to a passing footman. Though she missed Lily, Odette understood her sister-in-law's desire to avoid a crowd of this size. She'd seen it happen before in the theater as well. Some actors were fine in rehearsals and small groups, but they froze and all words and sense left their bodies as soon as they saw a full house for the first time. It happened in varying degrees to some. She didn't think less of Lily for it; in fact, she quite admired Lily's willingness to forego Society in support of her own nerves and comfort, as well as Shefford's obvious unwavering support of his wife's sensibilities. Though she hadn't known them all that long, she expected nothing less.

Meredith's familiar, friendly face was comfort enough for Odette. Through her and her husband, Odette had been afforded numerous introductions to members of the elite. She formed new acquaintances and was able to place some faces to the names from a few of the invitations and calling cards left at her home. Throughout the night, she made mental notes which ones she could outright decline and which showed the promise of a genuine friendship. For the most part, Simon stayed relatively silent by her side. His arm beneath her hand was a comforting presence, his handsome face looking fondly down at her was thrilling. He'd briefly left her with Meredith after his father had pulled him aside to lend support in a debate over something having to do with investments and returns.

"You certainly seem to have done wonders pulling Simon out of his shell," Meredith murmured and nudged Odette's side. Though her cheeks warmed, Odette knew she was right. Simon had been attentive, if quiet. He'd even asked her to dance three times that evening without any prompting. It had created a bit of a spectacle, but Meredith had assured her it could be overlooked since they were so newly out of their honeymoon. "There's no denying that he looks far less miserable than he has in the past at these things," Meredith added, mirth twinkling in her indigo eyes.

"I suppose it's reassuring that he doesn't appear miserable to be escorting me," Odette said in good humor.

"I think it's perhaps the first time I've witnessed Simon as the more amiable Stratford male." Meredith grinned and leaned in conspiratorially. "If you want my opinion—and you'll have it whether or not you desire it—he's rather smitten with the woman he's escorting this evening."

A full-fledged blush covered her face and crept down to her throat and her chest, sharing the carnation-pink evidence of her feelings for all to see.

Meredith seemed so confident in her assessment, but Odette wasn't so sure. Simon had been attentive. He'd remained by her side. She'd been able to feel the caress of his gaze upon her ever since he had walked into her bedchamber earlier. In fact—she snuck a glance over her shoulder and found Simon's eerily intense blue-green eyes completely focused upon her, like a hawk and its prey. She barely suppressed a delicious shudder and turned back to Meredith.

There was no denying the fact that Simon was attracted to her and they'd certainly grown closer over the weeks since their marriage, but she doubted he felt quite what had been unfurling incrementally in her breast. Every smile, every touch, every moment he allowed her a glimpse inside his mind and his heart, well…made it blossom a little bit more.

To tell the truth, Odette was gradually coming to accept the fact that she was falling more than a little bit in love with her husband.

Later in the evening, the punch caught up to the ladies. Odette and Meredith retreated to relieve themselves and pause in the powder room to make sure the heat hadn't undone their hair entirely. Odette was particularly nervous because she knew she tended to sweat an unfortunate amount—much more than the slim, elegant Meredith, no doubt.

The room set aside for the ladies had several tabletop and full-length mirrors scattered throughout, along with two chaises and a number of chairs and ottomans upon which women could rest their aching legs. The center of the room was partitioned by an oversized high back lounge resembling a two-sided clamshell. The furniture was quite remarkable and looked incredibly comfortable. Odette quickly fixed a few of her hairpins and, as Meredith continued to adjust the neckline of her seafoam-green gown, Odette took the opportunity to drop onto the lounge. There was no one else within sight, so she allowed herself to sink low and enjoy the respite.

Meredith met her eyes in the mirror. "These things are quite exhausting, are they not? Only another hour or so and then we can rest at dinner."

"I never knew one could enjoy themselves too much," Odette laughed and glanced down at the toes of her satin slippered peeking out from beneath the hem of her gown. How she longed to step out of the shoes, peel off her silk stockings, and rub the arches of her feet.

"It's clear the poor dear won't have much of a marriage with him."

Odette's every muscle tensed as a conversation began on the other side of the lounge upon which she sat.

"I've heard she's some sort of relation to that French actress—the one at The Mask and Lyre," another female voice chimed in and Odette continued to listen, her sense of dread growing, sitting heavy and leaden in her gut.

"No matter who she is, she's saddled with a rather unfortunate arrangement now."

"An earl's younger son would have been quite the match for many women, but him..."

Meredith frowned and turned to face her. "Od—" She was cut off when Odette held a finger to her lips and gestured for silence. Meredith quietly drifted over and sat beside her.

"At least he's quite nice to look at," added a third nameless voice.

"Yes," chimed the first; "but looks mean little if a man has a reputation for being so...so strange. His manners are shockingly lacking. The earl and countess must be so disappointed."

Odette's hands fisted in her skirts, her teeth clenched. Meredith's hand covered hers.

"Mr. Stratford is so rude and disinterested in polite Society—imagine what he must be like as a husband!"

Odette met Meredith's pained eyes; she was clearly upset for her.

But Odette...she was furious.

For Simon.

Meredith's mouth opened, but, before she could say anything, Odette stood and stomped around the furniture and came face-to-face with the trio of ladies. Slapping on her sweetest smile, Odette smoothed her skirts and greeted them.

"I don't believe we've had the pleasure," she began, glancing at each one in turn as Meredith came up behind her. "I am Mrs. Odette

Stratford." One of the women paled; the others looked more than a little uncomfortable. "I have always found it fascinating what people say when they believe no one is paying attention. For example, I can only assume others discuss your sour dispositions, judgmental attitudes, and pinched faces at every opportunity." One of the women gasped. "If you find that uncomfortable, then I strongly suggest you think twice about spouting such nasty words in the future." Odette advanced a step. "And I must insist that you keep my husband's name out of your mouths. You've no idea of what you speak and to do so is only to make yourselves more ignorant than necessary."

"Well, I never…" One of the women managed to splutter in outrage as Odette spun on her heel and quit the room in a flurry of skirts. She didn't stop until they were well down the dimly-lit hallway.

"Odette!" Meredith grabbed her arm. "You were brilliant!" she gushed. "That was—Odette?" She stopped when she caught the glimmer of tears in Odette's eyes. "Dear, are you unwell?"

Odette began to shake her head even before Meredith finished the sentence. "No. I'm angry. I'm so very, very *angry*," she choked on the words as the tears spilled over. Meredith steered her into a nearby room and held her as she sobbed. When it was clear that Odette's emotions were only growing more powerful, she slipped from the room with the promise to return as quickly as possible. Alone in the dark, Odette sank to a chair and wrapped her arms around herself.

How dare those women say such things about Simon? They didn't know him. They didn't know his brilliant mind and his soft heart. They judged him only by their own standards and very likely knew absolutely nothing more about him than his name and family. It was so vastly unfair that Odette believed she might be ill from the injustice.

Less than two minutes later, Meredith returned with Simon. His dear, concerned face set off a new wave of enraged, frustrated tears as Odette stood and immediately walked into his open arms.

"What happened?" he demanded in a harsh whisper.

Still unable to speak, Odette shook her head and buried her face in his cravat as he held her, supported her when her legs were weak.

Meredith could only watch in awe as Simon cared for and cherished his wife in a manner she'd never witnessed from him before. To say Simon could be perceived as cold was a plain way to put it, but this scene before Meredith was far from that. The tenderness and caring was of a depth that actually made her avert her eyes.

"Come, I'll take you home," Simon murmured into Odette's hair.

"You stay here with her," Meredith interjected. "I will have your carriage brought round and let the family know you'll be taking your leave. We will handle the excuses for you."

She turned on her heel to carry out the task when a deep, hoarse, "Thank you," came from behind her. Simon's blue-green eyes met Meredith's over Odette's hair and she inclined her head in understanding.

Only once they were safely ensconced in the dark closeness of the carriage did Odette release a final torrent of emotion. And Simon simply held her and allowed her to vent her frustrations. Her throat was tight and her face burned from the salt of her tears, but she couldn't stop. Each time she tried to stop, a new red haze washed over her vision, the women's cruel words echoed in her skull and her fists clenched. They were nearly home when her sobs finally calmed and she stilled in his arms. Simon crooked a finger and turned her puffy face to his.

"Will you tell me what happened?" His voice ached for her. "Did someone say something to you? About you?" She felt Simon tense around her and she shook her head.

"About *you*," she rasped from her raw throat. He sat back, clearly perplexed by her admission.

"I'm used to people saying things about me," he admitted evenly.

"That is the problem," Odette snapped. "That is precisely why I am so mad. You don't deserve it. No one deserves to be *used* to criticism. It isn't fair," she sniffled the last words. Simon said nothing. Instead, he cupped her cheek and pressed her close to the thumping of his heart. They sat together and rocked along in silence through London until she spoke again.

"I fear we may see a lessening in our invitations after the things I said."

And Simon laughed, a real, unbridled laughter from deep in his chest—a sound she'd never heard from him before—and then pressed a kiss to her lips, his mouth smiling broadly against hers.

The carriage rolled to a stop in front of the St. James's Place townhouse and Simon jumped down before helping Odette to the walk. He guided her inside and deftly told the butler that nothing would be needed for the rest of the evening before leading her up the stairs to the bedchambers. Odette's heartbeat picked up its pace as he shut the door behind them and turned the lock. A shiver of anticipation traipsed up and down her spine.

Chapter Seventeen

Much, much later, Odette and Simon padded barefoot together down to the kitchens. His stomach had released a ferocious growl after their second bout of lovemaking and Odette rose from the bed, tossed him a pair of breeches and pulled her nightshift over her head. The only solution to their problem of missing supper at the ball was a midnight trip to the larder.

The foray took twice as long to accomplish because they kept stopping to steal caresses and kisses in the shadowy halls, but they eventually made it back to the bedchamber, re-secured the door, and leapt onto the bed, their bounty spread out between them.

"Poor Cook will believe we have a thief," Odette giggled as she surveyed the array of bread and fruit.

"Or a very large rat," Simon added, popping a cube of cheese into his mouth. Odette barely stifled a burst of laughter with her hand over her mouth. She removed it when Simon held out a bite of cheese for

her and she gladly accepted it, her lips grazing the pad of his thumb.
The dark pools of his pupils widened.

"Look what I found," he said, revealing a small wooden bowl of
fat, ruby-red strawberries where he'd kept them hidden behind his
back.

A low hum of appreciation emanated from Odette's throat. She
adored sweet late-summer strawberries. "Those were intended for tomorrow's dessert."

"I can think of a much better way to enjoy them," he murmured dangerously. He selected the ripest one and held it between his long, elegant fingers by its leafy green cap. He nipped the tip of the berry with
his teeth and held the rest out to her. She parted her lips for the
morsel, but, instead, he surprised her by tracing her lower lip with the
berry, spreading its sweet juices and filling her senses with the heady
scent of lazy summer afternoons. Unable to resist, her tongue darted
out for a taste. The berry was quickly replaced by Simon's lips and
tongue. He kissed her deeply, but, before she could sink into it too
much, he pulled back and gave her a taste of the strawberry. Seeing
him lick his lips as he watched her eat was one of the more erotic experiences of Odette's existence.

He set the strawberry cap aside and plucked one more from the
bowl. "Another?" he asked, his voice so low she felt it in her chest
more than she heard it. She could only nod mutely and part her lips
again.

They took turns feeding one another until the caresses and kisses
began outweighing the actual sustenance. It wasn't long until Simon
rolled Odette beneath him, tearing off her nightshift and reverently
licking and trailing his fingers across every petal-soft hill and valley
of her body.

Only when he had her mewling and thrashing beneath him did he finally sink his thick, throbbing member deep into her quivering body, gasping as she pulled him deeper, cradled him with her body.

"Wrap your legs around me," he ground out and she immediately obliged, hooking her ankles together and canting her hips to accept every stretching, insistent inch of him.

He surged forward again and again, bathing in every cry of ecstasy, every bite of her nails on his shoulders, every graze of her teeth on his throat. This was like nothing he'd ever experienced before—it was more than just the bedsport. This feeling of closeness so intense it felt as if they were a part of one another heightened everything. Made it better. Made him feel so much more alive.

He finally understood…

This was what Jem had been willing to die for…what George had learned to live for.

This caring and sense of devotion, this woman who saw past his flaws and was the only person who hadn't tried to change him into something she felt fit better into her life.

Odette was beautiful and sweet and well-meaning in every action, and he'd grown quite used to having her as a part of his daily life.

And now he couldn't imagine life without her.

Odette was everything he'd been missing in his life; she made up for his faults, and then some. She was something he hadn't even known he lacked.

She pulled his head down to collide with hers in a bruising kiss; he met her greedy lips with his own. Angling his hips, he reached between their sweat-slicked bodies and stroked the pearl at the crux of her sex. Three deep strokes and her body clenched around him as wave after wave of her climax broke. It wasn't long until he followed Odette into oblivion.

*****

The next day, Odette was exhausted by the time luncheon was finished. Simon had been insatiable—not that she was complaining about *that*, of course, but she could have done with a few more hours' rest.

To be fair, he had offered to let her sleep when he rose to begin his day, but she'd been too mortified after he'd practically chased off Mary when she'd come by to make up the bed and help Odette dress.

"Simon!" she'd hissed with burning cheeks as he strode naked back to the bed, gloriously unashamed by his nudity.

"Don't tell me you're shy," he'd chuckled.

"But now she'll *know*."

"And you think she didn't know what we'd been up to before now?" She'd silently admitted that he had a point, but that didn't stop her flare of embarrassment. "We are newlyweds," he added very matter of factly; "it's expected." He then proceeded to kiss away her self-consciousness.

Exhausted and deliciously sore, she proceeded to go about her day when Simon finally released her to return to his work. If she'd learned one thing about her husband in their brief time together, it was that he applied his single-minded drive and determination to *absolutely every aspect* of his life…the bedroom included. He was brilliant and talented, to say the least. He didn't stop until he found what made her sob in pleasure and then he would continue until she was breathless and weak, as if her bones had been melted down to molten gold. As reserved as he was in the outside world, he unleashed a whole other side of himself when it was just the two of them behind closed doors. He was sensual and confident; unerringly talented and ravenous. It was amazing. Just thinking about it heated her skin fair to steaming.

"A caller has arrived for you, Mrs. Stratford." Odette jumped from her reverie when the butler arrived in the sitting room. Newly decorated in shades of emerald and cream, it was one of her favorite spaces in the house with its warm sunlight and comfortable furniture. The space beside the hearth also happened to be the very spot where she and Simon had christened their new home…

She had to avert her eyes from that spot to prevent another blush. "Who is it?"

"She provided no card and insisted her name would be sufficient: a Mademoiselle Auclair."

Odette sat a little straighter. "You may show her in."

What could her mother possibly want? Now that she thought on it, this was the first visit her mother had initiated in recent memory. It was perhaps less kind than a daughter should feel toward her mother, but Odette couldn't help but wonder what she wanted.

Mademoiselle Auclair, ever stylish and a force to be reckoned with, garbed in a Grecian dress of gossamer sky-blue material, floated into the room like Aphrodite on a wave of sea foam. Unbelievably elegant and perpetually youthful, she still had the power and presence to make Odette feel frumpy in even her new ivory morning dress.

A prick of uncertainty prodded at her mind. A part of her still felt bad about what she'd said about her mother's past relationships, but Odette still stood by the intentions behind her words. Her mother had trapped a good man into a marriage and stolen both Simon and Odette from a rightful choice.

Still…her mother's machinations had brought them together…and there was no denying that Odette was deliriously happy—much happier than she'd ever hoped for from a marriage.

"*Ta maison est magnifique!*" her mother sang, complimenting her home and greeting her with three kisses to her cheek as she held her in place by her shoulders. "I'd never dared to dream of such an address for you. Imagine, my daughter, neighbors to *ton*, and one of them!"

"Thank you, *maman*," Odette replied, gesturing awkwardly for her mother to sit. "We still have no idea as to the identity of the gifter, but we've settled in quite nicely. I'm happy to provide you with a tour should you desire."

Her mother waived away the offer. "Perhaps another time."

Odette found the declination a bit odd, but she didn't press. "Might I offer you refreshments?"

"*Merci, non*," she replied. "You know how I watch my figure during performances." She executed a familiar tilt of her coiffured head. "Though it looks as if you have settled into married life quite…comfortably."

Odette barely suppressed the urge to flinch. She'd gone how many weeks without being made to feel poorly over her appearance? Simon blatantly cherished every one of her curves in the same way she reveled in his body. She refused to allow her mother beneath her skin now.

"And how is the performance?" Odette smoothly shifted topics to one of her mother's favorites. "I haven't had a chance to read the reviews yet—is it being received well?"

"*Oui!*" Her mother clapped her hands in delight. "Every performance has been sold out so far! There is talk of this being my most brilliant performance yet."

"That's wonderful," Odette replied honestly. She knew how her mother's existence depended upon her looks and her ability to remain in demand and draw crowds. Nothing was better for business than an actress with stellar reviews.

"But I caught wind of a little performance of yours, Odette." Her mother arched one artfully-shaped brow. Odette's stomach felt heavy and her ears began to ring a warning.

"I don't know—"

"Please. Do not play the imbecile. Last night at the Haverford ball."

Odette's stomach plummeted further to the point of nausea. "How did you hear of that?" she eked out. She should have known her mother would catch wind of the outburst—the popular actress often claimed to have "friends" in most spheres—but it was nearly unbelievable that the news had reached her ears this quickly. Less than twenty-four hours later and her mother had shown up on her doorstep practically foaming at the mouth with her need to discuss it.

"Bah." Her mother dismissed the question with a flick of her fragile wrist.

"I was merely protecting my husband." Odette clenched her hands so tightly her nails bit into her palms, no doubt creating deep, crescent-shaped indentations.

"I commend you for having discovered your spirit," her mother answered coolly. "But I would not be a mother if I didn't caution you to choose your battles amongst the *ton* more wisely. The sister of a duke, the wife of a viscount, and the daughter of an earl would not make good enemies." Another wave of nausea gripped Odette and she suddenly regretted eating the fish at luncheon. She hadn't realized just who those women in the powder room were at the time…but, would it have changed the way she'd reacted if she had? Her answer was a resounding no. "It won't do to set yourself at odds with any of them, especially not when your position is so new."

"So what am I supposed to do?" Odette ground out. "Allow them to walk all over my husband?"

Her mother leaned forward, an animal cunning glittering in her bright eyes. "If there is truth to the words? If they are not said directly to your face? Then it is wiser to allow them to slide. This is how these titled Englishwomen operate. To make enemies could destroy you before you've even truly begun." The words were spoken in a tone so flat it gave Odette a chill. "The talk amongst those of quality is Mr. Stratford suffers from monomania. It is true, *non*? That he is so obsessed with his work that he sees nothing else? That the world can burn around him and he will not lift his head from it?" Odette's silence was all the answer her mother required. She nodded at her daughter in understanding. "Then let it be. The *ton* has allowed you within its fold as the wife of an earl's son; do not offend them and spit in their eye or you shall lose whatever foothold you have gained."

Simon stood rooted in place in the hallway outside of the sitting room, his skin icy cold and clammy. The door was ajar nearly six inches—plenty wide enough for him to hear every word being said inside. His entire body was taut and, despite outward appearances, his mind was running more frantically than it ever had before.

He'd been able to convince Odette to admit what had upset her so at the ball…but it was clear he'd been a fool to believe it was done and handled. As much as it irked him, Odette's mother was correct.

This was far from over.

If anything, it was just the beginning of what Odette would face as his wife.

And his crime? Simply being different and straying from the norm.

It wasn't fair to Odette to have to endure this. She shouldn't be forced to become his champion. He should be the one protecting *her*.

Fists balling tightly at his sides, Simon vowed to do just that. He would do absolutely everything in his power to protect Odette from the stain of his reputation. Whatever the cost to him, he had to do it. He needed nothing more in this world than to give her the space to realize her potential. And if removing himself from her world accomplished this, then so be it. He could not expect her to commit social suicide on his behalf, nor did he wish her to.

He would leave and finish his work elsewhere, and Odette would be free of his tainted shadow. He would make sure she had his family to look out for her in his absence—to make sure she had what she needed and that she entered the right circles. If he knew one thing in this world, it was that he could count on them. Odette already had enough going against her because of her background; she didn't deserve to have him hold her back.

Her mother was right.

Less important was the fact that his research had fallen behind… exactly like he'd promised himself it wouldn't. If he had any hope of finishing his paper—if Odette had any hope of fitting in—then there was only one choice for him to make.

Chapter Eighteen

That evening at supper, Odette was more than a little surprised when there were two settings at the table. Simon cleared his throat behind her and she whirled around. He was dressed impeccably—as was his custom when he was not working. His charcoal coat and silver waist-coat somehow made the vibrant colors of his eyes stand out even more brilliantly. Only weeks ago she might have felt self-conscious in her simple dress. He was so beautiful to her and she wanted to feel as if they were a pair; but, if Simon had taught her one thing since their wedding day, it was that she need only be herself for him to want her.

"Good evening." Simon greeted her softly and brought her knuckle to his lips.

"Simon!" Odette's heart fluttered. "I wasn't expecting you this evening."

"I do occasionally leave my office," he replied a little on the cooler side of warm. He helped her into her seat and then took his at the head of the table. Mary and their cook had prepared a supper of chilled pea soup, turbot in a light sauce, and roasted vegetables. Odette had come to truly enjoy the simple, rustic meals they prepared. She did not see the need for all the pomp and circumstance when it was just the two of them and a quiet night at home. In fact, she secretly savored the informality of their household, the relatively relaxed life they led behind closed doors. Odette was about to say as much when Simon spoke up instead.

"Sir Nigel Wright has extended an invitation to his home in Lincolnshire. The hope is that we can spend the last few weeks combining our efforts and crafting a final cohesive article for the journal in time for the deadline. The invitation extends at least through the completion of the work."

"I've never traveled that far north," Odette smiled and took a sip of her wine before stifling a grimace—they'd have to find a new vendor because the selection had been quite atrocious as of late. "How soon do we leave?" She picked up her spoon to take a bite of fish.

"I leave tomorrow."

Odette set down her fork, no longer hungry in the slightest. "*You* leave tomorrow?" she whispered, praying she had misheard him.

He stared down at his food, his thumb tracing the stem of his wine glass. "Yes. Early."

"Alone." It wasn't a question, rather, Odette coming to terms in terrifying increments that she was to be left behind.

"Yes."

"Do you know when you will return?" she asked, trying her best to remain cheerful. She wasn't the kind of woman who needed her husband beside her at every moment. She was slowly becoming more acclimated to the freedoms of a married woman. Meredith had promised to help introduce her to her friends and broaden her circle of acquaintances. She could make due just fine for a few weeks until Simon's work was done.

And then they could celebrate!

Cheered somewhat, her mind immediately began concocting a small celebration for Simon—something to show how loved and supported he was, how proud they all were for his revolutionary work.

"I know not."

His response collapsed any bit of buoyancy Odette had felt.

"Y—You don't know when you'll return home?" *To me…*

He gave a single shake of his head in response and Odette's stomach plummeted so quickly she actually experienced a wave of nausea.

"Simon. Whatever is the matter—" Her words abruptly died when he removed his hand from the table and out of her reach. He was a preoccupied man, often aloof, but never, ever icy like this. Not to her. "Was it something I did?"

"Not everything is about you, Odette," Simon snapped, making her jump so hard the silverware clattered atop the table. She had never heard him raise his voice, let alone at her.

"I didn't mean to insinuate that it was," she stammered, suddenly feeling more lost than she'd ever been in her life, not knowing which way was up and which was down in this world where her even-tempered scholar of a husband snarled at her with chips of ice in his eyes. "I am only trying to understand this change in you."

"Too much has changed, that's what." His voice was a low growl and he averted his eyes once more as if the sight of her was too vexing in that moment. "I cannot afford the distractions you pose. I've worked too hard for far too long on this project to have it crumble down around me because I was forced into marriage."

The words struck Odette like daggers to the heart. One after another, they pierced vital parts of her soul. She felt her heart weeping in pain. Her eyes began to fill with stinging tears. "I apologize if I have been intrusive. I only meant to take care of you, to help see to your needs so that you might better complete your work—"

"I am not a child!" Simon's fist slammed against the table. "And I'll not have you martyr yourself for me."

Odette's head snapped back in surprise as if the words had been a physical blow. "Martyr? What is it you think I do for you?" He opened his mouth to speak, but she held up her hand to silence him and ignored the tears burning her eyes. "It is not martyrdom to care for one's husband, to see that he is fed and cared for. It is *love*." Her voice broke, along with her heart, split raw and wide and vulnerable.

She swiped at her tear-blinded eyes in time to see Simon's eyes slide closed; his jaw clenched and its muscles flexed, as if her words were too painful to hear. His fist remained on the table and his knuckles were bleached a painful white from the force of his grip.

Then, abruptly, Simon shoved himself away from the table.

"I leave tomorrow," he reiterated in a strangled growl and stormed from the room. Only when she was alone did Odette allow herself to crumble completely. She sobbed, her head cradled in her hands.

What had she done? What could have caused such a deep fissure in their relationship from one night to the next? She'd believed they were on a steady path in their marriage; had felt that he might have even begun to care for her as deeply as she had him.

Because she did love him, she did.

And to have him push her away as he just had was like having her legs kicked out from beneath her. How could she have misjudged their relationship so terribly? And how could she convince Simon not to leave?

Odette did her best to take a shaky, steadying breath. She had to persuade him to stay. There had to be another reason he was leaving with no return date in mind. Having him travel was one thing; having him abandon her was something she refused to tolerate without at least giving it her best go of it.

Odette pushed back from the table and dropped her napkin across her plate. Food had lost all of its appeal at that point.

Stepping into the hallway, she glanced toward the front door only for her eyes to land upon a stack of trunks she hadn't previously noticed. Two of them were the battered cases from their dressing room. Pivoting on her heel, she went to splash cool water on her heated face before she sought out her husband, determination steeling her spine.

Simon sat alone in the parlor, silent in the dimly flickering light of the sputtering, low-burning hearth. The sun had set some hours before, lending the room a close darkness befitting of his mood. He'd long since removed his coat, cravat, and waistcoat and had perched on the edge of the sofa, elbows on his knees, head hanging low.

He knew he was doing the right thing by leaving—Odette didn't need the black mark of his reputation upon her and she deserved more of a life than a connection to him would give her—but the look on her face...her tears...had sliced him deep, shredded his soul. Her tears had severely cracked his resolve.

And her love...

It was unbelievable, but he couldn't deny what his ears had heard: she'd actually said she loved him.

That *broke* him.

If he were a man prone to imbibing in spirits, then he had no doubt he'd be three sheets to the wind at that very moment...but there was no stiff alcohol to be had in the house. Whether this was to his detriment or for the best, he had yet to determine.

He collapsed there in glowering silence, deflated and disheartened, when he heard the snick of the latch of the door behind him. It was a faint sound, but the quiet footsteps that followed were like the crack of gunshots behind his head. He knew the cadence of Odette's every breath, every step. He hated himself for it, but he did.

Odette said nothing as she crossed the quiet room. The faint rustle of her skirts was deafening; the tap of her slippers on the floor before they were muffled by the carpet made his anticipating rise to a dizzying height. She continued to approach until she stood before him, blocking out the gasping embers of the fire and silhouetting her curvaceous form in the failing orange light. Though they were alone, the entire room seemed to hold its breath.

Would she strike him?

Lord knew he deserved it.

Would she cry and scream?

Simon knew that would be appropriate as well. Any husband who willingly abandoned his wife, especially so soon after their wedding, deserved as much, if not more.

Simon braced himself, but she didn't move.

They waited in pregnant silence until Simon was the first to move. He sat back on the sofa with uncharacteristically poor posture and looked up into her face. Confronted by her slightly puffy eyes, he wished he hadn't.

His heart ached with immediate force so strong it winded him. His mouth opened to tell her he'd made a grave mistake, but no sound came out.

He was struck even more dumb when Odette spoke instead. "I love you, Simon." Her voice was barely above a whisper, but it held the impact of a guttural scream.

"I love you," she repeated. "And you leaving will not change the way I feel." She inched closer to him and his pulse quickened in like. "I've experienced these feelings for a while, so don't believe I am voicing them in a conceited effort to give you a reason to stay."

Odette then lifted the hem of her skirts and stole Simon's breath as she straddled his lap and stared down into his face. The warmth of her sex hovered just above his steadily growing crisis, her lush bottom rested on the fronts of his thighs with tantalizing softness as she braced her knees on either side of his hips. It took everything in him to not cup her bottom and pull her flush with him.

"I just need you to know. How I feel." She placed her palms on either side of his head to rest on the back of the sofa. "And I need you to know that, though you have decided to leave, that will not change how I feel. About you."

Odette leaned forward in increments until her lips grazed his. They rubbed back and forth in a delicate dance and he longed to tilt his head and extend his neck the millimeter necessary for the caress to evolve into a full-blown kiss. But he knew he shouldn't. He couldn't. It was one of the most agonizing experiences of his life, but Simon continued to hold himself immobile.

Odette's lips ran a faint trail down his cheek, to the hard line of his clenched jaw, the tender flesh where it met his ear lobe, and then down.

He swallowed convulsively when her lips traced the curve of his throat, the hollow there. He had to fist his hands at his sides to not grab her and haul her mouth back up to his. His control remained intact by a dangerously tenuous thread.

"I love you." Her breath against his throat sent chills through every one of his nerves.

"I love you." Her tongue flicked out to taste his hammering pulse and he nearly groaned aloud.

"*I love* you." His cock throbbed powerfully, straining against the falls of his breeches when she finally pressed an open mouth kiss to the underside of his jaw.

Simon's head fell to rest on the back of the sofa. Odette read the invitation and continued peppering her sweet, teasing kisses on his sensitive jaw to punctuate her last word.

She finally pulled back and met his eyes, the dark blue orbs boring into him with ferocious candor. "If you must leave, leave and do your work. Accomplish great things. But come home soon. To me." Her fingers brushed his hair back from his forehead and he was lost.

If only she knew how much he didn't want to leave her.

If only she was aware how weak and powerful she made him feel; she could knock him over with a feather and, yet, he felt strong enough to lift a building when she looked at him like that.

Unable to resist any longer, Simon reached up and finally allowed himself to touch her. He threaded his fingers through her hair and tugged her down to force her mouth to meet his in a bruising kiss. To be fair, she accepted every one of his kisses and licks with her own, successfully whipping his desire higher and chasing away his last shred of reason.

His other hand flew to the lush curve of her bottom, gripping her there and pressing her more firmly to his awakening arousal. He helped her find a rocking rhythm that teased his body and worked her own into a blossoming frenzy.

Her sensuous moan shattered his reserve. He reached between their bodies and ripped open the falls of his breeches. Unable to resist, he brushed his knuckles through the wet, delicate folds of her sex, thrilled with the knowledge that she'd anticipated their mating and had already removed her stockings, garters, and drawers. He traced her nether lips with trembling fingers, groaning when she gasped as he located that secret pearl at the crux of her sex. She was already so wet and pliant, so ready for him she dripped with need. He could wait no longer.

Firmly grasping her hips in his hands, he positioned her above his reaching member. Notched into place, he simultaneously thrust his pelvis upward and pulled her down flush with him, entering her in one great, swift motion that stole both of their breaths. Her nails bit into his shoulders through the thin lawn of his shirt, but he reveled in it.

Their mating was fast and furious, so filled with desperate need that Simon was brought to the brink in an unnervingly quick amount of time. From the tightness of her sheath, the thick wetness coating both of them, her rapid gasps at each grinding thrust of their bodies, he could tell Odette was near to her climax as well.

She leaned forward and changed the angle to one of delicious torture, bringing her bosom within his reach. He nuzzled the improbably soft pillows, licked the deep crevasse between them, savored the salt of her passionate sweat and the light hint of her own delicate musk. His hands spread wide on the globes of her buttocks, rocking her just so, until she stiffened in his arms and lowered her forehead to his, crying out, gasping in the rapturous joy of her climax. Even when her tremors eventually slowed, Simon remained relentless.

His fingers held her close in a bruising grip as he planted his feet and surged up into her again, and again, and again. He filled her, stretched her wide with every inch of his desire, trying to use his body to convey the words he would not, could not say. Their pounding flesh and Odette's soft cries of passion, finally drove Simon over that soaring precipice. He buried himself deep within her, nestled safe and hot as wave after wave of his release threatened to drown him. His mind was blank, his world went dark as he screwed his eyes shut and growled through his climax, but he didn't feel lost. And he realized he never felt lost as long as they were in one another's arms.

Simon stood in the front hall of their townhouse and accepted the proffered hat and cloak from his butler. He made certain the cream-colored envelopes still waited in a neat row on the small, spindle-legged table Odette had selected for the entryway. On it sat a simple crystal vase with a fluted neck; in it was a small bouquet of pink and white blooms. The hint of their perfume floated on the air and struck Simon like a punch to the stomach.

"See that those messages are delivered." Simon tilted his chin in the direction of the table. One each to Meredith and Lily, another to his father's solicitor who handled Simon's funds. A short note awaited Odette on her dressing table. He'd been torn about whether or not to leave it for her, but, faced with her naked sleeping form bared from the waist up where the sheet had slipped low, he simply hadn't been able to leave her with nothing.

Following their lovemaking in the study, he'd carried her up to their bedchamber and there, they'd shared the bed for the remainder of the night. He'd intended the second time that evening to be softer, gentler, something to savor, but he had failed miserably. Odette hadn't seemed to mind. She'd pressed back into his pounding thrusts, clawed at him to come closer when he flipped her over and covered her body with his. She'd wrapped her legs around his hips and locked her ankles to keep him deep within her as he spilled his hot seed deep, deep inside of her.

Simon couldn't lie to himself. He recognized in his bones that he did not wish to leave Odette; he simply knew that he had to. He couldn't allow his presence to drag her down. She'd deny it, but he knew it would eat at her gradually. She was warmth and light and Simon…his presence would only hinder her finding her place in Society.

"Of course, Sir," replied the butler, snapping Simon back to the present.

He nodded and walked through the open door and down to the hired carriage that would bring him to the far flung estate of his colleague. The luggage had already been loaded and the conveyance was weighed down with numerous trunks of papers, notes, and books.

As the carriage jerked into motion, Simon steadfastly refused to look out the window and watch the Townhouse—and Odette—slip away.

Chapter Nineteen

Odette lay abed long after she awoke the following morning.

It was her habit to bound from the mattress nearly as soon as her eyes opened; she'd been like this even as a girl, much to her mother's chagrin. This day, however, was one she did not wish to face. She loathed the rising sun, the chirping birds and cooing pigeons swooping and strutting through the light morning traffic in St. James's Square, even the laughter of children as they evaded their nanny's scolding and darted between the trees. Absolutely everything seemed to somehow bring her mind back to her husband.

She'd awoken alone; the pillow upon which he'd rested his head just a few short hours before was already cold. As much as she wanted to curl into the warm space he had abandoned, Simon hadn't even left her that much of himself.

In that dreamlike state between sleep and wakefulness, she'd almost been able to convince herself that Simon had simply risen without waking her and was busy collecting her favorite sugar-dusted pastries and other delicious treats with which they might break their fast together in bed. Her reasoning became more desperate as the minutes tipped by, however.

Maybe his delay was due to another early fencing practice.

Then, maybe he'd become sidetracked by a particularly riveting piece of his work or a book he'd come across.

But as Odette's mind grew more alert, she knew with fierce, cruel certainty what the reality was: Simon had left her.

Even after their lovemaking.

Even after he'd held her.

Even after she'd repeatedly told him she loved him.

Odette was wrecked by the thought of having to face this day without her husband.

Truthfully, it wasn't so much that she would not see him or be near him and more so that she didn't know when or if that would happen again.

When.

There had to be a when. She had to believe that Simon would finish his work and see past whatever obstacle he seemed to perceive lay within their marriage and then he would come home to her.

Odette screwed her eyes shut, inhaling one last deep, bracing breath, and swung her legs over the side of the bed.

Initially, she was rather proud of herself for maintaining her stiff upper lip. She didn't cry when she saw his toiletries were missing, nor when she didn't stub her toe on one of the trunks in the dressing room —imagine that—nor when she noticed his second pair of boots had also been removed.

Her facade all came crashing down, however, when she caught sight of the letter laid so carefully on her vanity table, propped up against her crystal scent bottle.

The folded note had no address—it didn't need one for her to know it was for her and just from whom it came. She stared at it for several minutes, like a chess player regarded an opponent, before swiping it up and unfolding the parchment. She both needed to know what it said and feared what Simon had deemed important enough to write down. He was an expeditious man and simply transcribing the words he'd already spoken the night before was something she was sure he'd deem superfluous.

Odette's eyes flew through his neat script, now so familiar to her from his journals. She hadn't believed her heart might possibly sink further than it had, but she was wrong. So very wrong.

Odette,

Below are the directions of where I am staying. I trust you to respect my work and remain here in Town while I am away. My family have been notified of my absence and, I feel safe in assuming, will be available should you require anything at all. My father and his solicitor have been asked to see that monies from my portion are disbursed to you to use as you see fit, but he will, I am sure, advise you should you have any questions in that regard.

You know me well enough by now to have come to the conclusion that I am not an eloquent man. Words and expressing my emotions through them do not come easily. I hope that you will discover joy and fulfillment in my absence, as I anticipate I will with my work. One thing you have always done is respect the place my passion holds in my life and now, though I suspect it will not be easy for you, I request that you continue to do so. It is my hope that our lives may run comfortably parallel; two roads traveling in a complimentary fashion, but

never interrupting the other. My work is my life, and now you have the
freedom of the Stratford name to discover yours.

Regards,

Simon

The finality of it all left Odette reeling. Her sorrow cut off her air as effectively as a hand to her throat; her chest was congested with a thick, choking fog of it. Tears began to dot the paper, the words blurred and swam in her eyes until she could no longer see through the torrent of emotion pouring from within her soul.

Meredith and Lily arrived before luncheon to find Odette still lying in her bed burrowed beneath the Simon-scented coverlet and pillows. After receiving their own letters from Simon, they'd brushed past the poor butler and worried maid to burst into her bedchamber in a flurry of skirts and pelisses, comforting words and hugs.

Like the true sisters they were, they made no comment or sideways glance when they found Odette too despondent to dress herself, too listless to eat. Instead, they set about making her more comfortable. Lily ordered strong tea and some sweet pastries; Meredith drew back the blinds and helped Odette into a clean shift and her wrapper. Together they piled onto the bed, sitting in silence or chatting, comforting her and holding her—whatever Odette needed at that moment.

Though they had no answers for her and needed to provide a steady supply of handkerchiefs, they reassured her again and again that they were going nowhere. A deep part of Odette appreciated their efforts, but she was first and foremost lost, vacillating between anger and hurt, sadness and mortification. What could possibly have changed so drastically from one day to the next?

Several days passed and Lily and Meredith remained as determined as ever to provide her the solace and reassurance that they felt she deserved.

The countess didn't intrude, but she consistently sent her well-wishes along with Lily and Meredith and included tins of biscuits and shortbread from their cook at Aldborough House.

Odette's mother made not a single appearance, though she'd heard a whispered conversation between her sisters-in-law that word had been sent to her without a reply.

It took hours of effort and quite a bit of coercion, but Odette was eventually convinced to dress and tag along for a mindless shopping excursion. She felt like a ghost as she trailed along in their other women's well-meaning wake. She couldn't even bring herself to smile politely when Lily made a particularly humorous observation about an unfortunate stuffed swan perched upon a hat in the milliner's window.

Though Odette went through the motions of tea and social niceties, she felt hollow. There was a soul-deep ache in her breast and she felt unmoored from it.

Two weeks passed before Meredith was able to convince Odette to join a ladies' reading society with her. It was apparently a rather exclusive group, but Meredith promised she could gain her entry if she so desired. It had been weeks since Odette had picked up a book and she was nervous that the material would be out of her depth, but Meredith insisted she would be welcome into the fold.

The first meeting of the reading society took place the third week after Simon took his leave of London. She knew Meredith was right —finding something to occupy her mind would be good—but it was one of the most difficult things she'd ever had to do. On top of the usual social anxieties where she wondered how she would fit into this circle, she now had to put on a pleasant face and pretend her husband hadn't recently abandoned her.

Meredith retrieved her in the elegant Sommerfeld carriage, reassured her several times over as they wound through the streets of Mayfair that all would be well, and they were deposited on the front step of the expansive home belonging to the Duchess of Moreton. It wasn't long before Odette was enveloped in a warm, welcoming atmosphere. A dozen or so women were clustered in the duchess's beautiful, airy sitting room, chattering and sipping tea, devouring an obscene amount of sweets curated by the duchess's brilliant cook. Their hostess and patroness was far younger than Odette had managed. She was breathtakingly beautiful, intelligent, and so clearly wise beyond her years. Meredith had whispered that the absent duke meant Lady Moreton could host these events and meetings without fear of interruption or censure of their oft-incendiary reading materials.

Odette recognized the duchess as having sent her one of the many invitations she and Simon had received, but it was not until that meeting that they were formally introduced. She'd been instantly taken in by the other woman's wide smile and frank manner of speech. Indeed, they seemed to share an unspoken connection as being women with husbands off minding their own pursuits. It was a rather pathetic club in which to be a member, but it was somewhat reassuring to have a woman as gorgeous and intriguing as the Duchess of Moreton among the ranks. It made Odette feel less alone, less like she'd failed horribly and had no idea why.

While all Lily and Meredith's efforts helped to bring Odette out of her head and the dark spaces within, she was still terribly alone at night. It wasn't even purely physical; she missed their late-night sessions in his study. She ached to curl up on the comfortable sofa and look over to watch him rake his fingers through his hair as he puzzled through a problem.

As the weeks progressed without a word, her anger-tainted sadness cooled to loneliness. She had immediately been sorry that she'd allowed Mary to change the sheets she and Simon had shared; they no longer smelled of his skin. She ached to bury her face in them and inhale deeply so she might pretend she wasn't so alone.

One afternoon, out of desperation, she riffled through the clothes remaining in the dressing room. After some digging, she was able to locate one of the comfortable linen shirts Simon sometimes wore during his fencing lessons. It smelled of him…clean starch and soap…a hint of his particular scent. It was silly and she'd likely be embarrassed about it later, but she couldn't stop herself from taking the garment to bed with her. She burrowed beneath the coverlet and curled her body against the soft linen, imagining her husband was there beside her.

The next morning, eyes gritty with tears and sleeplessness, Odette decided to write to Simon. He had, after all, left the directions to where he was staying. She wondered briefly if a letter would be considered an intrusive interruption of Simon's wishes, but she sent it off before she could overthink it.

Chapter Twenty

Simon crumpled another sheaf of paper and whipped it at the floor, barely resisting the urge to snap his quill in two. He'd been ensconced at Sir Nigel's estate on the coast of Lincolnshire for several weeks now and he had yet to complete a full draft of his essay.

If Sir Nigel had found it odd that Simon had so suddenly accepted his invitation to visit and finalize their collaboration so soon after Simon's marriage, then he hadn't commented aloud. A consummate bachelor of middling years, he'd never experienced the desire to take a wife or have a family. He'd inherited the small seaside manor from his mother upon her death as well as a sufficient income. As a viscount's second son with an elder brother who already had a passel of his own children, "What was the point?" Sir Nigel had chuckled. The wiry man with small, round spectacles and a bush of curly brown hair was more than content with his life. He ventured to London several times each year for Society meetings and lectures. Other than that, he was free to pursue his work in peace.

The Simon of several months ago would have been envious of such a life.

The Simon who had arrived in Lincolnshire was left deflated by it all. He had the nauseating feeling Sir Nigel was a version of himself had he not met Odette.

Though Sir Nigel had offered Simon free use of his expansive library and roomy study, the men spoke very little, often choosing to retreat to their respective spaces like the solitary creatures they were. When they did meet, it was for hours in a language of numbers and scholars many might think quite foreign. They coordinated their research and discussed their respective contributions. Gradually, painfully slowly, the essay came together and, with it, Simon's future. Great strides were being made in the field of mathematics, but Simon didn't feel quite as buoyant as he'd anticipated.

The solitary work Simon accomplished only took place in fits and spurts. Some days, he'd tumble into his haven of numbers and formulas for hours on end. There was no interruption for societal obligations…no one to remind him to eat. On other days, he would lose hours staring out the window at the wild landscape, contemplating how Odette would love the peace of the gardens and listening to the crashing waves against the craggy cliffs near the edge of the estate.

There was no denying how he'd been changed by his wife. Whether or not she'd intended to do so, Odette had given him something else with which to occupy his mind. His arms ached to hold her; his body yearned to possess her again.

As if following the track of his mind, the butler appeared one afternoon with a letter on a silver salver. The servants had been instructed to leave Simon in peace, but one glance at the sender and seal told him why: It was from his wife.

His heart choked him and he nearly speared his unsteady hand with his penknife as he broke the wax seal and prepared himself for the scathing admonishment he deserved for abandoning her.

Instead, he was shocked by the tender tone he found within.

He had to read the words several times before he believed them.

Odette didn't fully understand why he'd left, but she had to trust that he knew what was best. The last thing she wanted to do was stand in the way of his work.

She then inquired after his health—hoping that he was remembering to eat without her there to force-feed him or bribe him.

Simon smiled wistfully.

She went on to tell him how Lily and Meredith had taken great pains to care for her. She described a reading society she'd joined and had taken a trip to the bookstore for materials. She wrote of the mundane, but he was far from bored. He heard every word of it in her voice. And his heart skipped when he saw how she'd signed the letter:

Love,

Odette

He traced her signature with his fingertips and then allowed himself several more minutes of maudlin behavior to re-read it through once more. He then carefully folded the letter and set it aside.

Simon did his best to resist, but he wound up responding after putting it off for several days. He sent off the letter with the post and his soul felt both lighter and heavier for it.

Odette received Simon's response just as she'd begun to believe he'd never reply. She tore it open as soon as she was alone and found the words much like their author: straightforward without the frills and flowery composition so en vogue. Still, she liked to think she knew him well enough that she could sense moments of fondness within— perhaps there was hope there yet.

Simon inquired about her reading society and their current choice of works; he wanted to know how she was finding London life and whether they still needed additional furnishings for the Townhouse. She was unfolding the bottom crease of the page when a pressed purple flower fell into her lap. Amazed the petals had survived the brutal journey, she marveled at the delicate bloom still so vibrant and lovely. Curious, she found a scribbled post-script following Simon's signature:

These flowers bloom throughout the gardens here at Cliffton, Sir Nigel's home; I can see them from the window of the space in which I do most of my work. I thought you might like it.

Touched beyond reason, Odette pressed the note and the flower between the pages of her favorite book of poetry before sitting at her desk to pen a reply.

Several more weeks passed in this fashion. Simon would sometimes take a week or so longer to reply than was normal, but he would always reply. Odette knew the deadline for Simon's research and paper loomed close, yet not once had he mentioned or even hinted that he would return to London (to her) anytime soon. Rather, he mentioned how his colleague was discussing a trip to Germany to meet with a brilliant young scholar whose work would complement their research.

Her stomach had plummeted with foreboding, but she remained true to her resolve that she would allow Simon to do what he felt was

necessary to achieve his goals. She refused to be the anchor preventing him from setting his course, even if it pained her to do so.

Despite feeling poorly, Odette hated to cancel plans with her sisters-
in-law. They'd been so kind to her since Simon's departure; Lily had
even stayed in London longer than planned to be there for her. Truly,
these women had gone above and beyond to comfort her and ensure
she was alright.

This was why, when she'd awoken to a sour, roiling stomach the
morning she was scheduled to accompany them to help Meredith pick
a new gown for an upcoming event, she did her best to choke it back.
She hadn't been successful…but she did wind up feeling vastly better
after the fact.

"I should have listened to Cook," she moaned. She had mentioned
to Odette that she suspected the butcher might be selling them his
wares past their prime and needed a stern reminder of just who he was
serving. Odette had reassured Cook that it looked fine enough and to
cook and serve it anyway. She could speak with the butcher the next
time there was a delivery. "What do I know?" Her voice was swallowed by a moan; her stomach lurched when she thought of the meal.

Using water from the pitcher by the washbasin, she dampened
some toweling and wiped her face and mouth. When she was sure she
wouldn't be sick anymore, she scrubbed her mouth with tooth powder
and checked her pale appearance in the mirror. She could do this. She
said as much to her reflection and smoothed back her hair. She was
determined to follow through with her plans. Besides, she was already
feeling improved. Odette took several deep breaths and began to very
slowly, very carefully prepare for her outing.

And she swore to shove some of the butcher's own product down his throat and see how *he* enjoyed tossing the contents back into a chamberpot.

A short while later, Odette along with Meredith and Lily arrived at the modiste's. Aside from this extended visit to lend support to Odette, Lily rarely came to Town except to update her wardrobe. Her more relaxed life in the country allowed her to dress less formally, but that didn't mean she didn't want to stay current with trends and would also occasionally require a gown for a more formal celebration or dinner. She liked to say she still enjoyed dressing like a lady, even if she eschewed many of a lady's social obligations. Meredith was specifically in need of a gown for the ball she and the countess were to host together; she was under strict instructions that this must be *the* gown of the Season because this ball was to be *the* event of the Season. Odette already planned on wearing one of the new gowns she'd purchased for her wardrobe upon their return to London.

That day seemed so very far away now.

A lifetime ago.

And she'd been a different person; so much more optimistic. So much happier. So much less alone.

Tears began to sting the backs of her eyes as the thought of returning to that silent, empty house plagued her. Though living with Simon hadn't been the liveliest of existences, there had been something warm and comforting knowing he was near…that she had merely to walk down the hall and he'd be there for her.

Odette took another steadying breath through her nose and turned her attention back to her companions.

"Green and blue always look so striking on you," Lily commented as she held up several fabric swatches to compare to Meredith's complexion. Their group had been shown into a quiet sitting area set into the curved alcove overlooking the bustling street outside. After greeting them and passing them off to her assistant, the shop owner floated off to finish working with another set of customers—a mother and rather unfortunate teenaged daughter who looked every bit as miserable as Odette had felt whenever her mother had dragged her to the modiste. Odette made sure to cast a sympathetic smile to the girl. She wished she could tell her it would get better, that she'd come into her own and find her own voice and freedom to be herself, but she couldn't make those promises. No woman in their society could. She'd come to realize how fortunate she was to have met Simon; not many husbands in his family's social strata were as lenient as he when it came to allowing a wife to dress as she wished. Who understood what it meant to be allowed to be who she wanted to be.

"What do you think, Odette?"

Odette leaned back in the pink-striped upholstered chair and examined the swatches to which Lily was gesturing. There was a rather lovely emerald shade of satin with three swatches of blues in colors varying from cerulean to sky. To be honest, any one of those colors would look stunning with Meredith's indigo eyes and bright red hair, and Odette said as much.

"Of course they do, but that does little to help us narrow down our choices," Lily replied, feigning crossness.

"Both of you are of no help whatsoever," Meredith sighed good-naturedly. "At least tell me you've found some silhouette options in those fashion plates, Odette."

Her heart jumped when she remembered she'd been charged with flipping through the stack of plates to narrow down those choices. She frantically flipped through them until she found one that was pretty enough to be believable that she'd sought it out. "Here is one," she said, passing it along to Meredith.

Lily peered over and examined it as well.

"This is lovely," Meredith said with a smile. "I quite like the square neckline.

"I like it as well," added Lily. "But Mother will insist upon something far more extravagant for the ball." She flashed an apologetic glance at Odette, who then quickly turned back to the plates lying across her lap. She did her best to find another that would suit both the countess's demands and compliment Meredith's willowy frame. The second-to-last option was immediately stilled her fingers. It was a gown draped with Grecian folds and a wide band set beneath the empire waist that would accentuate Meredith's slim build. The short, fitted sleeves were cut such that they would mirror her elegant collarbone. A short gossamer train spilled in pleats from the band beneath the bust to trail behind the wearer. It was perfect.

"How about this one?" Odette passed it along for Meredith's approval.

Lily gasped. "It's perfect!"

Meredith's eyes glittered in excitement and gratitude. "I agree. Well done, Odette!"

"Now we just have the impossible task of choosing a color and trimmings." Lily resumed shuffling through the fabric swatches. "I fear we may need some lighter material to better display this gown," she added thoughtfully.

"What about ivory?" Odette chimed in, catching sight of another swatch peeking out from beneath a discarded plate.

"Oh, ivory could be lovely!" Meredith grinned.

"With gold trim!" Lily clapped her hands together excitedly. "Georgie will lose his mind; he's already utterly besotted as it is. To see you presented as such will drive him mad."

Odette didn't miss the way Meredith lowered her eyes and gave a small (but genuine) smile, a faint blush fading the gentle freckles on the bridge of her nose.

"Here," Odette began as she leaned forward and reached for the swatch she'd spotted. If she wasn't mistaken, it was a crepe which would suit the gown and the wearer quite nicely. Just as she stood to pass it along to Meredith and Lily, however, the room tilted sharply. In a split second, a cold sweat broke out on Odette's flesh and a nearly crippling nausea overcame her. She barely had time to hear Meredith ask if she was unwell—she'd gone quite pale in an instant. Odette's head seemed to float above her body and then everything went black.

Chapter Twenty-One

Odette awoke with no sense of time or place. She experienced a wash of panic and disorientation before her eyes landed upon both her sisters-in-law at her bedside, their eyes wide with worry. A glance told her she'd been brought back to her home on St. James's Square and she'd been tucked into her comfortable new bed.

There was movement in the corner of the dim room and Odette's heart skipped a beat at the dark clothing and masculine form…until she realized the man was too broad and not quite tall enough to be her husband. He approached the bed, a reassuring smile on his angular face.

"Mrs. Stratford," he greeted her, the barest hint of an accent playing with his consonants. His chestnut hair was tied back neatly and he wore a uniform of dark clothing.

Odette tried to sit up, but Meredith stilled her with a pale hand on her arm.

"You fainted, dear. Lily and I thought it prudent to call for a physician." She tilted her chin at the man on the other side of the bed. "This is my friend, Dr. Ian McCullom."

Odette looked back at the man. His kind eyes were framed with gentle lines and he appeared to be of an age with George and Jeremy. Despite his size, there was something calming and reassuring about the way he moved and spoke.

"How are you feeling?" he inquired. "Are you nauseous at all? Does your head bother you?"

She shook her head, but then a wave of nausea did strike her. Lily read the change in her pallor and was quick to haul over a clean chamberpot. The illness passed after she pressed her knuckles to her mouth and swallowed several slow gulps of air.

"Bad meat," she groaned, well past the point of being mortified about being sick with an audience.

"I beg pardon?"

"I think the meat at supper last night was questionable."

"Were you ill earlier this morning as well?"

Odette could only nod in response to the doctor's question. She gratefully accepted the cool cloth Lily offered.

"I managed to catch her," Meredith began to explain; "I don't believe she struck her head."

Dr. McCullom nodded. "May I?" he asked before taking Odette's wrist in his strong fingers. He stood and silently tested her pulse before moving on to check her eyes and throat, his strong, warm fingers palpated her neck. "Have you eaten today? Had enough to drink?" Odette nodded in reply. "Is it alright if I check your abdomen?" he asked next.

Odette felt like a lost child and couldn't help but look to Meredith for reassurance. Her sister-in-law gave her a small smile and a single nod. Odette agreed.

His large hands were surprisingly delicate as they pressed and kneaded, moving along her waist and stomach to her lower abdomen. "If I may ask, when were your last courses?"

"I—" Odette's cheeks caught fire as she stammered. "That is...I mean—"

The doctor gave her a kind flicker of a smile that wasn't the least bit patronizing. "I realize it's indelicate, but an inquiry was presented to your lady's maid. She's only been in your employ for a couple of weeks and had nothing to report. Just try to remember to the best of your ability."

Odette tried to think, to peer through the haze in her fuzzy head. Her life had been thrown upside down, righted, and then knocked on its ear time and time again over the past several months. It was hard enough to remember who she was, let alone when she'd last experienced her courses.

"Four weeks," Odette finally answered and then frowned.

Had it been while they were still at Bridleton?

No.

She'd still been living with her mother in the West End apartments. Her pains had been rather troublesome and she'd requested Alyssa borrow some of her mother's special tonic for the aches.

"Eight. Eight weeks." She added more confidently. Only then did what he was asking sink in. She'd missed her courses. He nodded once and Odette's eyes flew to Meredith as she remembered what she'd told her at Bridleton. Missed courses meant, "A baby?"

"It's not outside of the realm of possibility," explained the doctor. "Are your courses normally quite regular?"

"Yes," she replied in a whisper. Her mother had always said her courses were like clockwork and could plan a calendar around when her pains would begin.

"There's really no way to be certain until we give it several more weeks, but, given your fainting and nausea, I would say a child is a distinct possibility. I would, however, caution you that it's still very early. And, if you are amenable, I would like to check for any bleeding just because you did take a fall…even if Lady Sommerfeld was quick enough to catch you." Odette agreed and Meredith and Lily remained with her all the while, but she was in too much shock to be overly self-conscious. The quick exam was over even before she could ponder it, her mind was too far gone with the possibility that a new life grew within her.

"You have no pain and no cramping, no bleeding," Dr. McCullom summarized as he scrubbed at his hands in the nearby basin. "I suggest remaining abed for the rest of the day. Be sure to drink plenty of broth and tea; rest when you feel you need to. These first few months of pregnancy can be difficult for some women. Do not be surprised if your nausea increases, but that should taper off after another month or two. If it does not or if you experience any pains, please do not hesitate to contact me. I am in the process of opening my new office not far from here. I will leave my card with your butler and give instructions to your maid." Odette was still in too much shock to do more than nod. "Would you like me to speak to Mr. Stratford before I take my leave?"

Odette's head whipped up.

Simon.

He was going to be a father.

She was unsure how he was going to react to the news. If he'd traveled to the end of the country to find some peace to complete his work, how would he feel about the obligation and interruption of a baby in the household? It certainly tempered her excitement about becoming a mother, morphing it into nerves more than anything.

What was worse, how was she to explain her husband's absence to Dr. McCullom without eliciting pity she did not desire, nor making a villain out of Simon?

As if sensing Odette's indecision, Lily saved her from having to speak. "My brother is away attending to his work at the moment, but thank you. It's been lovely to see you again, Dr. McCullom." She rose and offered to show him out.

"Always a pleasure, Lady Shefford," replied the doctor and he nodded in Odette's direction. "Mrs. Stratford." He and Lily rounded the bed to head toward the door, but not before he paused near Meredith and, unexpectedly, placed a reassuring hand on her shoulder. She looked up and gave him a tremulous smile, her indigo eyes glistening and suspiciously bright. It was a very familiar gesture for a man to make toward a woman who was not his wife and, had she not known Meredith's true love and devotion to her husband, she might have questioned it. Clearly, Dr. McCullom was an old and close friend, indeed.

"Lady Sommerfeld."

Meredith inclined her head in thanks and Lily and the doctor took their leave, chatting amiably as they strode down the hall.

"I will leave you to rest," Meredith said softly and gathered her skirts to stand. Before she could move away, however, Odette reached out and grasped Meredith's fingers. Her sister-in-law froze.

"I'm sorry," Odette blurted. She didn't know if it was the right or wrong thing to say, she just knew she couldn't allow Meredith to think she didn't care. Odette couldn't help but remember how broken and sad Meredith had been that afternoon at Bridleton. She and George had been trying to start their family for years…and here Odette was so young and foolish that the thought hadn't even crossed her mind.

"Whyever are you sorry?" Meredith dropped back down into the nearby chair.

"Because I—" she tried to begin lamely, but couldn't finish. What could she say?

"Oh, my dear." Meredith readjusted her grip on Odette's fingers so *she* was somehow now the one comforting *her*. An unchecked tear escaped Odette's eye. "There is nothing for which you need to be sorry."

"That isn't how it feels. You said back at Bridleton how badly you wished for a child."

"Whatever my sadness may be, your joys should never be diminished because of it." She squeezed Odette's hand and swiped at a tear on her own cheek, and then another. "I shall never forgive you if you do not celebrate my new niece or nephew with the appropriate amount of pomp and circumstance," Meredith added with a watery laugh.

While Odette appreciated the sentiment, she didn't want Meredith to diminish her feelings either—they were just as valid as anything Odette was experiencing. "Just promise me that you won't pretend to be alright if you're not. You've held my hand enough times where the least I can do is be a shoulder and an ear for you."

"Thank you," Meredith replied and moved to perch on the edge of the bed and embrace Odette.

This is what it is like to have a sister, thought Odette. Tears filled her vision and clogged her throat, a warm wave of acceptance washed over her. She hugged Meredith back with every ounce of emotion bubbling up within her.

"I miss Simon," she whispered into Meredith's shoulder without intending it.

"I know…" Meredith rubbed Odette's back in a more maternal fashion than Odette had ever received from the woman who'd actually given birth to her. "When is he due to return?"

The question caused her heart to skip. She couldn't very well admit that she had no good answer to that question.

"Soon, I should hope." It wasn't a lie.

"Good. And you'll write to him of the babe?" Meredith asked as she sat back.

Odette could only force a small smile. It was noncommittal, but it didn't feel right to outright lie to the woman who'd been nothing but her champion since she'd been introduced to the family.

"Very good." Meredith patted her hand and stood. "I'll leave you to rest. We don't live all that far away; please do not think twice about sending for me if you need anything."

"Of course. Thank you, Meredith," she whispered sincerely.

"Think nothing of it."

Meredith quit the room, leaving Odette with a very important decision to make. She pressed her palm to her abdomen.

Should she tell Simon of the baby?

Was it right to distract him at such a critical point with news of this weight?

Either way, this was not a decision to take lightly.

*****

With a great amount of relief and anxiety, but very little pomp and circumstance, Simon and Sir Nigel shipped off the final draft of their essay with its dozens upon dozens of pages of calculations, explanations, proofs, and summaries of their research. By this time next week, the hope was that it would be on the desk of the head of the London Mathematical Society. With any luck, the Society would see the merit of the manuscript, it would be reviewed and published, and

Simon would be granted admission into the Society. His life would be on course and he'd be free to pursue his ambitions and work with the other brilliant minds in his field. His dreams were finally being realized.

However, as he tapped his celebratory glass of brandy against Sir Nigel's, Simon felt as if something was missing from the moment. The hollow pit in his chest told him exactly what it was.

He'd denied it to himself for weeks and weeks at that point, but there was simply no use in continuing to refute just how desperately he missed his wife.

All well-ordered statistics, complex analyses, and consuming research couldn't replace her touch, her taste, her smile. It was a lesson Simon had learned the hard way, and taken far too long to do so.

He was lost in his musings and snapped back to reality by Sir Nigel's voice.

"The weather should hopefully permit an uneventful crossing to the Continent next week," he said before taking a sip of his drink. "I'm so pleased you decided to join me. I think we'll find this to be quite a productive venture. There are some fascinating questions— and even more fascinating answers—being debated about..."

The sound of Sir Nigel's voice died away as Simon was lost staring into the depths of the amber liquid in his hand, seeing only Odette's eyes in the clear cut glass. He gave his head a little shake and pictured those eyes overflowing with tears; he heard her mother's words. Simon knew what he needed to do...where he needed to go...even if it killed him.

The arrangements for Germany were made. Most of the trunks had been packed and situated for travel.

Simon was going through his last piece of luggage, making sure everything was safely stored as it should, when a letter arrived.

He hated the thrill he experienced in his chest at the prospect of reading one more of Odette's letters. The mail was spotty at best on the Continent and the delay between letters could be upwards of a month. This might very well be the last letter he received for some time.

He split the wax seal without checking the address and was surprised to notice it came not from Odette, but his sister-in-law.

Simon,

I hope you know that I have always held a special place in my heart for you. We are two kindred spirits in that we were not always understood by the families into which we were born. The science that fascinates us confounds those we love. This is why I hope you accept the next thing I have to say with all the love in the world:

You are an imbecile.

I cannot pretend to understand the depth of your passion for your mathematics, but I know what I feel for George. Nothing in this world would keep me from him; not when he has supported me, not when he has seen me at my most vulnerable, not when he holds my heart and soul in his hands. Whether you realize it or not, Odette is this for you. You have shattered her heart and yet she refuses to speak ill of you. She remains your champion even in your inexplicable absence. To leave your wife for such an extended period of time is unconscionable; to refuse to return to your young, pregnant wife to support her during this time is unforgivable. You must...

The rest of the letter died away in a haze of smoke and noise.

Pregnant.

Pregnant?

He read the line several times over, stared out the window, and then read it several times more. His eyes hadn't deceived him.

Odette was pregnant?

Confusion and dread crashed over him in equal measures. Why had Odette said nothing in any of her letters? And how in God's name could he be a father?

A child was never something he'd considered. It was all admittedly stupid of him given the fact that he was highly-educated and hadn't done anything to prevent Odette from falling pregnant, but it was terrifying, nonetheless.

Simon hadn't experienced the best of boyhoods. The torture he'd endured had scarred him to that very day. How might he possibly be expected to coach a child through such experiences when he had none of the answers? Becoming a husband had terrified him. Being in charge of a small, innocent life petrified him to the point of numbness. What advice could he possibly offer a child? What did he know of fitting in and displaying acceptable behavior? And what if the child developed the same quirks from which Simon suffered? He knew he would never forgive himself if his child had to endure the same hellish childhood he had, filled with ridicule from his peers, punishments at school, and parents who shook their heads in loss and misunderstanding. He'd be solely to blame because Odette…Odette would be the most brilliant of all mothers.

The letter fell from Simon's numb fingers and he doubled over as a wave of nausea struck him like a blow to the gut.

A baby.

There was only one thing he could do.

Chapter Twenty-Two

Odette accepted Meredith's offer of more tea as she and her other sis-ter-in-law, Lily, enjoyed the relative peace of the Sommerfeld town-house. Jeremy and George had set up camp at a small table in a warm sunbeam to play a few hands of cards, throwing good-natured barbs all the while, interspersed with deep chuckles. Meredith's unique in-digo eyes would occasionally flit over to the game, but Jeremy had threatened to bow out if she played: "There's no beating her," he'd complained dramatically, though the kind humor never left his dark eyes; "At least with George, I have a chance!" Instead, the women formed their own triangle of chatter. Lily's sons, Vincent and Edward, were napping up in the nursery—a room Meredith was kind enough to keep readied for their visits even though Odette knew it likely gutted her that the babes it housed were not her own.

Not for the first time, Odette sank back into her chair and took stock of just how lucky she was. The familiarity of these siblings and their respective spouses was something to be admired; their kind regard and clear adoration for one another was something to which one should aspire. It was all something she'd never before experienced, let alone for which she'd never dared hope or dream. The warmth and openness had taken some getting used to, but she quickly found she very much enjoyed it—that it actually suited her nature quite well, in fact, despite its differences from her upbringing.

She'd come to recognize that her mother loved her in her own way. She had yet to call upon Odette once since the day after the Haverford ball, which served only to underscore how theirs was not a relationship of reassurance and nurturing embraces. Odette may never comprehend how her mother could possibly be so cool and calculating when it came to her own child and the lives of others…but a deep part of her soul recognized that she would have none of this without her mother.

Of course, there was no denying the noticeable absence from their little group.

Odette barely checked herself just before she placed her palm to her abdomen in an instinctive acknowledgement of yet another thing she could indirectly attribute to her mother's machinations—another way to remind herself that she wasn't really alone, no matter how sick her heart felt. She'd sworn Lily and Meredith to secrecy and it wouldn't have done to make such a gesture in front of the men.

Dr. McCullom had officially confirmed her pregnancy and gave her warm congratulations. Though she was certain his schedule was already quite full, he'd offered her his services should she ever have need of them. Odette had a strong suspicion his kindness was due in large to his long-standing friendship with Meredith, but who was she to turn down such an offer? It was yet another benefit to being a part of this powerful, well-connected family, she supposed. Even several weeks later…even after she'd felt the babe's first flutters in her womb…it was difficult for Odette to comprehend the tiny life growing inside of her…part her and part Simon…

The mere thought of his name caused the wound in her heart to open wider. She'd so fervently hoped time and distance would help her to heal, but it didn't seem that she worked that way.

Unfortunately.

Why couldn't she have inherited her mother's ability to walk away from a man and take with her only that which made her stronger?

She had yet to inform her sisters-in-law about Simon's plans to travel to Germany. She had gotten to know Lily and Meredith so well over these past few months that she didn't doubt what their reactions would be.

The last thing Odette wanted, however, was a husband who was forced to give up his dreams to be by her side. Simon had made it clear that this was where his heart took him, and she'd felt guilty enough over their forced marriage…to ask him to give up any more of his life seemed cruel. And she'd come to respect his passions over the short course of their married life. If this was what he needed in order to feel whole, then who was she to stop him? Though the thought of being separated from the man whom she loved so dearly for at least several additional months ate away at her spirits, she resolved to remain sturdy and confident. She had a new life upon which to focus her attention.

She had yet to write to Simon of her pregnancy and she'd lain awake late each night, her conscience tortured with just how to broach the subject. They'd never discussed a family, though a man as intelligent as he must surely have identified the possibility with all of their…activities.

In the end, she'd decided to send him a letter when he was well and truly settled on the Continent; in fact, she had (no less than a dozen) drafts of the letter tucked away in the drawer of the writing desk in her bedchamber. She planned to reassure him that he needn't rush back to London—that his family was taking very good care of her. She had more than enough funds to prepare and care for the child in Simon's absence, however long that may turn out to be. He hadn't ever truly given her a date for his return and, if history were any indication, it could be an endless, winding road of research. Once intrigued by a particularly fascinating bit of information, Simon could potentially drag out a project for years if it showed promise—his journals had proven that to her.

The pleasant chatter droned on around her, but Odette heard nothing beyond a steady tone, like the wings of a hummingbird. The details of the rose-colored room blurred and faded as tears collected in the corners of her eyes.

She could do this.

She *had* to do this.

She loved Simon with everything in her. If he couldn't (or wouldn't) accept it, then she'd transfer that same affection to the babe within her womb. She'd—

A sharp shout and the thunder of boots in the hallway shattered her unhappy musings. Jeremy and George shared a brief, startled glance before dropping their cards and rising to their feet.

The door to the parlor banged open with enough force to cause the tea service to tremble and clatter; an uncharacteristically disheveled Simon was followed closely by the panting, disgruntled butler.

"My lord—my apologies. M—Mr. Stratford—I could not—"

George frowned at his younger brother's appearance, but his tone was not unkind. "It's alright, Percey. My brother is always welcome."

The butler ran a hand through his salt-and-pepper hair, tugged at his lapel, and bowed before taking his leave, clearly still irked that he'd been brought down to such a lack of decorum.

"Well, brother," George began to address Simon; "what is all this then? I don't think I've seen you create such a scene in decades."

"Weren't you supposed to be in Lincolnshire?" Jeremy asked with a tilt of his dark head and then added; "Did you *ride* all the way to London? In this weather?" A chill had settled over England, heralding the official shift of the seasons from Fall to Winter. Frost coated the grass in the mornings and didn't disappear until afternoon.

Odette remained speechless on the sofa near the center of the room. She and the other women were situated between the door and the card table George and Jeremy had once occupied. She was helpless to do aught but stare wide-eyed at her husband; she barely managed to tamp down the urge to fling herself into his arms. To her, there had never been a more welcome—or handsome—sight.

Gone was the starched propriety of his usual demeanor. He wore no cravat—either out of ease or if it had been lost on the road—and, indeed, it did appear that he'd ridden hell-to-leather back down to London from Lincolnshire. His golden hair was tousled and his face was pink from the lashing winter wind and flecked with mud. At least three days-worth of dark blond stubble covered his chin and cheeks. His lean chest heaved beneath his soiled linen shirt, which was untucked from the waist of his dirt-streaked buckskin breeches.

"Simon?" George's voice finally began to reveal his concern. "What happened—"

"Odette," Simon croaked, effectively cutting off his elder brother. He cleared his throat and spoke more forcefully, his flashing blue-green eyes never leaving her face. Her pulse began to race uncontrollably. "Why did you say nothing?" he demanded, and she knew instantly to what (or, rather, to whom) he referred. "Why did you not tell me of the baby?" The ferocity in his tone would have caused a man to tremble where he stood, but Odette knew her husband. She had no fear of physical retribution, but she also knew how earned his anger was. She didn't know how he'd discovered the pregnancy, though that was beside the point.

He'd come.

And she could read the very real pain and fear in his eyes. This was a man who had come to accept his place in the world and was confident in the truths of his existence. And here she had shaken his understanding and wounded him deeply.

The room around them was so silent it was a wonder they didn't hear the wood and stone of the building settling around them. Everyone was so used to Simon's carefully-modulated behavior that the uncharacteristic outburst had all but struck them dumb.

Suddenly feeling rather like an actress on stage who'd forgotten to learn her lines, Odette stammered—not out of fear of her husband, but because she didn't know how to make things right. "S—Simon…I—I wanted…That is to say…" Her guilt rose up to choke her like bile.

There was a flash of fiery hair to her right and Meredith quite literally stood in Odette's defense. "I'm sorry, Odette, for breaking your confidence. I hadn't realized Simon didn't know and when I wrote to him…well, I was so upset because I believed he *did* know and still chose to stay away." George limped over to his wife and slid a protective arm around her waist.

Simon's wild eyes turned back to Odette. Setting aside Meredith's interjection entirely, he uttered one pleading word to his wife:

"Why?"

Where she'd previously been keenly aware of all the eyes on her, the room immediately died away around them so it was only Odette and Simon. She fisted her hands in the fabric of the skirts at her hips.

"I—I was postponing telling you because I didn't wish to interrupt your work." Suddenly, all the words began to gain strength from her frustrations and sadness of these past few months; they poured forth from her like a leak in a dam. "Why else would you have left in the first place? I was obviously an unnecessary distraction—and I can accept that; I knew having to share your home and your life with me was a diversion from your work. I was trying to respect your wishes."

All at once her husband's face crumpled; a strangled groan was wrenched from his chest as he lurched forward to close the gap between them and fall to his knees at her feet.

"I wished to protect you, Odette. That's all I've ever wanted," he choked out. He pressed forward into the cradle of her legs and wrapped his long arms around her waist. She barely registered his sudden nearness before he pressed his head into her lap and squeezed her to him like a lifeline.

"Come," Odette dimly heard Jeremy murmur to Lily as he helped her to her feet. "Let's give them some privacy. George and Jeremy then ushered their respective spouses out the door, though Odette doubted any of them went too far. She likely wouldn't have if she were in their position, truth be told, so she couldn't blame them.

The door clicked shut behind them, leaving Odette and Simon alone in heavy, anticipatory silence. She gazed down at her husband's strong form, literally brought to his knees by the news that he was going to be a father…and the sense of betrayal that she'd kept the news hidden from him.

Her appeasing nature made her want to take full responsibility for the fissures in their marriage—to fall to her own knees beside him and apologize—but she had been betrayed as much as he. Simon had abandoned her with only a poor explanation. She'd respected his wishes, but he'd left her hollow and lost. Her husband had absconded with a piece of her when he'd fled to Lincolnshire, and she'd allowed it.

No more, she decided. She loved her husband, but her own heart and joy needn't be sacrificed at the altar of these feelings. She deserved just as much care and consideration as she'd given to him. She had needs, as well.

And she needed her husband.

She cared not one bit that he was a filthy mess from his journey or that he reeked of sweat and horseflesh, she felt as if she might shatter if she didn't touch him that second—she was already on the edge of tears as it was. Dr. McCullom had cautioned her that the pregnancy might make her emotional reactions quite extreme, but she doubted he'd had this degree of drama in mind.

Hesitantly, her hand cupped the back of his head and her fingers gradually began to stroke his tangled hair.

"You left me, Simon," she whispered. His shoulders tensed and his arms gripped her a little tighter, telling her he was listening. "I needed you and you weren't here. I have done everything in my power to respect your work and your wants throughout this marriage, but I have wants, as well. I am a person, just like you, and, while I may not be as brilliant or as accomplished as you are, I deserve some concessions, to." His head nodded against her once. "What I require from this marriage is a husband who is there for me. I don't expect you to remain affixed to my side at all times, but I must know you are coming home to me. To us."

They sat like that in silence as Simon clutched her to him with a desperation just shy of discomfort, and Odette running her fingers through his sweat-damp locks. Gradually, the tension began to leave his body and he relaxed into the embrace. He half-laid upon her rather than simply holding her to him as if he was afraid she might float away if he didn't weigh her down in place. They sat there for several long minutes without a word passing between them, each seeming to savor the nearness of the other after long weeks of separation.

Finally, Simon heaved a sigh and turned his head to look up into her face. Odette's fingers stalled.

"How long have you known about the baby?" he asked softly.

"A few weeks," she replied, matching her tone to his. Odette weighed her words carefully before continuing to describe the fainting spell she'd experienced while shopping with Lily and Meredith, and then the care Dr. McCullom had provided in the aftermath.

"Why wouldn't you send for me?" She felt his muscles begin to stiffen in equal measures of indignation and concern, but she was quick to reassure him.

"Because there wasn't any serious cause for concern. Please believe I would have written or someone would have sent for you if there were any true problems."

She recognized in the grim line of his mouth that he didn't care for her answer, but he understood it. She could tell he knew it was his fault she felt she'd come to such a decision.

Then, for the first time, it seemed he realized where he'd laid his head. His eyes bore into her abdomen as if he could see the soul growing within. One of his hands released her back and moved to cover the spot at which he stared, but he froze as if too afraid to touch her.

Odette's lips tilted in a whisper of a smile as she covered his hand with hers and pressed it low on her abdomen just where the swell was beginning to show. The doctor had told her the baby's movements would become stronger and more noticeable as the weeks went on; a part of her was confident it knew its father was near.

Simon's hand was so large and firm against her—oh, how she'd missed his warmth these past weeks…how she'd craved his nearness with something akin to mourning. And now he was kneeling before her, holding her, touching her reverently, and it made her dare to hope he'd missed her as well.

An overwhelming surge of affection and contentment washed over her, but her heart skipped a beat when Simon next spoke.

"I never thought I'd be a father," he murmured so softly she might have fooled herself into believing he hadn't spoken…had she not seen his face. Her heart splintered at the sight of tears glistening in his stunning eyes, but it broke entirely with his next words: "Odette…I'm terrified."

Her own vision began to swim as she clutched his palm to her abdomen. It took her several tries before she could form any coherent words. "It'll be alright. I'm afraid, too, but I'm told most new parents feel these trepidations—Lily said as much."

He shook his head, interrupting her reassurances. "I'm afraid this child will be…like me." His eyes screwed shut, his brow furrowed in agony. "I spent my whole life wondering why I didn't fit in, why the other children didn't share my interests. You know I have difficulties connecting with people—even to this day I have precious few friends willing to tolerate my idiosyncrasies. I would *never* wish this fate upon my offspring." He opened his eyes and his unnervingly-earnest gaze met hers, stalling her breath. "That's why I left. You don't deserve to be viewed as an object of pity because of your marriage to me. I figured the more distance I put between us, the better, because I hoped you might have some semblance of normalcy in my absence."

Hot trails of tears carved unchecked paths upon her cheeks as she cupped his beard-roughened face in her palm. "I couldn't give two figs about normalcy—nothing in my life has been remotely normal… I'd rather have you, Simon."

Simon couldn't believe his ears as Odette continued speaking.

"I hope our child *is*, indeed, like you, because then he will be brilliant and driven, infinitely sweet and thoughtful in his own way. And, besides," her full lower lip trembled; "he will have your guidance, which will be the best blessing of all. I know this child will love you as much as I do."

Unable to resist any longer, Simon straightened and pulled Odette into his arms to kiss her as he'd been dying to do for every second since he'd left her side. He savored the familiarity of her soft curves against his body and, with more than a little male satisfaction, looked forward to learning how they would change in the coming months as her body swelled with his child.

He clutched her to his chest, pressing every inch of her against him that he could as she wound her arms around his neck and met his lips with each bruising kiss. Despite his exhaustion and the aches in every one of his muscles, he needed her with every fiber of his being. He needed his wife.

"I love you, Odette," he groaned in between furious kisses. "I'll never leave again, I swear it." His hands roamed downward to cup her lush bottom through her skirts and press her pelvis flush with his. Her gasp sent chills of lust down his spine, but he remained coherent enough to remember her delicate condition.

Panting, he tore his lips from hers and pressed their foreheads together. "Do you think…that is, it won't be harmful if we—"

She giggled in that delicious husky way of hers and shook her head, catching his meaning. "The doctor said it wouldn't be harmful to…indulge a little."

"In that case," he began with a wolfish grin; "I think it's time we return home." He caught his wife beneath her knees and at her back and held her high to his chest as he stood. He loved her laugh of surprise. He loved the way she trusted him. He loved how she felt against him. He loved *her*.

He began to stride from the room as Odette wrapped her arms around his neck. "But I simply refuse to get into bed with you until you bathe." She wrinkled her adorable nose in exaggerated disgust.

A loud bark of joyous laughter escaped his chest—the first such occurrence in months. "Don't worry, I'll have a bath." His eyes met hers; the fire she no doubt found there made her lips part in anticipation. "And then I plan on making love to my beautiful wife who—beyond all reason and common sense—loves me…and I fully intend to do so again and again until she either regains her sanity or neither of us can move…whichever comes first."

With only a little difficulty, Simon was able to open the door without having to set down his wife. Sure enough Simon's siblings and their spouses were mingling in the hallway, attempting (and failing) to appear as if they hadn't been listening near the door and then scattered once they'd heard his footsteps. He ignored their questioning looks and allowed Odette's shy wave to be their only farewell as he quickly strode down the hall and bounded down the stairs, leaving his family in their wake as they kissed and laughed together, savoring the new-found lightness in their souls.

Epilogue

Simon watched from the periphery of the ballroom as Odette spun across the floor to the lively steps of a popular dance—yet another that he'd not bothered to learn. Though he wasn't participating, he took immense pleasure in his wife's broad smile and the tinkle of her laughter to which he'd become so attuned he could pick out through the din of the partygoers. A single golden curl flew loose from her coiffure and his fingers itched to wrap the lock around them and revel in the familiar silkiness.

Odette seemed to have gained a foothold in Society, thanks in large part to that reading society of hers. Meredith and the Duchess of Moreton had welcomed her with open arms into their intimate circle of singular women, and neither Odette nor Simon could have been more pleased. It gave Odette a purpose and a sense of belonging in this world, and Simon loved nothing more than seeing his wife so content.

The only downside—for truly only one such as Simon could see it thusly—was that they were now more obligated to attend social functions such as this one. Truth be told, Simon had believed he'd mind the intrusions upon his time more than he actually had, which surprised no one more than he. It seemed that his world had well and truly been altered if he far preferred watching his wife's joy as she interacted with her friends and acquaintances more than he did his endless hours of solitude.

How could he have known the meek little woman he'd quite literally stumbled upon only six months prior would have so metamorphosed his life? Or that that same woman would come out of her shell to be a beacon of joy who shone brightly enough to catch one's eye in even a room as glowing and glittering as that ballroom?

Odette was so adept in these situations; Simon believed it a sight to behold. She recognized when his mind wanted desperately to be elsewhere and his wife effortlessly made up for his lack of social graces. She wove witty excuses when she saw he needed a break from the crush. And she never, ever made him feel as if he was lacking… though Lord knew even Simon was aware he fell far short of what he should be as husband and escort. Watching Odette was watching a work of art in motion; though Simon's favorite part of these evenings was, by far, at the end when he finally had the opportunity to return all the favors she'd paid him. It was like unwrapping the most exquisite of presents, designed only for him.

Even after all these months, he had yet to fathom her love and acceptance, but he had slowly learned to welcome it with open arms.

One night shortly after he'd returned from Lincolnshire, he'd lain awake holding her as she slept. Odette had been on her side, the length of her back pressed against his front. He had placed a tender hand upon her abdomen and listened to her breathing—for how long, he couldn't have said. A sense of contentment covered him like the warmest blanket. He'd whispered into her love-tossed hair how much he adored her and would love this child—that no matter how scattered he might seem or preoccupied he may get, she and this babe would be his whole world; and he prayed they'd never doubt it.

To his surprise, Odette had rolled to face him and kissed him with soft, swollen lips. Her words would stay with him to his dying day: "I know." Then, she'd drifted off to sleep, her body softening against his once more, but Simon could do nothing but lie awake.

She did know.

She knew everything.

She knew more than she gave herself credit for.

She knew him, she saw him, and still she loved him, and she'd never doubt him.

Simon continued to watch his wife twirl and dip, twining between other couples on the dance floor. So enthralled was he by the way the gentle swell of her stomach was just beginning to become visible against her skirts when she moved that he hardly noticed the arrival of a tall, heavy-set man beside him.

"And how is married life treating you, hm?"

Startled from his musings, Simon turned to find none other than the Prince Regent.

"Your Highness," Simon uttered hastily. His manners and training kicked in and he dipped into a low, respectful bow. For a man of his girth and health, the Regent certainly moved surprisingly stealthily.

"You didn't answer the question." He straightened as the Prince Regent bid him rise with a dismissive flick of his wrist.

Facing the dance floor once more, it wasn't all difficult for Simon to locate his wife again. His mouth tilted in a self-assured smile and he clasped his hands behind his back. "I've found it life-alteringly pleasant, Your Majesty."

A grunt of thoughtful approval from the Prince Regent preceded several minutes of contented silence between the two men as they gazed upon the dancers. No one approached them; even the Prince's closest companions remained at a respectful distance. The interaction wasn't unnoticed, however, and eyes kept flicking in their direction; heads tilted in murmured contemplation. For Simon to have caught onto such interest, it was likely blatant to others.

His wife must have rubbed off on him, for there could be no real explanation for Simon's next words other than the fact that there may never be another opportunity to express his long-held suspicions to the Prince Regent in such relative seclusion.

"I hope you will forgive us for our delayed conveyance of gratitude for our wedding present. My wife and I are quite overwhelmed with gratitude for the purchase of the townhouse." Simon didn't turn to face the Prince, but the weighty silence beside him told him nearly as much as the following grunt.

"And why is it you believe We know to whom your thanks should be awarded?" the Prince, using the Royal We, asked gruffly, though there was no anger there—more so resignation disguised as haughtiness, if Simon wasn't mistaken.

"The secrecy was intriguing," Simon began, deciding in that moment to be nothing but honest; "the ghostly imprint of initials on the letter, the intense secrecy and use of a tertiary solicitor to purchase and hold the property, the interest you seem to have taken in me and my wife—I am, after all, only a second-son of an earl and my wife the illegitimate daughter of an actress in the eyes of Society, though I see her as nothing less than a princess in my world." Simon followed this with an uncharacteristic pause for effect. "And you share the same eyes and smile."

To the last, the Prince Regent heaved a sigh. "You mustn't think less of her mother." There was some wry amusement on Simon's part that the Prince didn't include himself in that statement. "We did what We were able to from afar—she was always well cared for and attended the best schools."

"If you'll forgive me, Your Highness," Simon interrupted gently; "she and I both appreciate all of what she has been given, but I believe she would have cherished knowing her father far more."

The ensuing silence was pregnant. Who knew a man so round and soft could suddenly go so cold and hard? He recognized that he was pressing his luck, but Simon continued: "She'll be a mother come the New Year…and I've heard it said that being a grandparent is about as close as one can get to a second chance at parenthood. My only hope is that this might be taken into consideration…for Odette's sake, of course."

Simon didn't need to watch the Prince Regent's ice-blue eyes to know he, too, was following Odette's trajectory as she mingled with other guests.

Suddenly, the Prince gave a noncommittal nod and bid Simon a good evening. His next words, however, made Simon freeze mid-bow. "By the way, congratulations on your publication. We have heard your work has made quite the impression."

Not usually one for overt expressions, it was a surprise to Simon when the Prince seemed to take note of his shock.

"We have not read it, of course," the Prince amended, "but We hear it's quite good."

"I beg your pardon," Simon cleared his throat to give him another moment to regain his composure. "Of course, I am honored and flattered, Your Highness...I simply had no idea you might take note of such a thing."

The older man's eyes met his and there was a startling keenness Simon had never before witnessed. "We do pride Ourself on knowing everything to do with those in whom I have a vested *personal* interest, and that is a very small circle, indeed." With that, the Prince Regent took his leave and was very quickly swallowed back up by the hoard of eager attendants and others salivating to gain the attention of their portly Prince Regent.

"Was that the Prince?" Odette's breathless voice snapped Simon back to attention. A becoming flush caressed the apples of her cheeks and her blue eyes glittered even more brightly and clearly than the sapphires at her throat. Simon slipped his gloved hand into hers, savoring the glide of warm satin against his palm. "What did he say?"

"Only that he'd taken note of my research and the publication."

Her joyous little yelp of surprise caused the feathered headdress of a nearby matron to bob, affronted. "Oh, Simon! How wonderful!" She gifted him with a beaming smile more wonderful than any prize or award or accolades, combined. Forgetting where they were, she reached up and cupped his cheek. "I'm so proud of you, my love," she added earnestly.

Simon resolved at that moment not to reveal the Prince Regent's secret. He didn't want to be responsible for shattering Odette's joy if the Prince couldn't or wouldn't follow through with any promises or her hopes. Of course, Simon sincerely wished he would take more notice of this woman before him than just an illegitimate extension of the royal bloodline. Here was a woman who was worth so much more than all the gold in England's coffers—at least to Simon.

Until the Prince made a decision, Simon silently vowed to be all the family Odette needed for the rest of her days.

He squeezed her hand. "I believe I may be the only man here who has not had the pleasure of dancing with my wife." His smile broadened further when she grinned up at him. "You aren't too overtaxed to dance, are you?" He made a pointed look at her abdomen, but she shook her head and twined her fingers with his.

"Not at all," she murmured and allowed him to lead her back to the dance floor as the strains of a waltz began to swell in the air around them.

Did you enjoy Simon and Odette's story?
The Stratford siblings may all have found their happily ever afters, but what happens when a certain Scottish physician meets the sheltered sister of a powerful earl…and they strike a scandalous bargain?
<u>A Most Unsuitable Lover</u>, a spinoff of "The Stratford Family" series, is available now!

And receive a free copy of the Bonus Epilogue for <u>The Baron's Folly</u> when you sign up for my newsletter.

Follow Kelsey for updates:

Instagram - @authorkelseyswanson
Facebook - Author Kelsey Swanson

Acknowledgements

After one year of being a published author—of having my stories floating around the world and being able to share my characters with readers—I still need to pinch myself. I can't believe this is my life. So few people can realize their biggest dreams, and this past year, alone, has fulfilled several of mine (I finally became a mom four years ago, so he's been crossed off my wishlist for a while now). No woman can do everything alone (only 99.9% of it), so it's only right that I thank those who have helped me (and continue to help me) achieve my dreams.

As always, my husband and our son remain my biggest supporters, my most dedicated fans, my truest loves. You motivate me, drive me nuts, make me laugh even if I don't want to, and you are my shining stars when it grows dark.

Thank you to Ruta for helping make one of my oldest dreams a reality. Our London trip is something I will never, ever forget. Not only will our trip live on in my memories and the photos I look at practically every single day, but it has already colored my writing and will continue to do so forever. You are my supporter, my friend, my provider of levity. We can speak in inside jokes (better not run out of socks and underwear!) and I love and cherish every second of it. You and your family changed my life more than a decade ago and I believe I am who I am today because of it. (Tell Greg I'm still working on his character.)

Thank you to Amy, as always, for your years and years of unwavering support, your willingness to listen as I rattle off ideas, for helping Beta read this story, and for celebrating with me the very second I received my publishing contract for my books due out in 2025!

Thank you to my fellow co-founders and the lovely members of the Historical Hoydens group for helping me name Sir Nigel Wright! I adore the sense of camaraderie and community we have begun to cultivate.

And thank you to my readers. Writing can sometimes feel like shouting into the void but hearing from you makes it so much more tangible. I love the feedback and the comments. Learning how my stories and my characters have impacted you is truly moving for me. I wouldn't trade this life and this journey for anything. I've laughed, I've cried, I've stressed, I've experienced highs and lows, I've proofread until my eyes crossed, I've spent hours upon hours lying awake brainstorming plots and conversations, I've foregone sleep and sacrificed…but you all make it so, so worth it.

ABOUT THE AUTHOR

Author, wife, mother, animal lover, and owner of an obscenely large To-Be-Read book stash; Kelsey is an Illinois native. She fostered her love of reading and writing after a heart condition sidelined her childhood. Her passions continued to develop long after surgery restored her health. To this day, it's difficult to find her without a book in her hands. She dove headfirst into the romance genre (perhaps) a bit earlier than the recommended minimum age and became rather adept at disguising her reading material. Once exposed to the glittering world of historical romance, she was forever changed. Her love of writing and all things British translated into her future collegiate studies in both English (with an emphasis on Brit Lit) and History (mainly British and European). She would go on to earn Bachelor's Degrees in both English and History, as well as a Master's Degree in English. She finished penning her first novel fresh out of high school and has never looked back. When she's not reading or writing, she's usually watching reruns of her favorite shows, streaming just about any true crime show; obsessively collecting architectural designs, crafts, and recipes on Pinterest; or sketching, crocheting, cooking, and spending time with her family. She is a diehard supporter of the Oxford Comma and is glued to the TV whenever le Tour de France is on.

Kelsey loves to hear from readers! Find her on social media, or email her at authorkelseyswanson@yahoo.com. Reviews on Amazon and Goodreads are always appreciated!